BANDAGES 2

Joe McClain Jr.

This is a work of fiction. Names, characters, places and incidents are either the product of the authors imagination or are used fictitiously. Any resemblance to actual events or locales or persons, living or dead is entirely coincidental. From the mind of Joe McClain Jr.

DEDICATION

This book is dedicated to every woman who has been a victim of domestic, verbal, physical, or mental abuse. I want you to know that you are special and not to let the actions of the ignorant break your spirit. You were made to be great. Overcome and do great things.

ACKNOWLEDGMENTS

I have six nieces. Amaya, Ariana, Adaya, Alana, Zaviah and the most recent arrival as of January 28, 2017, Nariah. Each one of them has a different personality. Amaya, she was my first born niece. As a baby, she was as quiet as a mouse. Once she hit three years of age, she started to show her true colors.

Every time she would see me, it meant three things. Irritate Uncle Junior, torture Uncle Junior, and spend up all his money at the mall. She never shut up, but that was my baby and I accepted that. Now, she is 15 and a soon to be sophomore in high school. Then, there is Ariana. The princess is what I call her. She is beyond girly. She has always been involved in dolls, tea parties, and everything else that little girls were supposed to be into. I remember when she was about seven or eight. We were talking on the phone and she asked me a question that hit from the blindside. She said

"Uncle Mac? When I turn 16, can I wear heels?" That's when I knew I would have a problem on my hands. She is now 12, and will be a teenager at the end of this year. Then, there is Adaya, one half of the World Class Wrecking Crew (I'll explain that here real soon). She reminds me of my niece Amaya, except she is her to the 100th power. She's five, and always crawls over me, and beats me up everytime I see her. However, if you throw Disney on, she is as quiet as a gopher that just saw a snake. She is pretty much one big ball of energy.

There is her sister, Alana, the other half of World Class Wrecking Crew. Now, she is three, but everywhere Adaya goes, she goes. That's why I call them the World Class Wrecking Crew because they roll together to torture me equally. Now Alana, she is the quiet one. She'll play, but she won't be as turned up as her elder sister. And like I said, she is quiet.

She's sneaky. She's the type that if I mess with her at one in the afternoon, she will try to get revenge at midnight by putting an ether soaked rag over my nose (Not literally). As you can see, she will get you back. Then, there is Zaviah. Oh boy, this girl is something else. As a baby, she didn't like me. I'd hold her, she would moan and moan, until her momma or daddy came and got her. She only got comfortable with me when she was two. Once she hit three, she became a princess, just like Ariana. She is five now and loves to dance. I love it, but I always pester her mama when I see the pictures from her dance recitals. I tell her to make sure no one is looking at my baby's legs or I'll choke 'em. She usually responds with a

"Shut up Mac." Zaviah isn't as nutty as Amaya and Adaya, but she is an exciting child to be around. She always has a plethora of stories to tell me whenever I come around. Then, there is my newly arrived niece Nariah. I can't judge her yet, but if she ends up having the attitude of her mama (Love you Niya), then my hands are going to be full.

So why am I writing about my nieces? As you know, this book is a sequel to the original. Only this time, it is told from the female's view. I commend any woman who has made it to adulthood after suffering mental trauma and became a success story. I also know that the healing process takes a long time. Like most people, we have all had a case of molestation at some point in time in our families. We may have seen it directly, we may have not. I do know however that all families have a sicko or two. My family is not excluded, as a close female family member of mines was molested by a male member of my family. I didn't find out until I was 17. To say I was angry was an understatement. I wanted to kill the person. Like outright murder. What is crazy is that the victim was the one who convinced me to have forgiveness for the oppressor.

When I look at my six nieces, I always have in the back of my mind the thought of what would I do if someone hurt them? Now, I know all men say with their daughters or nieces that they will choke out any boyfriend of theirs. They will never like any boyfriend of theirs. The sayings go on and on. We say this because we know how bad we were when we were young men.

We would try to tell every female slick lines to get whatever we wanted out of them. Then, when we grow older, we do everything in our power to make sure no young man tries it with our young ladies. It's amazing how things change don't it? Before Amaya was born, I had three nephews. I was excited for when they would be able to tell me stories involving girls, going to parties, all that. When Amaya came, I prayed that she never grew up past the age of seven. It's funny when I think about it, but I don't laugh when I think that there are sickos out in this world who are ready to mentally destroy our young girls.

The psychological effects that occur from the actions of perverted men (and sometimes woman) are drastic. I usually don't apologize for any of my words, as I know that people will become offended even at the nice things you say. However, if there is a female who draws up traumatic memories due to reading my work, I humbly apologize. That is not my intent.

My intent is to tell a brutally honest story to show the world hey, this is what happens to our young women when we allow vultures to prey on them. It is key to be fathers and uncles to our young ladies, to ensure that they grow up into the queens that they were born to be. So to Amaya,

Ariana, Adaya, Alana, Zaviah and Nariah, Uncle loves y'all and wants you each to know that you are all queens. Never let any man tell you different.

1 MAY

"Uuuuhhhh." That was the little moan I let out as I lie in the bed, playing with myself, thinking about my husband Carl.

Masturbation is indeed healthy, especially when the thought process behind it is your best friend. I was waiting for him anxiously. It was something about having a man who worked out on the regular and kept his body tight that sent my hormones through the roof. "Uuuuuhhhh." I let out another moan, as I was beyond damn horny right now and ready to explode.

"Ok Star. Ok. Stop." I whispered that to myself because I didn't want to cum by my own hand. I needed my husband to make that happen. About a minute later, I heard those keys jingle in the door

lock. He strolled into the house on this crispy Saturday night, fresh out of the gym. California winter's weren't bitterly cold like the Midwest, but it did get a little chilly come nightfall. However, you couldn't tell these natives out here that.

They swore that when it hit forty degrees that a national state of emergency should be declared. There I lie, sprawled out on an oversized silver platter, surrounded with pineapple and orange slices, on top of our king size roller coaster of a bed. It was amazing what a woman could find at the thrift shop on a boring and dull Saturday afternoon. The lights were out as I heard him come in the house, with the exception of the light over the stove. He went to mess around in the kitchen for a minute, probably looking for some almond milk to drink because he was good for that.

"Baby," I called out, acting like I was sick.

"Sup?!" That was his typical response. Hell, any man's response for that matter.

"Can you come back here?"

"Hold on. Lemme hit another glass of milk."

I heard him put his glass down and I let out a faint chuckle. I knew my husband all too well. If there wasn't any almond milk in the house for him to drink as soon as he came through the door, he would freak out and probably murder the neighbor's dog. Hell, he would murder half of the neighborhood to be quite honest. He needed to hurry up, because he had some milk that I wanted to drink down myself. As I heard that glass get put down for the second time, I heard him making his way down the hall. My heart was racing. I needed Carl and I needed him bad.

"Babe, why is every light in here out?"
I didn't even respond. He hit the light switch once he entered the bedroom and the biggest grin in the history of mankind came across his face.

"Come here," I told him, directing him with my finger at the same time. You could tell he wanted to turn into a kid on Christmas, but he did his best impression of trying to look hard like he wasn't excited. He came over and I stopped him as he got to the edge of the bed. I rose up off that platter. I didn't say a word to him. I just crawled over to him ever so sexy.

"Sup baby?" He tried to sound cool. He did alright, but he was happy as a pig in shit and the acting like he wasn't excited came to cease. I gripped his manhood in one hand and rose up on my knees to kiss him. Our tongues flickered inside each other's mouths. His hands caressing my face, combined with me rubbing my favorite toy was driving me crazy inside.

"You like this?," I whispered to him.

"Yea," he responded, after biting his lip. I dropped back down and started to loosen his belt up. I wanted to put some nastiness into it, so I pulled it off with my teeth. Once I got those Tru Religion jeans down, it was all over for him. I didn't even start off how some women do, and that's being all slow and steady. I went to town from the jump. I inserted his manhood all the way into the back of my mouth and just held it there for a few seconds. I came back off and began droolin' and slobbin' all over my favorite toy. My eyes were watering from his dick hitting the back of my throat. I just took it and gagged like a good wife was supposed to do. I then began to multi task on his ass.

I was sucking him up while massaging his football player type ass in the process. To keep him going crazy, I switched it up. I let my left hand go and felt around for the belt on the bed. Once in my grasp, I just held it up. He got the idea of what I wanted and grabbed it. He wrapped it around my head and began pulling ever so right that he was fucking my face.

I could tell he was enjoying this because those baby ass moans were coming out. As for me, this shit was getting me wetter by the minute. I loved pleasing my husband. It was what a wife was supposed to do. There was nothing in this world, that I wouldn't do for him. He kept in control as I began to play with myself while sucking him up.

"Babe slow down. You gone have me explode."

I moaned once he said that. I began to go harder. I felt his meat throb in my mouth as his breathing started to get deeper and uncontrollable. He had lost control of that belt by now as I had him damn near in outer space. I knew it was almost time for him to explode, so my moaning and sounds of nasty sucking got louder. It was turning me on more than him.

With a few more flicks of the tongue, he began to shoot off. It was damn near like someone cutting on a fire hose at full throttle. It was more than a lot, but I handled it all. I slowly came up on my knees with my mouth full, with some oozing out from between my lips. I looked him dead in his eyes as I played with his cum in my mouth.

I cocked my head back and gargled it. I closed my mouth and crawled back over to the platter full of fruit. He was going on deployment soon and every time he looked at his dick, I wanted him to think of me. I bent down over the food and let his cum ooze out all over the fruit. I looked back up at him, as he was staring at me in complete disbelief.

"What the fuck girl?," he asked, breathing as if he had just got finished running six full courts back to back.

"What?," I said as if I didn't know why he was asking me that question. He knew I was a freak, but he didn't know the half of what I was capable of. I always thought up fresh stuff to keep our bedroom life spicy. I didn't like repetitive, basic and standard sex that would eventually become boring and uneventful. I grabbed a pineapple covered in his juice, put it in my mouth and chewed it up.

"This good baby. You want one?" He started busting out laughing as I had no choice but to join him.

"Babe, I can't say shit. You got me. You've done some shit in your day," as he wagged his finger. "But this shit here. Whatever you need, I got you." I smiled and grabbed another pineapple covered in his man juice and ate it up.

"So I take it you enjoyed this like I did huh?," I asked him with a smile on my face. He smiled right back, sitting there rubbing his stuff so he could get it back up and fuck the soul out of my body like he always did. My nights sleep was compromised with dream after dream after dream. From the erotic dreams I had of me and my husband's final time having sex, to the past hurts that I tried to rid my mind of, I saw everything as if I were back in the time that it happened. My foster home with the many sisters and brothers that I had was one dream. The crazy thing about all of us in that foster home is that we all came from similar backgrounds. That background was abuse. Whether it was verbal, physical, or psychological, we were all prone to it. Dorian. Tyrell, Nikita, Ashton and Lorita were their names. They were literally all I had. Hell, we were all each other had.

How in the hell did the state grant permission for the folks we had to care after us? I still scratch my head to this day looking for the answer. Mr. and Mrs. Ronnie Gilman put on the act of acts. They should have been Oscar nominated for their roles in duping the state of Kansas out of thousands of dollars. They made Denzel Washington and Angela Bassett look like amateurs. They didn't give a shit about us. They just enjoyed the extra money that we brought in. We lived in a three story, six bedroom brick house in the slums of Wichita. To the rest of the neighborhood, it was a crown jewel. To us, it was hell on earth. We ate as if we were prisoners and were treated much of the same way. At times, it seemed like the homeless were in better living conditions than us. We all suffered. However, there wasn't much any of us could do. All of our previous situations made this situation look like heaven, and it was no way in hell that any of us wanted to go back to where we came from.

One by one as the years passed, my siblings became victims of our circumstances by either the jailhouse or death. Ashton, who was two years my senior, died from a drug overdose at the age of 16. I was fresh out of school the day he died. I was feeling useless as usual. I got to the house, seeing neither the tan, nor the rusty blue Chevy outside. I slowly stepped up the wide, yet cracked out concrete steps of my home with caution. I had a feeling that at any given time, that concrete would give out from underneath. I stood there in front of the door, staring up into space. There was a feeling in my spirit that was telling me that something wasn't right. I opened up the door to the house.

"Hello," I yelled. I got no answer. "Dorian?!" I got no answer from my brother. I didn't call out anyone else's name because I truly didn't care about them. I looked down to see a few spoons on the bare wooden floor. I picked one up, analyzing it, looking at the residue that was left behind on it. I looked around the house with the spoon in my hand.

Things had begun to get real creepy. Up and down the stairs, room to room I went, but I found no one. As I got back to the living room, I saw the basement door cracked open. The first thing that came to my mind was that some dope fiends had broken in and were downstairs getting the high of highs.

I was a frail 14 year old. If someone was down there, there wasn't much I could do against them. I went back upstairs to grab a black Louisville Slugger from my foster father's closet. He called it the black panther, as he said he kept it just in case any crackers wanted to come in and test how much he loved being black. I walked over to the basement door and then proceeded to slowly creep down the basement steps. With each step I took, I tried to remain as quiet as possible. Knowing heroine addicts, they were probably passed out on the floor.

Once I got to the bottom step, I hit the light switch. That is when I saw my brother Ashton. He was sprawled out across the cold concrete in a dirty wife beater, some ragged jeans, with one reebok show untied on his right foot. A lump appeared in my throat as it was my first time seeing a dead body. I put the bat down and slowly walked over to his deceased corpse. His eyes were wide open and a cloudy white color covered his pupils.

Next to his body, I saw an empty syringe that still had a lone drop of residue dangling from the needle. His facial expression is what frightened me the most. His mouth was wide open as if he were yelling for someone to come help him escape the misery and anguish that he was facing. I will never forget that look. It became etched into my cranial for all time.

Then, there was my brother Tyrell, who got caught up in the street life, trying to be the next Don Juan. His robbery and sexual exploits of girls his age saw him land in the young adult prison system at just the tender age of 13. He wasn't heard from again. For all I knew he was still locked up, or worse off dead. Then, there was Dorian. Dorian, Dorian, Dorian. I really didn't know where to begin this story. Out of everyone that I was in that house with, we were the closest. He was born in March just like me, only three days apart. We were the same age. Like me, he was a victim of abuse, but the type of abuse that he faced was on a level that I couldn't even fathom.

He was five years old when he became introduced to the foster system. He was the only child too some drug runners who had migrated to Wichita from Compton. His parents had taken him on a road trip to Houston to meet up with a bunch of other high profile dealers, suppliers and runners who were preparing for a huge score that would see them all net a profit of at least $200,000. Just like black folks were good at, they used the kids for entertainment.

In Dorian's case, he was the kid, since he was the only young person in the house that night. They addressed him as "my lil nigga," "nigglet" or "boots," in reference to his daddy wearing Timberland's all the time. As the story goes, he was in the house with 40 something other people. He watched as people snorted coke, played cards, drank the hardest of liquor, loaded up guns and fucked right in front of him.

As he sat in the middle of the living room, coloring in a book, all of a sudden, the doors of the house were kicked in and all hell broke loose. Nine to twelve masked gunmen entered into the house, dressed in all black, armed with AR-15 assault rifles and began unloading a hail of bullets among the occupants of the house. When it was all said and done, all 40 something people who were occupying the house at that time were marinating in a pool of their own blood. You know these guys had to be professional hit men because not one of them got hit. When the smoke cleared, the gunmen stood around Dorian, who was lying face down in the living room. He wasn't even crying he said because he truly did not comprehend what was about to happen or what had happened.

"LEVANTATE! LEVANTATE!" That's the spanish word meaning "get up." He slowly rose up to his feet and looked around the living room, observing dead bodies on the couch, an adjacent room and on the steps. As he looked up at the group of men hovering over him, he said that they talked in Spanish and let out menacing laughs that reminded him of the devil himself. One of them suddenly handed their assault rifle off in exchange for a smaller pistol and placed the barrel right into his forehead.

"Are you going to kill me sir?," he asked them. Right then and there, he said the gunman just held the gun there. He was motionless and silent, as were the other men. A few seconds later, he lowered his weapon down by his side. They were staring at him. Just then, the gunman gave him a dollar. He said to Dorian,

"Te doy un dolar por ser el joven mas veliente aqui. Que Dios se apaide de tu alma. **VAMOS!"**

With those last words, they all stormed out of the house. That is what you call punishment and pain to the highest degree. Someone lets you live but kills everyone around you. I don't think he ever fully recovered from that. Now, I didn't know where Dorian was at, or whether he was still alive. I just know that it would be a dream come true if I found my long, lost brother. He meant everything to me.

As for Lorita, she became pregnant soon after turning 18 and was rumored to be tricking off in the streets of Wichita. She was always the stuck up, bitchy one out of all of us. In her mind, her shit didn't stink and if you put syrup on her shit, it was pancakes. You never think that you will be the one to make it out of a situation in which many people are enduring troubling times. However, God's favor poured over me something serious. Why? Well, you'll just have to ask Him yourself.

I woke up bright and early before seven o'clock. The sun was starting to make its way above the clouds and the birds were already singing their tunes, sounding like the animal kingdom's version of Keith Sweat. I sat up on the edge of the bed focused and in my thoughts something serious. This was more of my closeout game of the NBA

Finals and I was about to get my Kawhi Leonard on.

Instead of 22 points and 10 rebounds, I was looking for the ultimate stat, and that was redemption. This would be the last encounter with the man who took everything away from me. This would be the last encounter with the man who stripped me of my being. The last meeting of the man who killed my mother in cold blood like she didn't mean anything to this world.

The horrendous memories of my life started to play back in my head. The fan was blowing and the light started to creep through the small slits in the room curtains. Star, the rehabilitated woman was slowly disappearing. The angry spirit of revenge began to grow inside of me. Inside of my soul, the evil bitch of the Midwest had erupted and was on the verge of showing her ass. They say anger is a deadly sin and that vengeance belongs to The Lord. Today, I could care less. God was going to take a seat and eat His popcorn with this one. I eased up off the bed and let out a stretch. I did the regular of brushing my teeth and washing up.

I threw on my red bandana, beater and red basketball shorts, and headed down to the hotel gym. Red was Carl's favorite color, so anything that reminded me of him brought me inner peace. The gym was empty upon arrival, which was more than pleasurable for me. I had all the room in the world to let off some steam and get focused. I pulled out my phone and set it too Waka Flocka's "Luv Dem Gun Sounds." I didn't advocate for violence at all. However, I needed raw and ruckus music to get my mind right when it was time to get those GAINZ.

I started with push ups, 90 to be exact, divided up into six sets of 15. Dead locked on my reflection in the mirror that I was literally a foot away from, I told my biggest competition that you will not defeat me. This was only the beginning as this served as my warm up for a massive slaughter session. From there it was bench and incline dumbbell sets. I murdered my chest as I cranked out max reps for three sets. Cross cables came next as I pushed myself as my muscles screamed for me to stop. Fuck them muscles is what I was thinking. They were gonna get this work, because no great body ever came from being a pacified pussy in the gym. I followed that up with eight sets of tricep dips to the max. Finishing off everything with a 30 minute elliptical session, and I was more than done. Sweaty, exhausted and beat beyond belief, I gazed at my body as I analyzed the results of my workout.

They have this myth that girls who workout are bulky. I can tell you that myth is the biggest crock of ass crap in the world. I was in great shape. Carl got me this way. He not only re-trained my mental, but my physical as well. I looked at the long scar that I had on my leg from when they had to repair it. A broken femur and tibia were the results of the accident that fateful Halloween night. I was a sight for sore eyes, but it reminded me of what I had made it through. I lifted up my shirt, looking at my stomach that held life, but was not yet showing. Becoming a mother is something that I never thought would happen, but by the grace of God, that moment was on its way. God I missed Carl.

I thought about how my body became his in every way. I yearned for how he made me feel like his personal project when we were in the bedroom. How he dug me out while I was on my stomach, while firmly gripping my chin, letting me taste his fingers ever so slightly. He made sure I felt good, yet dirty at the same time. I loved how he'd grab my breasts as I strapped tight on his saddle, losing my mind at the thought that I was being penetrated by my best friend.

No woman will understand the art of sex until they have it with their best friend. It's like a whole new ballgame. Men come and go. That best friend love is the most passionate, erotic and dirty love that you could ever have. If any woman who claimed that their man was their best friend, and didn't please him in every way possible, then she was a fool. She was only inviting the possibility of another woman doing the job that she should be doing. I still tripped on how some grown women didn't like to give their man bomb, sloppy head and we were in the 21st century. I guess they would learn when another woman came into the picture and sucked his dick for them. I finished up and walked back to the room for a more than refreshing shower. It was easy to take the elevator, but with what I would have to face later, I needed all the time in the world to think about what I was going to do. It would be a long three hour drive to the prison and I had to have myself together. Unlike the first time I went to see him, there wouldn't be any nervousness. I kept playing in my mind how things would go, but I truly wouldn't know until I arrived. It was Him vs. the daughter. The final showdown was coming. It was going to be ugly. However, before any of that was to occur, I had to make one stop.

As humans, we look at the cemetery as a place where the dead spend eternity. It also serves as a fearful place in the eyes of many, due to the fact that we all know that it will be the last place we all visit on this earth. However, I saw the cemetery for exactly what it was. It was a place where the richest people that roamed the earth resided. Am I talking money? No, not at all. I'm talking about all of the rich ideas, thoughts and brilliance people had that were buried along with the physical form.

My mom was one of those people. I knew that she had so much more to give to this world, seeing that she was only 33 when she passed. It was the same age that Jesus was when they beat and tortured Him on the cross. I always thought that was ironic the older I got. I knew my mom wasn't a Jesus type figure. In my eyes, however, she had the impact on me like he had on all of His followers.

She remained strong, even in the midst of turmoil, abuse and other atrocities committed by him. Mom was always there for me no matter what. She knew about the abuse I suffered and God honestly tried everything in her power to escape it. From the threats on her life to the beatings she obtained when she tried to pull him away from me, it was difficult to formulate any plan of action to get us out of the situation that we were in. Some are wondering why she didn't go to the police. It's simple. Fear. It was sad that her freedom would come in the form of giving her life. Now, it was time to see my mom again. I drove into the cemetery noticing nothing out of the ordinary.

There were groundskeepers cutting the lawn. Gravediggers were digging more plots for new additions. It was normal business as usual from what I was seeing. Finally, I stopped on the road about 200 feet from where she was resting for eternity. I reached into my purse on the passenger seat and grabbed the pregnancy test that read positive.

It was the same one that I showed Carl before he left on deployment. Most people come with flowers, bears, wreaths, and all that other mumbo jumbo. Me? Nah. This was different. I was different. I wanted to give a gift to my mom that was more than meaningful. I exited the car, taking my time as I indulged in this beautiful mid afternoon day. The breeze was just right, the temperature was a nice 74 degrees and the sun was on its usual tip of being beautiful. I walked over to my mom's headstone and knelt down in front of it. For a good 30 seconds, I just took the time to look at it, reminiscing on the great memories that we once had. I took my right hand and ran my fingertips across every inch of her headstone, reading every word inscribed.

"Anita Jennings. Beloved mother, friend, and person. 1967-2000." Below those words was a picture of herself that was placed into the marble stone. I didn't cry, because I had done enough of that since I was eight years old. I just stayed there and took in the fact my mommy was gone forever. I pulled up a little bit of the grass from in front of the stone and dug out a small hole in the underlying dirt.

"Hi mom. Guess what? You're going to be a grandmother." I said it looking directly at her picture, hoping that she would smile back and start screaming with joy. I placed the test into the ground and put dirt back over it.

"If it's a girl, her name will be Anita Jackson. If it's a boy, his name is gonna be Clinton. Love you mom and I wish you were here to see the woman that I have been molded into. It's not what I was when I was a teen. I'm past that phase and I am doing what I am supposed to be doing in life. Advancing and being a great wife to a great man. More importantly, I am being a great woman for myself. I love you always."

I touched her picture one last time, leaving my hand on there for maybe two or three minutes. In that time, it seemed as if her energy had transferred throughout my body. Great memories started to cloud my thoughts and for a moment, I smiled.

"Goodbye mom," I told her with watery eyes. As I got up and began walking back to the car, I heard what I thought was a crow. I turned around and saw that a group of crows were flying above. Suddenly, one swooped down and landed on my mother's headstone. It kept squawking, making that sound that crows love to make. To most, a crow is a symbol of evil and death. However, I remember what made a crow so special to me and my mom. I don't remember too many major instances from one to eight years old. When I was four, however, my mom took me to a mini carnival. It wasn't anything major. It was just a small two week festival at a local

Catholic Church where people could come, have fun, win prizes and eat some good food.

"Now baby, throw the ball, and if it lands in a fishbowl, you can win a prize." I remember her giving me the ping pong ball and my frail little four year old arm throwing it with all of my might. To my surprise, I landed it in a bowl.

"Yea baby!!! See, you won a gold fish."

"I don't want the fishy mommy. I want that." I was pointing to a plush bird that was sitting behind the man running the game.

"Oh baby," mom said. "I don't think that's a prize."

"But I like it," I responded. Just then, the man behind the booth smiled.

"Young lady, here you go." He handed it to me and began to whisper a fable to me.

"Now, this is a magic crow. His name is Jimmy. Jimmy will bring you joy all the time. Keep him near you when you are at home and he will always protect you. Okay?" I shook my head up and down. My mom was laughing.

"Thank you sir."

"No problem ma'am. You and your beautiful daughter enjoy."

Now, all these years later, I was watching Jimmy the crow sitting on my mom's headstone. It kept squawking and looking all around until it looked dead at me.

"I LOVE YOU MOM!!!," I yelled out. Right then and there, the bird flew up into the trees and became one with the rest of its group. I now know that my mother had heard me. That old man might have said Jimmy was protecting me, but I know that crow that was looking down on me. Its name was Anita Jennings.

The drive to the prison was slow and serene. I took in the typical Kansas outdoor scenery of flat plains and silos through my shades. This was home. I couldn't complain. The same way New Yorkers loved their tall buildings, or South Dakontans loved their Black Hills, I loved this state. No matter what had transpired in my life, I would always be a Kansas girl with Jayhawk blood flowing through my veins. Slow jams from the 70's era helped put my mind at ease while traveling. Teddy P, James Brown, The Temptations, The Whispers, The Delfonics, The Isley Brothers and The Chi Lites were just some of the groups that I was listening to. All of these singers were ahead of their time. I would listen to my mom play them on occasion when she wasn't getting her head bashed in by him.

I used to sing along with her as she washed the dishes or did the laundry. It was rare, but those were the times that were filled with the most joy. It was also the time he was gone away from the house. Either he was at work or somewhere else with another woman. I missed her dearly. Had she been here, I felt like things would've been totally different. At the same time, I probably would've stayed curled up under her and not expanded myself to do bigger and better things.

I continued traveling up 35 North, still a good ways away from the prison. I was about an hour and forty five minutes into the trip when that bathroom itch started to creep up. A rest area was coming up in a few miles and Lord knows that I needed to hurry up before I flooded this vehicle. I threw on some old Frankie Beverly and Maze to take my mind off of peeing, but it only lasted for so long. The rest stop was now just two miles away, but it was a long two miles. I ditched the 70's records and threw in some Wale. I took in every word of his song "Bad" with Tiara Thomas. It was once a reflection of me and I could definitely relate to it. It was crazy that I had to always remind myself of my past. But for me, it worked. It allowed me to not go back into it. I know that doesn't sound normal, but everyone has their different methods for coping with the things life throws at them. Reflection of the hard times was certainly mines.

I arrived at the rest stop right on time. This pee was knocking at the door and ready to storm in like the FBI on a drug raid at the trap house. As with most women, I didn't trust public bathrooms. I would rather hover like a genie out of its lamp than to sit on any public toilet seat. I was well prepared, though. A while back, I had purchased a traveling toilet seat. I could sit my ass down on it and release in peace, without all the threats of germs. I swear it was the greatest invention ever made. I sprinted into the bathroom as if I were Usain Bolt at the 2012 Olympics. Sitting down, it was like someone had drained the Euphrates River dry. I handled my business and I felt like a million bucks. Finally relieved, I walked into the small convenient store of the rest area. I had an itching for some Vitamin Water, fruit snacks and some white cheddar popcorn. I know it sounded odd, but that's what my stomach was craving.

I sat in line behind the old white lady who was moving so slow that Jesus would be back by the time she was finished getting the money out of her purse. I respected the elderly, but I swear I wish they could have their money ready when they got to the register. Having a huge purse wasn't helping either as she was digging through old dinosaur fossils and Egyptian burial grounds to get a few dollars.

Finally, after what seemed like two centuries and the invention of flying cars, I finally was at the register.

"How you doing today Ma'am?" His voice got lighter and lighter with each passing word. He then stopped completely, giving me a look of shock. He was locked in. No words, no a nuthing.

"Ummm...are you okay?," I asked him.

"Star, It's me. Dorian." I stood in absolute silence. My heart began to take off like a cheating man who had just got caught in bed with the side chick. I couldn't fathom what I was hearing right now. **"RICO!!! TAKE THE REGISTER FOR ME FOR A MINUTE!!** Let's head outside yo?" I completely ignored my cravings, leaving everything on the counter and followed him out the door, into the parking lot. We were almost an arm's length apart. I was studying his facial features to see if it was really him. Through the dreads and the crispy goatee, I could see that this was very real. It was indeed him.

"Sis," he said. I smiled as we embraced in the biggest hug ever. It was like clutching on to your lifeline for the very first time after you had flatlined. My emotions began to pour out. My brother and I were reunited.

"Will you stop crying girl?," he managed to squeeze out as I almost took all the breath out of him.

"Boy hush," as I squeezed even tighter. We let loose and sat down on a nearby bench talking.

"Where have you been all these years?" He just gave me a look that said more than any words could ever say. I knew something that I didn't wanna hear was coming.

"Well sis, after you left, I was still in the house. I know ma and pa dukes wasn't our real joints, and they didn't care two shits about us, but they was really the only parents I knew. Long story short, about a year after you went to the Navy, he offed her, and then offed himself. This all while I was in the upstairs room chillin'. I didn't hear any arguments, screaming, name calling, none of that. Just two pops and that was it. I paused for a good minute in the room. After I didn't hear anything, I walked into their bedroom and observed something out of the movie Scarface. Only this time, it wasn't a movie."

I sat there in stone silence, trying to be immune to what I just heard, but it was damn near impossible. I didn't know what to say to my brother. I mean, I hated both of them, yes. In spite of my feelings, I would never wish death on either one of them. The only person I had ever wished would die was myself, and that was because I felt dead inside as an individual. Now, I sort of felt bad that I didn't have love for them in my heart.

"Where'd you go after that?"

"I bounced around yo. Homeboy house to homeboy house. Minimum wage job after minimum wage job. Finally, though, I buckled down and got on my grown man shit. Through a connection, I managed to get into a nursing school free of charge. Don't ask me why or how. But, I become a certified registered nurse next week and I won't have to scan no more items for anyone."

My mood instantly flipped. Dorian had buckled down. It was something that many didn't do until it was absolutely too late in life. He had seen the light. I was proud of him. I couldn't ask for anything more but to see the best come out of everyone I knew. I was a positive person now and that's all that I wanted around me was positivity.

"So how you manage to get through nursing school for free since you told me not to ask you?" He laughed for a few seconds.

"You might not believe it, but I was fucking the dean of students the whole time I was up there. What can I say sis? Ol bitties with old titties need loving too." I tried not to laugh, but I couldn't hold it in. We talked for a little while longer, exchanged numbers and it was back on the road for me, headed to Leavenworth to see him. Before seeing Dorian, I was full of hostility, anger, and just the female version of the devil. Now, I was trying to bring myself to grips with the situation I was facing and actually conjure up peace. In other words, I was just trying to be cool, calm and collective.

My foster parents' death stung because forgiveness was something I never gave them. I let them live in my head rent free and now the chance for amendment was gone. As crazy as it sounded, I now wanted to try and help the old man who raised me for eight years, even if he did leave me mentally scarred. The drive turned into something very different as I cut all of my music off and just stayed focused. Road trips do something to you. Besides giving you a scenic view of things you probably wouldn't see on the regular, they allow you to just think. Scenarios started to run through my head of good times, something that was rare in my childhood. Yet, at the same time, some parts that I wish I could forget came back into play for me as well.

It was a crisp October autumn day. The beginning of my senior year was two months in and I for one was happy. It would be the last year I was stuck in school for anything. I was who I was. By this point in my life, I had embraced it and was truly not giving a damn what anyone thought of me. I didn't like anyone to tell you the truth and I just preferred to stay to myself. During October, the holiday "Sweetest Day" arrived.

This was supposedly the men's Valentine's Day created by Hallmark. It was where the woman was supposed to send the man a gift, but it never worked like that, seeing that the girls got most of the flowers and carnations. I was sitting in my fifth hour chemistry class doing a bunch of nothing. When I say a bunch of nothing, I mean simply wasn't paying attention, seeing how Mr. J was always trying to preach some shit about life. Halfway through 5th period, a couple of students came into class with carnations. One by one, names were called and flowers were passed out.

"Willie!!!" Willie signaled for them to bring em over.

"You got six man," said his road dog Joe.

"I expected more, but six bitches is good." I swear on my life I hated this dude. He thought he was the shit because he was the star quarterback. Everyone loved Willie. Me, I wasn't expecting anything. I was a loner, had a bad reputation and I knew that no one liked me at all.

"Star?" I couldn't believe that my name was actually called. My eyes shot up with a look on my face like I had seen a ghost. I guess the rest of the class thought they had seen a ghost as well as all eyes became focused on me.

"I guess pigeons are pissing in toilet seats now."

"FUCK YOU WILLIE!!"

"No thank you Shorty. Already did that a few times." The whole class started oooing, instigating shit like teenagers were known to do.

"Good one my nigga," said bum ass Joe as they dapped up. They always called themselves trying to roast somebody. I just rolled my eyes at both of those niggas.

"The hell you rolling your eyes at me for? I ain't fuck you."

"And believe me Joe you never will."

"That's cool. I don't want any pussy that I can put my leg in." The class started laughing again, and I was through going back and forth with his dumb ass. I couldn't stand either him or Willie. I couldn't wait to get out of school. I literally snatched my flower from the four eyed nerd who handed it to me. Mr. J wasn't saying anything. He was just looking in my direction, shaking his head. This whole class was full of nuts. He just let us do us sometimes. The bell rung and everyone took off for the final period of the day except for me.

"A Kel, leave her ass alone. Quit being captain save a hoe and come on."

"Will stop man. Leave her alone."

"I really don't need your help so go with your funky ass friend." He then just gave me a look and backed away. Kel was a sincere guy, but I really didn't wanna be bothered by people telling me how great I was. If I was so damn great, then why did God screw my life like He did? Him and Will left out as I now sat in class alone, trying to think of who in the world would send me such a thing. I didn't have friends, so that made it even more awkward. I opened the small envelope attached to the yellow carnation and read the card inside.

"I never see you with anyone, so I figured you needed a friend. Hope this carnation makes you smile."- Anonymous

It didn't make me smile, nor feel good in any type of way. I thought that I would go out into the hall and there would be another bum ass dude trying to get into my draws. I had gotten used to that and this didn't make me feel any different.

"Are you alright Ms. Jennings," Mr. J asked me.

"Yea, I was just leaving."

"What's wrong besides the obvious nut cases of Joe and Willie? I know my students. I have been teaching for over 30 years, so trust me. I've heard it all and seen it all." I didn't want to really talk to him for the simple fact that I didn't trust him. However, I sensed something within myself telling me that I should listen.

"Go on Mr. J," I said, as I dropped the flower to the floor, slingin my backpack over my right shoulder.

"Look I notice things," he said, picking up the flower off the floor. "You don't talk much in class. You isolate yourself a lot around school. And it's okay, because everyone is not meant to be cliqued up and follow a crowd. Let me tell you something. In ten years, all of this. The clique, crew, groups, or squads or whatever people want to call it, it won't matter. All that will matter is your family and the ability to sustain yourself so that you can keep food on the table, a roof over your head and clothes on your back. Now, I know your situation is different than most, and I can never fully understand it or tell you that I know what you're going through. However, if someone took the time out of their day to send you a simple carnation, then smile about it. People always say if God loves me, then I don't need anyone else. Between me and you, that's the biggest crock and utterly most complete bullshit I have ever heard in my life. God put people on this Earth to help you in times of need. Whether it's good times when you need praises, or bad times when you need comfort. Right there, that flower right there that you let fall on the floor, that tells me someone thought about you. Someone is actively thinking about you. So chuck it up and smile. As a matter of fact, do you mind if I see the card?"

I handed it to him, my facial expression still cold and unemotional.

"Anonymous I see. Well, just take it as that you're cared for. Smile one time, at least for me." Mr. J smiled and I cracked a semi one.

"Good. Now go to last period and learn something new. I'll give you a pass saying that you were with me so your teacher won't go crazy for you being late. Who do you have for sixth hour anyway?"

"Madame."

"Oh wow. Yea. Let me definitely write you a pass, because that woman is nuts sometimes. Don't tell her that I told you that." That actually did make me laugh as I couldn't even deny that one. Madame was the French teacher. She could be cool, but in the blink of an eye, she could snap, kick you out of her class and tell you that you will never be allowed in school again. Yea, she was crazy.

I walked out of his class going about my usual. In the back of my head, I really did soak in what he had told me. Someone did care for me. It was hard to imagine because no one in this life ever cared for me, let alone expressed that they even wanted me around them, besides my mother. For the first time in my life since my mother had died, I think I was grateful. I felt obligated to whoever the boy was. If I ever met him in this life or another one, I owed him severely.

Finally, after three plus hours on the road, I pulled up to the prison and just sat there for a good while in the parking lot. Visiting hours were from 6:00-8:00 and it was just 5:30 in the evening. I tried to lay everything out on how I would go about things, but nothing ever goes as planned. This trip would be somewhat simpler, however. Unlike the first time, I didn't need a hookup to come in and see him. He was expecting me due to my relationship with one officer. Now, I was gonna give him the shock of his life. No phone interview. This one would be straight face to face, no bullshit, no chasers. The time ticked by slow as my anxiety started to run amuck inside of my head. My eyes closed for a hot minute, thinking about the pain that the past had brought me. There I was, clutching onto my stuffed teddy bear as always. I was four years old and not truly knowing the meaning of what I was hearing.

"SHUT UP!! BITCH SHUT UP!!!"

He was on his usual rants that were aided by pints of liquor that sat in his stomach. I was too young to fully understand it all, but I knew it was bad.

"STOP DONTAE!!! PLEASE STOP!!!" My mother's cries and please for help were no avail as I could hear his hands connect to her face with a sound that made a gunshot seem like mere handclaps. It continued on and on. The cries of my mother grew louder and louder. They didn't mean anything to him as he insisted on laying his foot down and showing her that he was indeed the alpha male. I cracked my innocent head through my slightly opened door to see him strike her once more. Blood was oozing from her nose and there was no stopping him. He was in a zone and I honestly thought that my mother was gonna die.

"Daddy," I called to him. His foot stopped dead in mid air as he turned to look at me.

"Baby, go to your room. Mommy just had a accident. Isn't that right mommy?" As he helped her up, literally snatching her up from under her arms, she was clearly distraught when he spoke.

"Y-Y-Y-Yea baby," she mumbled. "Mommy is okay. Go back in your room and rest okay." Wiping the blood off her face with her hand, he put his arm around her, helped her off the floor and waltzed off into a different part of the house, making sure to look back at me, saying with his eyes

"If you ever tell, you'll be next." That was before the physical abuse I endured. That was before my mind was completely screwed. That was before I started to give myself to men, all in the search to feel loved by the one person. Ho status wasn't even the word to describe me. I was more of a shattered mirror that was shaped into a human being. My skin simply held this broken glass skeleton of mines together.

Before the age of 17, at least 30 different men had pierced what was supposed to be my innocence. About the same amount had pierced my mouth. I consumed more kids than the diamond trade in Sierra Leone. All for what? All for the chance to feel loved. I had to face my shame at school, being the outcast, known simple as "that girl." I was a girl without a name. Star didn't exist until someone wanted to get in between my legs.

And when I think about it, Star doesn't even really exist at all, because I truly didn't know who I was.

Foster care was more like the psych ward. It only gave a shit about you when you went crazy. By then, it was too late for therapy. When I left Wichita, I said to myself that I would never come back. I didn't trust anyone here in this city. I didn't trust God. I didn't trust life. Then one day, a man simple called me ugly as shit, and he put on a path to show me how beautiful I was. I hated him at first. I couldn't stand the sight of him. However, he looked past the pain that I tried to hide. He looked past my snobby attitude. He looked past the fact that he could never be my first, second or even third. Hell, I had even lost count. What he did have was the power to give me the ability to say that for the first time in life, I truly loved a man.

This, the person who I was, it wasn't what anyone called wifey material. Yet he gave me the chance to become his wife. He saved me in more ways than one. When he first penetrated me, I felt like I had never felt before. I never made love to any man and he indeed did that to me.

My emotions came out of hibernation. My soul became rejuvenated with each touch of his fingertips. The words "I love you" and "I'm here" bandaged my open wounds and made me whole again. It may have taken 20 plus years, but it happened. I think we've all been through that. Our eyes close and we start to think about everything that has transpired into making us the people that we are today. It seems like life is taking forever, but at the same time, it's going by fast. As a matter of fact, too fast at times. I opened my eyes back up and was really wanting to get this over with. I pulled out a book from the glove compartment. It was full of poems that Carl had written for me over our time together.

I became misty eyed instantly. It was literally like I could hear his voice through the pages reading the words to me. Ironically, my favorite piece he had ever written wasn't for me. It was the one he wrote in that small green notebook, right there on the Boardwalk Pier in Imperial Beach, California. He wrote it right before he was going to attempt to take his life.

I remember vividly crying my eyes out as I flew down the 5 freeway that night. His cousin Snap was his lifeline. Once Snap was gone, he was gone mentally. I literally followed my heart all the way down there. I remember when I pulled up to park at the beach. I was double, maybe even tripled park outside of the lines, not giving one bit of care in the world. I got out of the car and saw him step up to the second beam.

"CARL!!!," I shouted, but to no avail. He was so zoned out that he didn't even hear me. Not to mention that I was a good ways away from him. I mustered up every ounce of strength I had and ran to get him, knowing that my life depended on it. The only other time I had ran this fast in my life was when I was trying to escape him when he was coming after me as a child.

My heart was racing a mile a minute. I really thought that I was gonna have a heart attack. Finally, as he started to lean, I dove out with every fiber I had in my body and managed to grab the back of his shirt by a small handful. It was like everything went in slow motion. It was like being in that movie scene where the dramatic rescue was occurring, yet the crowd didn't know what would come to pass.

That dive was enough as I managed to pull him down to the pier. He may have hit his head on some cold, hard wood, but it was better than him hitting the freezing San Diego waters in the middle of the night and not ever being seen again. I may have hurt my whole right side, but it was better than not having him by my side. If there was anything worth me risking my life for, it was definitely me taking that risk to save him. It changed me into a completely different person. I was upset with him after that. Then, when I had time to sit back and think about it, I realized that he was upset with the person I was at one point, yet he stuck with me regardless. See love is nothing but a constant cycle of forgiveness, fights, make ups and overcoming of trials. Indeed, we had a combination of all that and I wouldn't have wanted it any other way.

Six o'clock hit on the dashboard clock and I took a deep breath. I recited the Lord's Prayer three times in preparation for what I considered the biggest moment of my life. I stepped out of my vehicle and made the walk towards the prison. I got to the gate, buzzing my way in. I got to the second gate and did the same. This time, there was no officer from my past to help me. I was here dolo and had to do this on my own. I made it into the main building to a female officer sitting at the desk.

"Name please?"

"Star Jackson."

"Write your info down and inform me of whom you are intended to visit?" I wrote all of the details requested with no problem. However, when I got to the portion labeled "INMATE NAME," I hesitated. Seeing his name or hearing anyone with his name always put me in an uneasy mood. That's why I always referred to him as him. In my eyes, his name wasn't even worthy of being mentioned. Here goes nothing I thought. I spelled out each letter slowly. D-O-N-T-A-E J-E-N-N-I-N-G-S. I swore I felt like dying at that moment, but I couldn't bring myself down. I had anticipated this moment, so I had to be strong, even if it was the hardest thing for me to do. I slid the paper to the officer, waiting for her to give me the okay to go through the metal detector and into the reception area.

"Dontae Jennings," she said. "What is your relationship with him?" I would've taken this as a normal question except for the look she was giving me and the tone that she was speaking in

"He's...he's my dad." She stood up, placing her hands on the desk, giving me a stern look. I didn't know what I did to this lady, but it was obvious I struck a chord somewhere.

"Come through the metal detector. Then, we gotta talk." I emptied my pockets and obliged, nervous as all get out. It was just me and her, so that made things even more eerie.

"Come over here to this room," she signaled to me. I walked into an office not knowing what was going to go down. I knew this was a maximum security prison, but I was ready to fight for my life if push came to shove.

"Shut the door behind you please." Again, I obliged to her orders. We stared at each other with no emotion on our faces. I honestly was scared to death, but I wasn't gonna show it. All of a sudden, she smiled and crossed her arms.

"You know I remember the first time when Dontae told me you were born. He was so happy, jubilant and joyful. He had a daughter and wanted to spoil you to death. He always bragged about wanting to have a daughter, and then he had you.

He swore up and down that he would do whatever it took to make sure that your life was better than his sisters. His two sisters were molested by their dad, until one of them, his sister Karla, stabbed him to death in his sleep at 14. I don't know what happened between then and when you were born, but he became a clone of his father. I was in New Jersey for over a decade when your mother was killed."

"Whoa, whoa, whoa. How do you know all this? I'm not gonna lie, you starting to creep me out." She again smiled. "Star, I'm your auntie. Your Auntie Diane." Everything completely stopped in my world. I never met his side of the family. The people he brought around were the evil people in his life that he called his family. They were all drug dealers, gang bangers and low lifes. I see now that his actions had shunned away his whole family.

"Tell me you're not joking? Promise me you're not joking? I've been through too much shit to have my life played with."

"Baby girl. One thing I don't do is lie. Now, can I hug my niece for the first time ever?" I began to breakdown and she consoled me. It truly felt genuine, so I knew it was real. I couldn't believe this. I came home for merely one thing and now, so many wounds were being healed that I had completely became oblivious to over time. God was indeed working his magic.

"Auntie," I said muffled because of my emotion. "Can I go see my dad?"

"He's not here. He's in ICU at a nearby hospital." My heart dropped through the floor.

"Why?" As she took a deep breath, I knew it wouldn't be good.

"Your daddy developed cancer sometime back. Maybe around a year or so ago. His condition was getting worse and worse as time went on, so we transferred him up out of here and into a permanent hospice care. For prisoners, just picture a halfway house meeting a nursing home. I can take you to him if you'd like."

I was now confused. I didn't know what to do. In one instance, I wanted to see him. In another, I didn't wanna see him in the condition that he was in. It was quite possibly the hardest decision that I ever had to make.

"Ok auntie. Take me. I have to do this." "Let me get someone to cover for me and we'll be on our way." Immediately she called for another officer to take her position as she was gonna escort me to the hospital to face what was left of my dad. It was crazy that he was now my dad and not just him. We made the drive to the hospital, which wasn't too far away.

Auntie talked life into me the whole way. I needed her words because I had that eerie feeling that a part of my life was about to be gone, even if it was a negative part of my life. After about 20 minutes, we pulled up to the medical center.

"Now before you come in sweetie, I want you to take a minute or two to gather yourself and your thoughts. I'll be right inside when you're ready."

"I got you." Auntie got out and left me to be by my lonesome. I didn't need to gather myself. I just had to prepare myself for what I was about to see. As she waltzed through the doors, I immediately bowed my head and prayed.

> *"LORD,*
>
> *All I ask is for the spirit of forgiveness to enter inside of me and I ask that your healing powers be active. In your son Jesus name I pray. AMEN"*

I arose out of the car and took slow steps to soak in this whole experience. The sky was still pretty, but it was getting darker as the sun was starting its descent. An ambulance was out front, with two EMT's sharing a laugh over I don't know what. Over to the east of the entrance, I heard the wails of a woman being consoled by her family.

"MY BABY!!! MY BABY!!! LAWD, WHY DID YOU TAKE HIM LAWD???!!! WHY???!!!"

I couldn't even imagine her pain. No parent should have to bury their child. Also, seeing death is something that I didn't do well with. Before I walked through those doors, I took a deep breath. *"God, be with me,"* I whispered. With that, I walked in and found my auntie. She was the law, so there would be no questioning us walking through the halls.

We went on our way, headed to see my dad. As we hit the elevator, she pressed number 3. I always thought of three as a lucky number, so I was hoping to see something good. The doors of the elevator slid open to the Intensive Care Unit and I immediately paused upon taking my first steps out. It was an eerie feeling on this floor.

"You alright baby?"

"I'm just trying to keep myself together auntie. I hate hospitals."

"Face your fear," as she grabbed my face to let me know.

"It ain't nothing but chewed up grass." I shook my head in a positive nod and we made our descent down the hall until we reached room 3802. I hadn't even walked inside yet, but a feeling of death came over me.

"Are you ready sweetheart?"

"Yea Auntie. I can't get any more ready than this. Just let me go in by myself."

"You sure baby?"

"Yea. I gotta do this for me."

"Ok baby. You have to do this for you and I respect it." I wiped the remnants of tears from my face. I walked in my dad's room and slid the curtain back, seeing a mere shell of a man. Along with that, there were a hoard of nurses around him.

"Daddy?" Everyone turned around and I saw him cut his eyes. He was out of it, but I think he was coherent enough to know who I was. I walked up to his bed. The nurses had parted like the Red Sea, not interrupting or trying to stop me at all.

"He has never had this look in his eyes," said one of them. They weren't lying either. For someone with tubes running down their throat and all throughout their body, his eyes were doing a lot of talking. It was literally like he had seen a ghost. I leaned down over him and put my hand on his forehead. In his weakened state, he tried to raise his left hand. I softly gripped it. I didn't know what to say. I was steady stuck in this moment.

"Do you want to say something Dontae? Here, write." One of the nurses held up a notepad while the other nurse held a pencil in his hand, helping him get a semi decent grip. Dad's eyes were still locked in on me. I didn't know if his worst nightmare had come true, or was it a meeting he prayed for. In this instance, I understood why.

"Dontae. Do you want to write?," the nurse asked him again. He didn't look good and I feared the worse. Suddenly, he cut his eyes towards the notepad. With assistance, he got his hand up into the writing position. The pencil hit the pad and he began to scribble. It was sloppy at most, but he made out the word "I'm." He continued on, looking weaker and weaker. It was sad to see that doing something so simple such as writing was causing him an extreme amount of pain. I started to cry as this was one of the most unbearable things that I ever had to witness. The letters started to form. S-O-R-R-Y. Then, the pencil dropped. He looked at me with his cold, barren eyes. His right hand began to lift as if he was trying to reach out to me. The waterworks were on Niagara Falls at this point and my emotions were on high. The moment was here and this may have been my last opportunity to mend what was a terrible relationship between us both.

"Daddy? Daddy?" Then, the worst noise any human could possibly hear came ringing through my ears. He flatlined.

"**DADDY!!!**," I screamed. One nurse snatched me away as the others tended to him, trying to bring him back. I was fighting to get back there, but it was to no avail. Auntie had grabbed me as well and these two sisters had death grips on me.

The way I was kicking and screaming, you would've thought I was a five year old being abused again. It's funny how life goes doesn't it? The same way I fought my dad to keep him off of me was the same way I was fighting now to be with him when he needed me the most. I kept screaming and screaming for my daddy to the point that my voice sounded like a demon was trying to escape my soul. Finally, I was on the floor with them both on top of me.

"Calm down baby. It's okay," I heard my auntie through my demonic screams. I just began to cry uncontrollably as the pain of his passing hit me. My aunt had drug me out of the room and the nurse came over for condolence. All of a sudden, another one of the nurses came out.

"Karla, I'm so sorry. He's gone." The demonic screams then went to full out exorcisms. I was wailing in my aunt's arms in disbelief. She was crying, I was hysterical and my daddy was gone. The worst part about all of this is that the words

"I forgive you" never had the chance to come off of my lips. I hesitated. My emotions had caused me to miss out. I didn't want to forgive my dad for him. I wanted to forgive him for me. That way, maybe there was a chance that I could build up a love for him again. I cried tears for I don't know how long. It was obvious that my aunt had been up here several times to see him before, because they knew her and knew her well.

My soul was now an open wound that was going to fester at some point. I put the bandage on the wounds that my dad caused me many years ago. Now, I would have to live with an infection of taking too much time to make things right. All had finally started to calm down. They had covered my dad's body up. I didn't stick around a second after that, as I chose to go back to the car and sit in total darkness. I continued to cry my eyes out as I felt like the lowest piece of human scum. I felt alone again in the world. Auntie finally got back to the car and joined me after a half hour or so.

"Star. I love you. I know right now is hard, but I'm gonna tell you something that you probably didn't realize in there. What's my name?" I kind of looked at her weird. "Diane," I said with a muffled voice.

"What did I tell you your daddy's sister Karla did years ago?" I tried to fathom it, but my mind was in a million places and I couldn't think straight.

"Think about it niece? Think about long and hard?" After a good two minutes of silence, I began to breathe normally and really think. Then, my head whipped around.

"It was you. You killed your daddy."

"And every day I live with regret for doing it."

"But, but auntie. How'd you get away with that?"

"We were in poverty, just like you growing up. The projects can be the most beautiful place and at the same time the most long suffering place on earth. Daddy ran drugs, prostitutes, moonshine and whatever else you could think of that could make money. People were always in and out of unit 8B. It just so happened that the same night I killed him, a dope fiend came kicking in the door looking for him. He walked in right past us. When I say us, I mean me and ya other auntie Kelly. We were hiding in a closet, in the hallway that was leading to the bedroom. We were terrified. Not for the dope fiend, but for what we knew he was gonna find. Just as we heard him scouring through the bedroom, we made a dash for the front door."

"**HEY!,**" he yelled. Neither one of us turned around as we burst through the front door and dipped down the hall.

"**COME HERE G** DAMMIT!!!**" I heard his footsteps behind us as we hit the stairwell. We were going as fast as our young teenage legs could go.

"**HE KILLED ROACH!!! HE KILLED ROACH!!!,**" my sister started yelling out loud as we hit a group of brothers shooting dice in the stairwell.

"**WHERE THEY AT???!!!,**" one of them said as we kept booking it. After two more flights down, we heard the distant commotion a few stairways up. That was followed by a series of gunshots. That's when we stopped. We were transfixed in place long enough to watch the nine or ten bangers who were hustling down the stairs themselves. They rolled past us without a care in the world.

"Let's go up," Kelly told me. "I didn't want to, but I obliged. When we got to the spot where we passed them bangers, there we found him. They had put a good eight shots in homeboy. In simpler terms, they fucked him up. We then proceeded to head back to the apartment. I had stabbed my dad in the bathroom while he was shaving. Fourteen times to be exact. The bathroom door was wide open, letting me know that he had found my dad. It put his fingerprints on the door knob and saved me and your auntie's ass. I never told anyone that story until this very day. I never wanted anyone to know, but I feel that with you, I would be disrespectful not to share it. I told you upon meeting you that my name was Diane. That's my middle name and that's what I go by. Karla died that day along with my daddy and I wanted her to stay dead." I really didn't know what to say. I was in utter disbelief. My auntie. A murderer?

"Where was my dad at?"

"He had already ran off from home many moons ago. He had so many fights with daddy it was ridiculous. He got tired of that shit and figured that he could do bad by his damn self. So he left and lived as a runaway at seventeen. I knew where he would be, so did your auntie. But our daddy didn't know shit."

I leaned back in that seat trying to take everything all in. I was an emotional wreck. I wanted to run into the arms of my husband, but I couldn't, seeing that he was ten thousand miles away. This here was the shit that nightmares were made of. I felt like dying right now. Auntie pulled off and drove me back to the prison. Once there, she just sat with me in the car.

"Baby, you know if you need to you can stay with me tonight."

"I'm good auntie. I need to just be alone and absorb everything that happened tonight. I'll be okay. Once I hit the open road, music will calm me down."

We hugged outside of that car for what seemed like eternity. It was much needed at this point in time, seeing that she was the only family I had. We exchanged numbers and it was time for me to head off back into my own world. After stopping at a local eat joint to put some food in my stomach, I finally started my three hour journey back to Wichita at 12:47 a.m.

The drive was long and quiet. I left the music off, just trying to focus on the road and getting back to the hotel. I was wired up emotionally, so I wasn't worried about sleep trying to sneak up on me. Two hours into the trip and everything was moving along at what seems like a snail's pace. My phone began to ring and an unknown number popped up.

Me: "Hello"
Carl: "Love. How are you?"

Me: "Not too good hun. My dad passed tonight."

Carl talked with me the entire way back to the hotel. He did his best to comfort me in my time of need, but it wasn't enough. It felt good to hear his voice, but I yearned for something more at the time. He was in Hong Kong, living it up, enjoying the life of a sailor. Things had been going good on his end from the few weeks he had been out to sea. Just like always, the usual had already happened. Somebody had gotten caught fucking on the boat. People had acted out in Hawaii on the very first port visit and the Samoans beat the shit out of them.

The quality of the food had diminished aboard ship as the powder eggs, block ham, and everyday chicken and potatoes had become the norm. Yea, that was the Navy for you.

The letters say it all. U.S.N.A.V.Y. **U S**tupid. **N**ever **A**gain **V**olunteer **Y**ourself. I had been there and done that. It was fun, but it wasn't anything that I would do again. I made it back to the hotel a short time before four in the morning. I was dead to the world at this point. All I wanted to do was see the bed and plop down on it.

I hit the elevator and it seemed like it took forever to arrive on the 7th floor. Once those elevator doors opened up, I drug myself a few doors down to my room. I entered the room and just fell out on the couch. I didn't close my eyes, because I didn't want to fall asleep there. I needed a full mattress with the day that I had. Also, I knew if I didn't take my clothes off, I would wake up with them sticking to me. Once I got my second wind, I undressed all the way down to my bra and panties, and got under those sheets with the quickness.

"Fuck," I said. My crazy ass had to get back up to cut out the lights. It was only eight steps away, but it seemed like eternity. I drug myself to the switch and came back to the bed. I tried to go to sleep, but my emotions quickly took over as I continuously cried my eyes out. I wanted to stop, but I couldn't. I was now stationary for good and everything was hitting me all at once. It was a terrible feeling. A lonely and empty one.

I felt like this was the year 2012 all over again. I was going into a situation on a solo tip and I didn't have any backup. Shit had hit the fan and the fan wasn't running out of power any time soon from the looks of it. By the time I looked up, the clock had read 5:02 a.m. I couldn't cry anymore, because I was all out of tears.

"Thank you God," I whispered as I closed my eyes. Why would I thank God in a time like this you ask? It was simple. It was easy to thank Him when things were on the up and up, and going well. However, the true test of any individual is

when they can thank Him or give Him some praise in the midst of a storm. No matter how hard it was for me to say what I said, it had to be done, and that was all to it. There was no ifs, ands or buts about it. I was now headed into dream world, hoping to wake up ready and anew.

Tomorrow came and I woke up renewed and refreshed around two in the afternoon. I called my job back in San Diego and they allowed me to extend my vacation, as a private service for my dad would be held in the prison chapel. He was still serving time upon his death, so he would be buried where the other prisoners were laid to rest. It wasn't like any other funeral. The people of the state paid for it. The casket was a simple wooden box. It wasn't extravagant, but it wasn't something that you would be disrespected by. His viewing was three days after his death. My auntie came and picked me up from the hotel and drove me to the prison. Trust me, I was grateful because that was one drive that I didn't want to make again. And believe me, anyone who would drive a total of six hours for a family member was someone I owed a lot too. I was flying back the next night and this would be the absolute last memory I would get of my dad.

We got to the prison at 7:30 p.m. sharp and headed straight for the chapel once inside. Upon arrival, we stepped through the double doors. I had to pause for a minute and soak in the experience. It was crazy to say the least. It reminded me of the churches in the black neighborhoods across America. Here at the prison, the prison was just that. A prison. However, the chapel looked like something carved out of the side of a giant emerald mountain.

In the hood, the buildings and homes could look like they were hit with a nuclear blast. The church in the same community would look like a billionaire's mansion. I never understood that. If the church loved God so much, why did they let their surrounding neighborhoods fall apart?

"Embrace this moment," my aunt told me.

"Yea. I got you Auntie." I heard her, but I was still in awe. Struck from all the green emerald everything that seemed to line this place. When I came back to reality, things got back into focus real quick. There I was, standing in the aisle way, looking down at the casket. This felt eerily similar to a book I read entitled "The Writers Block." In it, the main character's girlfriend had passed. Like me, he was standing at the doors, looking down at his deceased loved one. I took a deep breath, soaking up any emotion that was left inside of me. Don't cry is what I told myself. I felt my aunt's hand come upon my shoulder.

"Go," she whispered. I looked over my shoulder at her. She just shook her head up and down. I turned around and began walking down to my father's casket. With each step, it became harder and harder to soak up the emotion. He had a white sheet over him, covering all except for his head and part of his neck. I got up to his casket, staring down at him, not believing that this moment was real. I turned around to look for my aunt. She was gone. Nowhere in sight. At first, I wanted to run. Then, I remembered. He's dead. I don't have to run anymore. And truthfully, I didn't need to run from this moment. I turned back around and stared at him once more. I touched his forehead, withholding my tears, because it's only so much you can cry.

"Dad, if you can hear me, wherever you are at, know that deep down. I forgive you, and I love you." Years ago, those words would have been impossible for me to say. Now, I was mature mentally. I finally felt like God had truly forgiven me. They say He can't forgive you unless you have the power to forgive. That's a true statement, but many look at it in a shallow text.

What he is really saying is to be loved by me, you have to love yourself. What I mean by that is this. Forgiveness is done out of good heartedness and love. If you love yourself enough as Jesus loves you, then you are willing to exonerate that love to someone else. We all fall short of each other as a people. Let's take God out of the equation for a minute. Love brings life. In life, people hurt us.

Hate brings death. In life, death brings misery. You have to decide what you would rather live with. Forgiveness of the heart and expressing love to your fellow person. Or, grudge holding and bringing death upon yourself. Not in the physical sense, but in the spiritual sense. I for one enjoyed my life and I hoped my dad was enjoying his.

"Goodbye Dad," as I gave him one last glance. Those were my final words and I placed a kiss to his forehead. As I was walking out of the chapel, I heard what sounded like a bang coming from the overhead. I whipped my head around, looking for whatever made that noise. The first thing I thought about was the show "Ghost Adventures." It freaked me out. However, when I looked back down towards the casket, maybe it was my eyes playing tricks on me, but it seemed as if my daddy was smiling.

Indeed, he had heard me and I believed he had told me that he would see me later. I walked out into the waiting arms of my auntie and hugged her for what seemed like eternity. Kansas, it had been real, but it was time to get back to San Diego. This month was damn near done and I for one was glad. The lesson was learned. A wound can heal on its own. If you put a band-aid on, however, the process can occur quicker, decreasing the risk of infection and future pain.

2 JUNE

The month of June rolled around faster than I had expected. My last call from Carl was on the first of the month. He told me that they were preparing to enter The Persian Gulf. Sitting on the other side of the military now, I was definitely scared.

It's one thing when you're in. You're surrounded by a bunch of other people with all sorts of skills. You know that whatever goes down, a ship is somewhere in the vicinity, having your back, ready to blow the draws off of any adversary who dares come at you. As a military spouse, however, it's fucking mind wrecking. You know every danger that your husband and 6,000 other folks are gonna face. But, because you can't experience it, your mind goes on a field trip every 30 minutes, contemplating about what is going on. You have the times where the communications go down and you won't hear from your loved one for days or sometimes even weeks. You have the news, but they will never give you the actual factual on a story, so you can't rely on them. To sum it all up in simpler terms, the shit was nerve racking.

Despite all of it, I couldn't let it stress me out to the point of all out depression. My husband needed me to be mentally strong and hold things down on the home front while he was holding it down out there. I wanted to get out and about. I hadn't really taken any personal time for myself since Carl left.

Between a growing fetus in my belly, work, my dad and just handling personal business, I really didn't have the opportunity to indulge in some genuine good times. I figured I might as well get it in before I became bigger than a house. It was Saturday morning and music was on my agenda. I cleaned up the house, blasting some old Plies. I know he wasn't the world's first pick for a rapper, but dude did have some joints. I know my neighbors were upset, but I could give two cares. This is what you did on a Saturday morning. Clean the house and blast your favorite music in the process. It was the black folks way.

I scrubbed, vacuumed and all out deep cleaned the house. Hell, I could've put my place up for auction on Home and Garden if I wanted too. I finished up everything around 11:30 and just bummed out eating peanut butter ice cream, while watching an old college football game of when the Jayhawks were actually good. It was the classic where we loss to Missouri while ranked #2 in the nation.

Desmond Briscoe, Aqib Talib and Todd Reesing had the state on fire. I wish they could've stayed forever, because we ain't be relevant since, and probably won't be for the next 50 years. This game and others lasted for the next couple of hours, as ESPN Classic took over my life. Then, I woke up. I didn't remember falling asleep, but I do know that when I looked up at the clock, it was 5:48, and the Texas-Texas Tech game from 2008 was showing.

"**SHIT!!!**," I yelled out loud. I didn't mean to do this, but I did. And now, I was hungrier than a hostage. I jumped up in the same beat up t-shirt and sweats I cleaned the house in, grabbed my keys and shot out to my whip. It was a quick ten minute drive to Lefty's Chicago Pizzeria in Hillcrest. This fat girl needed 2 pizza puffs and an Italian Beef. Actually, I really didn't need all of that, but the pregnancy cravings were kicking in. At least that's what I thought. So if I had to indulge, it might as well be with some real Chicago style food.

I took my time while there. Sitting down at the furthest table in the back, I could take time to myself. Once my food came, I smashed everything. It was almost better than sex at this point. That's how hungry I was. After an hour of eating and drinking God knows how many sweet teas, I rose up and made my way towards the door.

"The Cubs are going to win the World Series in 2016 Star. Remember I told you here first." That was Brendan, the owner of the joint, talking to me from behind the counter as I was walking out. I chuckled at him.

"Yea right. And Donald Trump is gonna be the President of the United States."

"Be careful what you wish for," laughing as he waved goodbye.

"Have a good one Brendan."

"You too Star." I started the drive home and saw Hillcrest for what it was. A hidden gem. Along with the North Park section of San Diego, this was the area of the city where you could guarantee that you would get some good food and that no one would bother you. Many, in spite of their love for food, were skeptical about coming to this side of the city because it had the highest gay population out of anywhere in the city. I had no problem with any of them.

They didn't bother me, so I didn't bother them. As long as they treated me well, then I treated them the same way. I arrived home and let out a huge yell on the couch from being stuffed. It was only 7:04, but I didn't operate on black folks time or like a normal woman. I liked to be ready ahead of time and inside of a place when I planned on being there. I soaked myself in a nice, strawberry scented bubble bath with candles lit all around me. It was soothing to my soul, my body and hopefully the fetus inside of me. The water was good and hot, just how I liked it. Carl personally hated taking baths with me. The first time he experienced one with me, I got inside first and watched him let out the biggest yell ever when his foot hit the water. He couldn't handle it.

It was funny to me, but he was literally traumatized. It took him a good ten minutes before he even eased all the way down in the tub. He would always ask why in the good hell would I run bath water that was 4,000 degrees fahrenheit. He would always talk about how I was trying to boil the sin out of my soul and dirt off of my skin.

Men just didn't get it because, well, they were men. If they could, their simple asses would simply soap up a rag, wash their balls off and go on about their day. But let our entire body, including the love box not be clean, and they weren't trying to do anything with us. I got out, dried up and headed to the bedroom so I could let the fan finish the drying off process. I eventually got up and got my gear ready for the night. A simple black dress with black heels. It was only 8:17, so I had some time to blow. I got dressed in the huge mirror located in my bedroom.

As I got my dress on, I stopped. The reflection in the mirror was as if I were 17 years old. I simply stared at myself. After a good minute, I realized one thing. I was always beautiful. I let the words of others and my own personal trials tell me that I wasn't. The crazy thing is that I believed it. Now, I was all grown up and I knew that my beauty lie more than skin deep. I threw on my heels and headed to the bathroom for one last brush down of the hair. It was all mines and I was proud of that. I didn't knock women who wore weave, but it felt good to have some naturally good shit on your head.

I glossed up my lips and that was it. I wasn't too big on make up. Quite honestly, I didn't need it. Every now and then, you may catch me using eye shadow. For the most part, I preferred to keep it 100% me. No, I wasn't looking for a man because I had one. However, I understood their plight when it came to us. We wear heels, falsifying our height. We wear fake hair, with a lot of us damn near bald when it comes off. We decorate our face, with some of us doing it too much to the point where we look like a circus clown. We got push up bras that push our titties up, making them look bigger than what they actually are. Yea, I totally understood men. We say we want a real man, but we sure as hell do a lot of false advertising. To each its own though.

I left the house, jumped in the car and headed down to the Four Points Sheraton off of Aero Drive. Jazz night was in full effect and that music was soothing to my soul. I let John Legend take me the 10 minutes up the 163 until I arrived. I got there right before 9:30 which was perfect. It was already people here, but not enough to where you couldn't get a seat.

The show had already started. I was already getting the stares from the men as I know damn well I was drop dead gorgeous. Not having a ring was going to be my downfall tonight as I know there would be at least one man in here that tried me. Hell, even if I did have a ring, that didn't mean a damn thing nowadays. That was an invite to try even harder. I sat down in the far corner of the venue, drinking on a glass of cranberry and pineapple juice that I got from the bar. I was soaking in the entire atmosphere as the big boy on the drums was getting it.

He was a heavy set brother who from my guess, weighed at least a good 350 He was bald and black as some licorice, but he was kicking ass up there. You could literally see how hard he was going with the sweat bubbles that were congregating and boiling on the top of his dome. I jammed along with the rest of the crowd as the band began to play a rendition of Mark Morrison's "Return of the Mack.

"Excuse me miss, another drink?," the waiter asked.

"No thank you," I said, as I kept jamming by myself. People were now up dancing and I for one wasn't sitting down any longer. I jumped up to the dance floor, immediately getting my two step on. An old man quickly jumped up in front of me and started grooving with me. I didn't mind this seeing that he was at least 50 years my senior and I didn't have to worry about a man that was probably close to his death trying to holla at me or anything else. We were all grown in here and that's how I preferred my outings.

Grown and sexy. The night was a blaze from that point on. All throughout the night, renditions of old school 70's, 80's and 90's jams were played to the max. The singers who hit the stage did a great job as well. I couldn't remember that last time that I had this much fun by myself. The night wrapped up for me around 1 a.m, and most of the crowd had the same idea as they were heading towards the exit as well. I was getting to the point where I needed to catch me some sleep. However, I took advantage of the departing crowd and had me a few more cran' and pineapple drinks before I left for the night.

As I got to my car, I leaned the seat all the way back and just closed my eyes, silently embracing the great night that I had. My heels were somewhere in the back as I had taken them off well before I even walked to the car. As I reflected on this great night, I also reflected on the dancing me and my mom used to do.

"Baby what you doing?"

"I'm twirling mom."

"No no baby. Let me show you this two step that I learned while your mommy visited Chicago."

"What's Chicago mommy?"

"It's a big city where people have fun. Now, grab mommy's hand." I was five at the time. My dad was gone from the house and had been for some days. His disappearance actually lasted three weeks. On a cool, breezy Saturday in November, my mom taught me the art of two stepping in our living room. I didn't have a clue as to what I was doing, but in my mind, I was getting it.

"Your good baby." I smiled. I had the approval of my mom and I was a dance princess. Then, she let my hand go and took a step back to look at me.

"Look at my baby. I'm so proud of you. Keep dancing and mommy will be back. I kept doing the five year old broke two step for the next five minutes, until I started to wonder where my mom had went. I went to the stereo and hit the power button on it, cutting the music off. In the distance, I heard what sounded like muffled cries. I walked in the hallway and noticed that her room door was shut. I pressed my left ear to the door. That's when

I heard her bellow out in a loud scream that didn't sound good at all.

"Mommy," I said in a soft tone as I opened the door. She looked up at me, wiping her face.

"Come in baby." I went in the room, shut the door and joined her on the bed. As her sniffles continued, she put her arm around me.

"I want you to remember something and never forget what I tell you. Mommy may not be here one day. And if mommy isn't here, I want you to remember that you never trade a good car that's proven to drive for a great car that runs on looks."

"Are we getting a new car mommy?" She laughed a little bit. "No baby no. Mommy wishes. But remember I told you this."

"Do we have a good car mommy?" "Yea baby. We have a good car. But mommy once had an old car that ran great, until I traded it in for something new on the lot. I'll always regret it."

"I'll buy you a new car mommy."

"You will baby?," she asked with a smile, with her tears almost non existent.

"Yea. I'm gonna get one million dollars and buy you a nice car." She hugged me and I hugged her back, not realizing that there was a deeper message in her words.

"Come on baby. Let mommy show you how to make some grits." I was ecstatic. Grits were my favorite meal. I didn't know what a grit was at five years old, but I always knew that whenever my mom   cooked them, I would always eat two bowlfuls. When she showed me how to make them that day, I vividly remember one thing that stood out.

"Now baby, it doesn't matter what you put in your grits. You can put bacon, shrimp and cheese in them. You always flavor them with butter and salt. **BUT DON'T YOU EVER PUT SUGAR IN YOUR GRITS!!!** People who put sugar in their grits are spawns of satan." That ended up being one of the biggest life lessons that I ever retained. I shot down Aero Drive and bent the corner until I hit the 163 South. I was fully aware of everything around me and I could tell that I would rest easy. As I hit the 8 freeway, heading West towards Rosecrans, I saw that everything was chill for a Saturday night. There were two cars in front of me up in the distance and it looked like it was going to be a stress free ride home. Suddenly, one of them swerved to the right and veered back left, plowing into the center divider. The other car had just avoided that one and was now literally parked in the middle of the freeway.

I sped towards the right lane and parked on the shoulder, parallel to the accident on the opposite side. Immediately, I called 911, as I know this wasn't going to turn out to be good for whoever was in that car. It literally looked like The

Incredible Hulk balled the car up and tossed it in a fit of rage. I was literally screaming into the phone for someone to come help while watching the man who swerved to avoid being hit get out and run across the highway to help whoever was inside. I was at the point in life where tragedy of any sorts affected me deeply. My weakness wasn't my emotions. My weakness was death. No matter how strong I had gotten since being with Carl, it was something that I still battled with on a regular.

I was more emotionally attached to the dead than the average person. I don't know if it was due to what happened to my mom, or some of my foster siblings, but death or the fear of it did something to me. How my now husband stuck with me with all of my mental baggage, I had no idea, but I was indeed grateful. I sat in the car waiting for the ambulance to show up. It was obvious that whoever was inside that balled up vehicle was dead.

I watched in horror as the man in the other vehicle, along with another person who stopped were trying to pull the individual out of the car. The way the car was bent up, however, it was damn near impossible. I started to rub on my leg. The surgical scar that was there reminded me of the night in which my life took one of the most dramatic turns for the worst. That Halloween night of 2013 was one of those nights where neither one of us thought anything could go wrong. That's how perfect things had gone. We had a great time on a yacht. The interaction with different creeds and personalities was amazing. I was his Cat woman, literally and figuratively. He was my Julius Caesar. My king for the night and more importantly, my king for a lifetime.

We danced the night away. Our smiles and eyes told a story that others could only guess. This was more than a party. This was life at its highest peak for the both of us. 1:30 in the morning came faster than we had both expected. That's how life always went when you were having fun. The boat docked back on Harbor Drive, and at that point, all we wanted to do when we hit the car was hop in, head home and go to sleep. We both had to go to work in a few hours. Pacific Highway was dead to the entire city of San Diego at this hour. From what I remember, we were the only ones on the road. Music was blaring as we were laughing and engaging with each other wholeheartedly.

"So when we get married, let's say." And with those last words from Carl, our world went black. *"Carl,"* I whispered, as I was dazed and confused, not knowing exactly where I was at. There was an eerie feeling as the wind howled and nothing illuminated anything over here except the lights from Jack in The Box. Through my blurred vision and blood pouring from my forehead, I could see the remains of what was the car. That once sexy black Chevy Impala sittin on dub deuces was now a dead duck sitting on it's top. I managed to fight through my disillusionment and roll to my side.

"**FUCK!!!**" My leg was in excruciating pain. As I reached my hand for it and looked down, I could clearly see a big ass bone sticking out. The adrenaline, if I had any, had worn off. I wanted to scream for Carl's name, but I was going too much into shock at the sight of my body. I started to weep tremendously as I thought this was it. I was gonna die right here on the spot from blood loss and trauma. With all the shit I had been through in my life, it was going to end on the side of a road. I couldn't hear any ambulance or emergency services in the distance. No one was here to save us.

"**STAR!!!**" His blood curdling scream in the distance shook me to my core. He was severely injured, crawling, more like dragging himself over to me. He was obviously in terrible condition like myself, if not worse. I couldn't do much but cry as I dropped my bloody left hand on the concrete hoping he would reach me. I wanted to help him so bad, but I was helpless my damn self. I watched him fight with every ounce of strength he had to reach my hand, screaming with every inch that he moved.

If the concrete was thirsty, it would have been full off of our blood. After what seemed like forever, he finally reached me. He extended out to me with the little strength he had and clutched my hand. That touch made me flash back to our first moment together where I literally told him to fuck off. I was just so happy that he didn't listen to me.

"Baby it hurts," he told me.

"I know babe. I know. Hang in there for me. For us." I wish I could've said it louder, but it was cold and my body felt like it was shutting down.

"Carl? Carl?" I wasn't getting any response. "Carl?" I began to cry as his head was planted on the concrete. I started to fear that he was dead. In that moment, I felt empty. I wondered what Jesus was gonna look like. Then, I flashbacked to him. That man. That man who was supposed to be my daddy. He was laughing at me as I was down and out, helpless and vulnerable. I hadn't made amends with him back then and I still hated him with a passion.

His evil face seemed like it was right in front of me, laughing at me with a demonic tone. Fuck that, I thought. If I was gonna die, then I was gonna go out a fighting bitch. My adrenaline rushed as I mustered up the strength to turn over and cover him. Screams assisted me as this was the most painful shit ever. I felt my leg snap, crackle and pop, but I didn't care. I was going to be there for the man that loved me and saved this once useless piece of human life. I whispered *"I love you"* repeatedly to reassure him if he could hear me. I used the little strength that I did have to shake him. Suddenly, I saw his fingers move.

"Star," he whispered.

"Yes baby?" His head raised ever so slow and his lifeless eyes looked up to mine. I just knew that whatever he was about to whisper would be the last words that he would ever speak. As I started to hear the sirens coming up the streets and drawing nearer, he said something that etched in my heart forever.

"The first time I saw you. I knew. I knew you were the one." He passed out right after that. I wanted to shake him, but I was completely out of energy. Then, my world went dark once again. I woke up in pain and saw nothing but bright lights. This was heaven I thought. It didn't look like I had expected it too look. It had brown ceiling tiles and loose wiring. There was a 32 inch television on the wall.

The Bible had said that God prepared mansions for his people. I must have just made the cut and got placed in the section 8 joints on the far Eastside of The Holy City. I guess this was the price I had to pay for my sins. I was out of it something serious. I turned my head, but it hurt like hell, so I immediately returned it to its original position. I was high as a kite and didn't remember much about how I had gotten here. I cut my eyes to see that my leg was elevated in the air in a full cast. Tubes were up my nose and an IV was stuck in my arm. Simply, I was done for. My eyes closed and I slipped into a long sleep.

"Ms. Jennings? Ms. Jennings?" I opened up my eyes slowly, trying to make out whoever these folks were surrounding me.

"W-W-Where am I?" I got a smile from a bald head brother with glasses who looked like Tommy from Martin. I guess my mans did have a job.

"You're in recovery ma'am. You had successful surgery." I didn't even fathom what he said. "Could you say that again sir?"

"Ma'am, you were in an accident. A very serious one. You are lucky to be alive. Just rest up and take it easy. My nurses will check on you throughout the night to ensure all of your needs are met." My head was pounding and the mention of the word surgery made my headache even worse.

"Doc. What about my boyfriend? What about my husband?" He smiled at me.

"Nurses, could you give us a minute alone?" They stepped out, and it was me and this stranger all alone. Luckily for me, I maintained a level of sanity and didn't go into a state of fear. The last bald headed man that I was left alone with was of course...him.

"Ma'am, he's okay. At the sight of the crash, next to the deceased drunk driver, a box was found. It was wrapped in a bow. Tight I may add. Here."

Through all the pain I was enduring, I clamored at this treasure that he pulled out of his pocket. It was a ring box and the word emotional was an understatement. A tab was attached to it. I never was big on anything material wise, seeing how materials were the least of my worries growing up. I opened it up, only to find nothing. Instead of being shocked, I immediately looked at the tab.

"*His and Hers. Yours and Mines. Ours.*" My eyes began to water as I couldn't believe what I was reading.

"Doc, where are the rings?"

"We don't know. The only thing that the EMT who brought it to me found was the box and its top. The jewelry? Well, it's somewhere out there." I looked down into my hands, staring into this empty box which was a representation of my soul right now. It was empty. Not for any missing jewelry. It was empty because the love of my life wasn't here in this room with me.

Memories of that night still haunted me when I saw the sight of any accident. I sat there in my car, looking at the flashing lights of the fire trucks, police cars and the flares that were on the ground. I clearly seen the medics pull out an individual and put a sheet over their body. Damn, I thought. Another one bites the dust. They probably died prematurely as well, not even getting the chance to excel at life. The cops, nor the medics paid me any attention as I slowly drove off and headed back towards the house.

My mind was going a million miles per hour as that accident really took me back to a place that I didn't want to be at. I got in the bed that night, trying to let it go, but I couldn't for the most part. I cut on the fan, played jazz music, but nothing worked. Finally, I just said screw it and cut on the television. Instead of me watching it, it began to watch me. Infomercials were all that came on during this time of night. I was too lazy to turn to anything else. I rubbed my belly, just grateful that it wasn't me and my baby inside of that car. I couldn't even fathom losing the life inside of me. I was lucky just to have a life growing inside of me. To think that many years ago I was told that I would never be able to bare children. Now, I was almost three months pregnant, expecting my first child in some time.

I quietly began to smile. I wanted four. Four kids for the four lives that I felt never got to see life truly. My mom, my younger self, my teenage self and part of my adulthood. I know that sounded crazy, but that's the honest to God truth on how I felt. I felt like three separate people inside of me missed out on a lot because of my situation.

I owed it to myself and to my husband to give someone else the chance. I no longer thought about myself, because it was no longer about me. And truthfully, life isn't about any of us as individuals. Life is truly about giving to everyone else. I had to learn that the hard way. See, it's a difference in giving to feel complete and giving from your heart. What I gave men years back was to achieve a false sense of feeling complete. However, when I gave from the heart, which was giving Carl my heart, God rewarded me in ways that I couldn't believe. So whether or not you believe in God, or you clown those for believing in something you can't see, what holds true is that you reciprocate what you put out.

Do good and good will come back to you. I truly believed that and it definitely showed. I cut the television off and looked at the clock. 3:37 a.m. I decided to get up and walk across the street to 7 Eleven. It was a brisk cold night, and I know Carl would kill me for walking alone at this hour. However, I just needed to clear my head.

As I entered into the plaza off Midway in Point Loma, my first sight was that of a homeless man. He looked like he was sleeping pretty good as he had a twin sized box spring and a mattress, with a thick comforter. I know homelessness sucked, but he was making it look like the life to have. I continued walking until I got to 7 eleven. Right as I got to the doors, I stopped. What came over me? I truly could not explain it. I walked away and headed back towards the house. I jumped in my car and headed down two blocks. The Body Shop strip club was letting out, as it seemed this was old white man night. I pulled up to the drive through of Cotixan.

"Good morning. Can I take your order?"

"Let me get a surf-n-turf burrito, with extra shrimp, no pico de gallo. That's all."

"$10.37 at the window." I drove up to the window and waited patiently for a go to meal that I had fell in love with since the moment that I had moved out here.

"Here you go ma'am."

"Thank you." I peeled off and turned back on Rosecrans. The smell of this masterpiece in my passenger seat started to bring me back to a happy place. As soon as I got back to the house, I grabbed a plate and sat on the couch. With the first bite, I fell in love with something that wasn't named Carl.

I fucked that burrito up. The way I inhaled it, you would've thought it was Carl and not a stuffed tortilla. I threw everything away, put the plate in the sink and went to get in the bed. I looked at the clock to see it said 4:22. Yea, it was a late night, but I got through it, thanks to some Mexican food in a city that shut down every other city in America when it came to Mexican food. I got under the covers, smiled and closed my eyes. I was going to sleep with a renewed sense about life in general. All thanks to one delicious surf-n-turf burrito.

I woke up Sunday afternoon, at 12 o'clock on the dot, feeling good as ever. I didn't even wanna cut on the stove like I usually did on Sundays. Catfish and grits weren't on my agenda today. This morning, it would be Frosted Flakes with some almond milk. It took me back to watching Saturday morning cartoons when I was a little girl and my mom would say "I don't feel like cooking this morning. Eat this bowl of Tony's."

I poured me a nice, big bowl. When I say big bowl, I mean the man portion bowl. Carl ass would piss me off pouring over half of the box in a mixing bowl like Cube did on Friday. Now, I found myself doing the exact same thing. I carried my oversized bowl and went to pull the paper from the front door. Everything was fine. The weather was nice and the sun was magnificent as usual. I sat on the couch, whippin my paper open and indulging in this sugary madness. My focus immediately left off of my cereal bowl and to the headline that I was now reading. *"BELOVED NAVY CHAPLAIN DIES IN HORRIFIC CRASH."* My worst fears were confirmed as I continued reading. It was Father Dan, the same man who married me and Carl. My heart and world literally stopped. It was like seeing Floyd "Money" Mayweather lose in the boxing ring. You knew it could happen, but you doubted that you would ever see it. I continued reading on.

During the investigation, it was determined that one of his tires had blew out and he lost control of his vehicle. All I could do was sit back and say damn to myself. Why did the good always die before their time? I mean, we all gotta go, but it sucks when the ones who truly made an impact in people's everyday lives bounced out early. This Sunday had now turned into a very somber one, yet I couldn't sit in the house feeling sorry for myself. I finished off my bowl of cereal, jumped in the shower, threw on a beater, some shorts and rolled out in the whip. I wanted to just indulge in a drive and take in everything that made the city of San Diego special. My first stop was La Jolla as I took a chill pill at the shores. Up here, this is where the rich seemed to get richer.

This was the area of San Diego that many people dreamed of getting too. I took in the early morning sunlight and just reminisced on how good it felt to be whole again. With each breath, any part of the old me that was left was slowly disappearing. They say that pain is weakness leaving the body. Well, I embraced this pain.

Leaving the shores, I rolled over to the mall in the same area. I walked around, not too interested in buying anything. I was just there to people watch. I left a short time later and hit the 5 towards Mira Mesa. I had to get my Souplantation on.

I know I had just eaten a big ass bowl of cereal not even two hours ago, but this was my life. I was a fit girl with a fat girl appetite. I swear I could eat all day and not gain a pound. This was a relief as I didn't have to worry about losing my shape. I murdered three bowls of their wild mushroom soup. I know it was odd for a woman to love mushrooms, but I was weird like that. Hell if you give me a sausage and mushroom pizza, that thing wouldn't stand a chance.

I finished up a little bit after 12:30 and took the 25 or so minute drive down to Southeast San Diego. It was much different over here. There was the San Diego that the world knew with Sea World, The Zoo and Balboa Park. Then, there was the San Diego that most of the world wanted to ignore. Most people got the wrong impression about this side of town.

Chicago and New York had the high rise project buildings. Los Angeles was just Los Angeles, with its Blood and Crip lifestyle flashed all over television. Here, it wasn't your typical looking inner city. It was cleaner than most. Not a sparkling gem, but not filthy like many places. It had a more relaxed feel than most. However, that's where people got it twisted. They say never judge a book by its cover and they were most certainly right. Southeast was poverty stricken like any other hood in America. Blacks and Latinos were the primary around here as with the case of most inner cities. This part of the city had seen the worst of the worst in its heydey. From the infamous Syndo Mobb, to the Piru's who ran Skyline. San Diego had a dark history. I jumped off the 125 at Jamacha and took everything in. From Skyline, O'Farrell, Lincoln Park, down Logan Avenue I went. I passed by the world famous Imperial Barber Shop, which was the one barber shop that reminded me of the movies, because it felt more like a family session than getting your hair cut.

I passed Huffman's on my journey. It was a once poppin' soul food joint that was now closed. All that was left was the sign with the one missing F. Market Creek Plaza had the Food 4 Less that seemed more like an oversized night club with food rather than a general grocery store.

Family Dollar on 54th was the old FAMMART. I wasn't out here when that was in existence, but from the old stories people would tell me, the shit was poppin'. People used to line this place up with souped up cars in the parking lot. Local rappers shot videos here, people hustled here, all of that. Not to mention that Church's Chicken was right across the street, so you could eat that grease in a box and genetically modified chicken all while doing you. Right across from it was Tina's. Oh shit, lemme tell y'all about this place. So Carl went up in there one night. When he came home, or more like escaped back to the house, he was traumatized.

"**BABY!!! BABY!!!**" He came in the bedroom screaming.

"**WHAT???!!!,**" I turned over and yelled at his ass for waking me up outta my sleep.

"Babe, I swear on my momma. I went to that place Tina's and oh my God. Those old geezers tried to rape me. It was like…like...like a buffet, and my black ass was the last piece of food."

"**CARL SHUT THE FUCK UP AND BRING YO ASS TO BED!!! I'M TIRED!!! I DON'T WANNA HEAR THIS SHIT!!!**" He tried rubbing on me to woo me over, but he was off limits that night. If it's one thing I hated, it was being woken up out of my sleep for stupid stuff. However, I ended up going into Tina's one night and I swear his words were true. Those old cougars were really grabbing on everything that was 35 or younger. If you were in the age range of 21-35, you were liable to wake up handcuffed to a bedpost and smell grits, eggs, sausage, ham, toast and pancakes cooking. It was really serious like that.

I kept on rollin' down towards University. I hit a left at the light and shot on down towards Hillcrest. Hubby's barbershop was down this way. I stopped in and holla'd at his barber Rico to see how he and his wife were doing. Ladarius Green of the Chargers was in E Dubb chair. Marshall, as in Marshall

Faulk, the NFL Hall of Famer who owned this joint, was choppin' it up with Steve in the opposite corner.

Things were normal in here. Rambo was running his mouth while slicing someone up. Tony was just Tony. Mellow and laid back, handling his business with the clippers as usual. I finished up the convo with Rico and left up out of there, headed back to the house. It was almost four in the evening and I was now exhausted. I simply planned to come in the house and relax for the rest of the night. I made it home and plopped down on the couch. Before I would indulge in anything on my TV, I cut my computer on to check my e-mail. I smiled when I seen my baby's name in my inbox.

Hey love. I know you are holding down things back at home and I appreciate it. As for out here, things are about to get hectic as you know we headed to the gulf. The only good thing about that Middle East life is that tax free. But, you know that. What I am really writing you for besides the obvious is that I am a lil confused. This old civilian who runs MWR on the ship came up to me a few days ago asking me about you. Of course, I got a lil defensive, seeing that he was relatively new to the ship, and wondering how he knew my wife and what was his business. He stated when he first got out to Cali, he seen us out and about. He was nervous and scared. He didn't wanna approach and didn't know how to approach. Any who, he is in his early 50's, a vet and HE IS CLAIMING TO BE YOUR FATHER BABE!!! I'm trying to figure out what the hell is going on. He told me details about your life that only you have shared with me and he did get real emotional when talking about you, seeing that he harped over and over about trying to find his daughter that was taken from him years ago. I truly don't know what to believe. I know you been through a lot, but I can tell you my love that he is not bullshittin with the way he explained himself to me. His name is Donald Thurman. He's originally from Manhattan, Kansas. I will give you his e-mail address if you want it so y'all can rap a taste. I will say though, ever since he found out, I been getting taken care of real nice on this joint. I just want you to remain calm, be easy and let time run its course. I'm not saying he telling the truth, but I'm also saying that he may not be lying either. I LOVE YOU ALWAYS BEAUTIFUL.

CARL

What in the good hell do you say after receiving something like that? What are you supposed to feel inside as a person after hearing something like that? How do you react? I mean. Really? How do you just continue on with everyday life after hearing something like that? I cut everything off and just began to cry. Here I was again, back at square one. The minute Carl left, it seemed like everything in my life started to fall apart. This battle wasn't easy and I was now stressing something serious. My dad. Wait? I don't even know if he was my dad anymore. What if, I thought. What if I was hearing the truth? My dad was dead now. Or was he? The pastor who ultimately helped me in my most needy time of life was dead. My husband was gone. My mom was dead. I was pregnant when I thought I would never be. All I could do was sit there and sulk. I basked in the quietness of the house.

Carl had gotten me into the art of writing, as it was his way of de-stressing. I had nothing but the pen and paper now. I had folks to call if I needed to talk, but I liked keeping my personal business in house as much as possible. I went back to my bedroom and grabbed the notebook that I had in my closet. It was still in good shape, seeing that I only wrote once in it.

I carried it over to the bed, opened it up and smiled. What I wrote in it was a poem. I wrote it the night after me and Carl got back together, days after he attempted to take his own life at The Boardwalk. The love making that night was beyond incredible and I put my feelings on paper after I rocked his ass to sleep on our third go round.

<u>PENETRATION</u>

How he entered

Was uncommon than most

He broke in, obsessed with thievery

Stealing my soul, holding my heart hostage, for a ransom of love

I didn't wanna give in to his demands at first

But as I hurt, he ransacked my pain

My possessions were tossed, broken and scattered about

He grabbed me with both hands, asking, demanding

"WHERE IS IT!!! WHERE IS YOUR HEART???!!!"

I told him I don't have it, knowing it was hidden

He continued to ransack my place, searching high and low

Angry and gentle at the same time

Then he finally found it, I said

"DO WHAT YOU WANT WITH IT, JUST LET ME BE!!!"

He said

"I CAN'T DO THAT!!!"

He then proceeded to analyze it, bandage it up, make it beat a tune of B.B. King's blues

And right then and there, I knew what it felt like

TO BE A WOMAN

The words brought me joy, but it was very short lived, as I had another dilemma to deal with. Feeling as if I needed to get away, I slept and put myself in another world. I hoped that somehow this was a nasty dream and I would awaken just as normal as I was when the day first began. Unfortunately, it wasn't. More unfortunate was that it was 7:30 on the dot when I arose.

I didn't mean to sleep this long. I knew it would be hell trying to go back to sleep tonight as a sister had work in the a.m. My mind was still racing a mile a minute. Truthfully, I was lost. There was only one place this time of night where I would find out whether I was fit enough to fight this new battle. It was a place that brought me pain a long time ago. I had to revisit it in order to truly see what I was made of. I grabbed my keys and hopped in the whip.

"God, don't let me fall." Those were my last words as I peeled out of my parking spot and headed towards one of the darkest places in my life. There I was. 8:43 p.m. was the exact time. Monday was near and no one was out, seeing that everyone was probably preparing for bed to make that bread in the morning. I just stared into the darkness which was dimly illuminated by the lights up and down the pier. Indeed, I was back. However, I could take my time. I didn't have to run to save anyone. I just hoped that no one would have to save me. "THE BOARDWALK." There it was.

The words that shook my soul to its core. They were lit up in their usual bright neon lights. Tonight, it was myself vs. myself. As I got out of the car, flashbacks of when I was running to save Carl played over and over in my head. My hair blew in the breeze as I contemplated my action. I began to take slow steps towards the center of the pier. Even though I was alone, it felt like a million eyes were on me.

Every step I took seemed to feel like my last. Finally, I made it to the exact same spot where I dove out and saved my husband's life. I stood there and just closed my eyes for a minute, taking in the sounds of the ocean. The waves were crashing a little bit louder tonight. It almost sounded like the dead souls of a million people with shattered dreams were howling for another chance. I opened my eyes back up, looking out into nothing but darkness. I looked back towards the beginning of the pier. There was nothing. I looked towards the end of the pier. Besides the restaurant that sat at the end of it, nothing. I took a deep breath and looked towards the sky.

"Prep my soul Father in case I can't fly." I stepped up to the side of the pier. I planted my right foot on the middle beam. Grabbing the top beam, my left foot followed in the right's footsteps to join it. I looked down at the ocean while steady grasping the top beam with my hands. I wanted to feel what my husband must have felt the night that he attempted to take his life.

I wasn't at that particular point, but this string of unfortunate luck and circumstances had me wanting to face death head on, all in the name of appreciating life. They say that you have to face your fears, and I indeed was doing that. Slowly and steadily, I got my balance and placed my right foot on the top beam. I slowed down once doing so, seeing that my heart was beating on Mach 3. With extreme caution, I placed my left foot to join it. Staggering and lucky to catch my balance, there I stood. Somehow, I managed to bring my heart rate down. Why in the good hell was I doing this? I thought it was to face my fear. Once up there, I truly had no clue. All it took was one good gust of wind, an asshole coming behind me to push or just me getting nervous and falling. It would be a wrap for me.

The flashbacks of my life started to play in my head once again. My life was appearing in a fast paced, feature film movie. My pulse now began to increase. I began to sweat furiously. A tear ran down my left cheek like a slow caterpillar crawling along a branch. Amazingly, I was still standing perfectly on the top beam.

Finally, after a good minute and a half at least, I jumped back down to the pier. I don't know what caused me to do what I did, but it wasn't me. It was like something had taken control of my body. I for one would never just risk my life like that when I had the will to control myself. I was keeled over by the waist, crying my eyes out. I was lonely inside and out. The life had been sucked out of me once again. I fell down to the cold hard wood on my knees and elbows, screaming in agony from my experience. Then, in that moment, with water filled eyes, I looked back towards the beginning of the pier. Still down on the wood crying, I saw through my watery vision a white figure. I couldn't make it out completely, but it was glowing and had a steady, brisk walk. I rose up slowly, trying to make light of what I was looking at. Either I was trippin', or this San Diego night air had something in it that was causing me to hallucinate like a heroin addict. As the figure got closer, I made the figure out to be a woman.

"**MOM!!! MOMMY!!!**" I knew it was her from the body shape and the long hair that was draped past her shoulders. I was done crying and in a state of complete awe. The closer she got, the more I knew it was her. "**MOMMY!!!,**" I yelled out once more. That's when I noticed it. We were about 70 feet apart and I noticed that the figure didn't have a face. I was stuck in a trance, looking at this blank faced figure continuously walking. The figure passed me. I no longer was shouting mom because this wasn't her. My mom would've talked to me. I didn't know who this woman was or what her purpose was of being on this dock. I followed her with my eyes. As she got about twenty steps ahead of me, she all of a sudden stopped. The little wind that was out on this night seemed to stop, as well as the sounds of the ocean. They both became dead silent. I ain't gone lie. The term fearful was an understatement. I was almost at the point of pissin my pants. However, I stood my ground. Next, on some Damien Omen shit, her head turned around slowly as her body stayed in the same position. The piss started to run down my leg like the NIle River and the lump in my throat made it hard to breathe.

The woman then started taking slow steps towards me. I was transfixed and couldn't move at all. Each step created a thunderous sound that shot through the old wood. The waves began to crash with huge thuds and the wind suddenly got fierce. It was like a giant wind fan was on me, blowing hot air. She was now face to face with me. I was looking into a blank canvas, scared shitless. The woman's right hand began to raise and I no longer could feel my body. I was literally paralyzed standing up. The figure touched my face, running the fingertips of her fingers across my jaw. Then, her face came into form.

"**MOM!!!**" In a flash, she smiled and disappeared. The warm wind dissipated and the waves went back to sounding normal. I was again alone. I kept blinking repeatedly, just to make sure what I had observed was real. I felt my pants. Yep, they were pissy as all to be damned. The lump in my throat had disappeared and I could breathe normal again. My body no longer felt like it was locked up in a paralysis state. It was time to get the hell up out of here. As I turned around, I noticed a manila envelope on the deck beneath my feet.

Now, things had gotten beyond creepy. This was something straight out of a Stephen King novel. I picked it up, analyzed it and made my way to the car at a furious pace. I didn't stop for anything or anyone. Once I got in, I sped all the way home. Hell, you would've thought I was Flash Gordon on wheels. As I returned to the house, first thing was first. I had to drop all of these clothes and get in the shower. I hadn't pissed on myself since I was six years old. As the water hit me, I could still tell I wasn't myself.

I was still traumatized from everything that had happened earlier in the night. I marinated in the water as I felt that it was washing my sorrows and fear away. That shower ended up being 25 minutes long. I finished up and dried off under the fan in my bedroom. There was no flat ironing the hair or any of the usual woman tendencies tonight. I just wanted to sleep.

I headed into the living room and sat down on the couch, next to the manila folder. I saw the folder was now open. As if things couldn't have got any creepier. Immediately, I went for the gun in my safe under my bathroom sink. I can't speak for other women, but this sister here knew how to pump lead in someone's ass. Was anyone in the house? No. It didn't feel that way. However, paranoia was screwing with my mind something serious and I wasn't taking any chances tonight. I made a roundabout throughout the house on some James Bond shit before heading back in the living room. Picking up the folder, I was anxious to see the contents which I were holding in my hand. As I pulled everything out, I was left stunned and speechless. In it were three black and white photos. One was of me and my mother. I couldn't have been more than ten months old in the pic. She looked beyond joyful. It was a look that I could not remember seeing her have too much as I was growing up. I was knocked out to the world with a pacifier in my mouth. All of my baby pictures disappeared the moment I went into foster care. Seeing something like this made me grateful.

The second pic was of me at thirteen years old, sitting on the porch of my foster home, desolate and alone. I was looking off into the distance at something. From the looks of it, I was very depressed, and it was accurate. I hated that house and I'm sure it hated me. The last pic was of me and Carl on our wedding day. My crutches were visibly off to the side. Instantly, I began to cry, as this had become the best memory of my short life. The biggest question I was pondering was who in the good hell had prepped all of this for me? I thought that was it for the surprises until I got to searching through the folder even more. That's when I found the white envelope. I opened it without hesitation, not being surprised at what its contents were gonna be, seeing that I had already caught enough surprises for the night. I opened it up, pulled out the paper and began to read.

To Star,

I don't know if this letter will find you one day, but if your eyes ever see this, pay attention to the things that I am saying to you. Believe half of what you see and nothing that you hear. This is me, your father. My name is Donald Thurman Jr. I have only seen you three times, and that's when you were too young to remember. I was born and raised in Manhattan, Kansas. After I graduated high school, I enlisted in the Air Force. I got stationed in Oklahoma for my first station. It was kind of cool being that close to home at such a young age. Well, long story short. I was home on leave one night, when me and a few of my fellas decided that hey, we gone take us a road trip to Wichita. I reconnected with your mother at a local spot down there and we hit it off again. One thing led to another. After about three months, I received a call from your mom, saying that she was pregnant. I didn't wanna believe her, but I didn't wanna take the chance of missing out on my child's life. I humbly accepted responsibility and upon your birth, I was there. I named you Teresa Thurmond, after my great grandmother. The first two weeks of your life were happy ones, as I slept with you in my arms every chance I got. I went back to Oklahoma, thinkin everything would be ok. I was making preps to move your mom out there, just so I could be close to you too. Then, she hit me with a blow that I could never forgive. Turns out she got with another guy midway through her pregnancy. The next time I went down there, she berated and belittled me, claiming that she didn't want me in their lives. That man obviously had influence over her. He came outside. We argued and eventually, a fight broke out. Scrapping and tussling, I didn't see the knife that he had hiding. With one swipe, he sliced my hand open. Thriving in pain, I remember him getting on top of me, going for the death blow. That's when your mother grabbed his arm and he flung his fist back at her. "GET OFF ME BITCH!!!," was the words he told her. He came back over to me, kicking me a few times in my face before heading off to wherever. When I came too, because I was knocked unconscious, I woke up face down in the grass, dazed and confused. I never went back. I reached out to your mother numerous times on the low, but she shattered me with her words about how I was so far, and how he was always there to comfort her and you. I know the story. I know the abuse. Just know that was not your father. I was dealt a hand that unfortunately, I had to play. However, I hope the hand you're dealt now can result in us reuniting for a lifetime. A father and daughter. If you are reading this, please know that I love you.

Donald

I must have cried my eyes out for what seemed like an eternity. I didn't want to believe this, nor was I gonna believe this. I ripped that fucking letter to shreds, screaming with every tear. I balled up the pictures. I didn't want to see this shit. I didn't need this shit. Someone or something was trying to screw my life up again and I would not be having that. I was at a place that I had never been in my life and that was stable in the mind. I wasn't going to go back to what I was or who I was. I finally stopped crying. The anger started to subside. The only thing I could think of to relax me at this point was to sit in the tub. I went to the bathroom and ran the water a little bit hotter than I usually did. I wanted it right on the brink of hot and what the fuck. I figured since the devil was trying to pull me to hell that I would at least feel the fire to become immune to it.

I sat and I sat and I sat. I wasn't even washing myself. I was just trying to soak and put my mind at ease. As bad as I was trying to let this go from my mind, I couldn't do it. The pain was too much and It was nerve wrecking. I closed my eyes, wondering what life would be like if I wasn't here. I slowly slid beneath the water and let life have its course with me. I thought nothing of this. I was simply trying to calm my mental. Then, I saw the guy who I called my father. He was pinning me to the bed, laughing in a horrific tone.

"Daddy's back sweetheart." I tried to fight back, but it was to no avail. I saw him unbuckling his pants with one hand while he had a death grip on my neck with the other. He then proceeded to tear my pants off. Suddenly, I was halfway naked and scared.

"Guess who your real daddy is?" The whispering of his words was actually scarier than if he was yelling it. He pinned me down and slammed his shaft inside of me. I screamed for help, but no one was coming to my rescue. I shot up out of the water, damn near out of breath and panicking on a level that was off the charts.

Tears mixed with my bath water. I sat there and cried, holding onto the sides of the tub as if my life had depended on it. I was out of it. My mind was completely fucked. I looked like the girl from The Grudge. I probably had no life like her as well. Worst of all, I had no one to lean on physically. I felt myself going back to a dire place in my life in which I did not want to return. This isn't what life was supposed to be about.

My time of pain had come and gone. It wasn't supposed to come back. Then, I had to remember one important thing that we all learned in life. Pain and prosperity is nothing more than a constant cycle. Good and bad intertwine like the yin and the yang. The birds and the bees. The sun and the moon. I wasn't immune to it. I had to face it head on and take whatever came with it. Life had indeed come back around to remind me that I was indeed living. In order for me to live with a sane mindset, I had to recognize I wasn't anyone special.

I got out of the tub and dried off. Unlike my usual, I didn't head for the fan. I sat on the toilet with the towel wrapped around me. Another towel was on the floor, catching the remaining drips of water that were coming from my hair. I got up to cut the light out in the bathroom and went right back to sitting on the toilet. I ended up sitting there for over an hour.

Finally, I proceeded to the bed where I stared at the ceiling, talking to my mother for God knows how long. My last words to her were *"Tell God to come in my life more than ever now."* Those words were followed by wet eyes until I began to drift off to sleep. I hated all of this crying shit. I wanted to be strong like my husband. Yea, things affected him, but you would never know it. I was just a crier. Deep down, I felt that it made me weak. Somewhere in the middle of the night, and I knew I wasn't trippin, I heard three knocks on my bedroom door. I shot up, breathing deep, looking at the door. I looked over to my clock and seen that the time was 3:37 a.m. My gun was still on the living room table, so I was royally screwed if a burglar was in the house.

I shot up from the bed and flung the door open. There was nothing but the darkness contained in the hallway. I looked down towards the living room, only seeing parts of the sectional that was illuminated by the moonlight coming through the blinds. I shut the door back and walked back to the bed, sitting on the edge. I just started to chuckle. I got back under the covers, smiling. I wasn't a psychic, but I was pretty sure that I let God in, just like I had asked my mother to tell Him.

Two weeks had passed and it was the middle of the month. Life was back to somewhat normal. All of my husband's emails were normal, as no family members from my past life had jumped out of a crack in the wall and said "Hey, how you doing?" It was a chill hump day the 18th. I had been at work for about an hour and a half, reading e-mails and preparing myself for the new clients I would have the privilege to speak too.

"Star?," as I turned around to see my co-worker Carla peeking her head in my office.

"Your 9:30 is here."

"Thanks Carla. I'll be out in about 15 to get them." This was my bread and butter. I helped military people who were going through their own mental trauma. My own personal experiences made me want this career. True, I could've probably made more money somewhere else, but I loved working with the military. I never worked since I been here. When you love what you do, you never work a day in your life.

"James Pierce?," I announced in the waiting area. He raised his hand and arose. Immediately, I clutched my clipboard a little bit tighter.

"Hello Mrs. Lady." Wow, was my first thought as I shook his hand. He looked distraught, but his frame was monstrous. From my guess, he was a good 6'4-6'5 feet tall. He was very muscular and it looked like he had been lifting semi trucks his entire life. I'd say he weighed between a good 245 and 250. His CT Fletcher type beard looked like it trapped souls of naysayers inside of it. His dark skin with the barely visible tattoos made it look like his arms were full of extra veins and not inked on stories. To sum it all up, he was an intimidating presence. I always analyzed people when I met them, especially men. Men had this shock and awe feature about them.

Now, it had nothing to do with the laws of attraction. You'd get these big, burly men who were emotional as women. Then you would have these skinny, frail men who spoke as if they had the heart of a beast. You would be amazed at how much you could learn about a person by just looking at their physical features, demeanor and walk. We walked in the office and began our session.

"So Mr. Pierce. First off, welcome. I like to open my sessions with just asking my clients to give me a brief synopsis about who they are so I can get a better idea of who I am talking too." He just sat back in the leather chair and twiddled his thumbs, not taking his eyes off of me. It was kind of creepy, but I wasn't intimidated. I had dealt with many service members who had some sort of mental issue. He continued to stare at me with a look of no life in his eyes.

"Mr. Pierce?" He leaned his head back, still staring a hole through me.

"Ma'am. Imagine for one second, that everything around you was good to those on the outside looking in. Inside though, it was mere hell. One minute, everyone is there. The next, you're carrying someone's mangled body to safety, while others are lifeless. Half of their bodies are blown up. Arms, legs, blood, all showered over you. It's everywhere. Do you know what it's like to have everyone leave you and feel as if you are alone in this world?" I soaked in his words and the emotion that he spoke in.

"Yes I do," I responded so calmly. He placed his face in his hands and began to weep uncontrollably. I handed him some tissue and gave him time to just collect his thoughts. I could see that whatever he was about to explain to me was more than traumatic. Once he got himself together, he told me one of the most horrific stories you could ever imagine.

"I had been dealing with the stress of the bullshit war in Iraq. How they sacrificed our lives for some fucking oil and money. The same way they got my niggas in Afghan dying for some fucking Opium, so they can keep flooding the streets with heroin. Seeing people die wasn't the worst thing. It was the many nights that I contemplated suicide.

My inside was torn apart. I regretted my military decision ever since I had stepped foot over there. I get back home after almost a year over there. I missed my twins birthday. They turned six. One boy and one girl, named Kevin and Kiara. I had just called my wife the day I returned stateside to Virginia. I didn't tell her I was stateside. I would be flying home the next morning, but she still was under the impression that I was flying out of Iraq in a week.

I was gonna surprise her and the kids, and give them the biggest shock of their lives ever. My flight landed at 7 a.m. San Diego time and a friend was there to pick me up. He actually was my neighbor too. He dropped me off and headed off to work. It was like 8:10, or some shit close to it. I looked at my home from the outside and everything looked normal. Nothing was out of the usual. My truck was out front clean as a whistle, as she always kept it like all of our cars.

However, the lawn was well taken care of, which was odd because she never cut the grass or watered it. I just assumed she sucked it up and hired someone to do some landscaping while I was gone. I mean, you know, cause the base did provide services like that. The flowers were in my hand. I didn't ring the doorbell or anything. I pulled out the extra sets of house keys I had and just opened the door.

I walked in and smiled, closing my eyes and taking in the smell of my home. I noticed my kids toys weren't scattered everywhere. That was a sign that they were either at their grandmother's staying the night, or one of the neighbors' homes. I was thinking cool. As much as I loved my minions, I had been gone for a year. I needed to get in some guts and give her the death stroke. I headed upstairs. The bedroom door was shut. She was still sleeping I know. As I got to the door, I started hearing faint noises coming from my bedroom. I placed my ear to the door. I could hear her and another man engaging in sexual acts. The rage inside of me started to boil. I calmly walked back downstairs and out the door. I paced around my driveway, thinking how in the fuck a woman could be so damn evil to do such a thing to a man who was faithful to her and did everything for their family.

The devil then got a hold of me as I went back in the house and straight for the kitchen. I grabbed the serrated knife that you cut steaks with. This had numerous teeth and would do damage to a muthafuckas insides. The sounds were now louder and unbearable to my ear drums. He was knee deep in my wife. I calmly walked back up the stairs to the bedroom and just stood at the door, listening to the now ear deafening screams.

I began to count slowly. One, two, three, four, five. On five, I kicked in the door. There he was. He was digging my wife out from the back. Both of their heads whipped around and they was stuck defenseless. I didn't hesitate as I stabbed him repeatedly. Thirteen times to be exact. My wife was screaming loud as ever as his blood had splattered all over her, the bed and the walls.

"Baby, Baby please. Let me explain" she said to me. I thought to myself, what in the good fuck could she explain. What explanation would be good enough for cheating on your husband? Fuck you Rhonda I screamed at her, as I slammed the knife into our dresser set. I told her to explain God to that nigga, cause he was damn sure about to meet him. I stormed out of my house and called 9-1-1."

(The 911 call)

Dispatcher: *"9-1-1, what's your emergency?"*

Me: *"I JUST CAME BACK FROM THE WAR!!! WALKED INTO A MAN FUCKING MY WIFE AND I FUCKED HIM UP!!! Y'ALL BETTER HURRY UP BEFORE HE BLEEDS TO DEATH!!!"*

Dispatcher: "Sir what did you do?"

Me: *"I STABBED HIS ASS!!! THAT'S WHAT I DID!!! COME GET HIM BEFORE HE DIES ON THE SHEETS IN MY HOUSE!!! LET HIM*

DIE IN YALL HOSPITAL!!! I KNOW I'M GOING TO JAIL!!! TELL THE COPS I'LL BE OUT IN FRONT WAITING PEACEFULLY!!!"

I stayed outside of the house, bloody knife in my hand, sitting on the curb, like I told the dispatcher I would. Four cop cars descended down the block and scattered their cars everywhere once they arrived at my house. I raised the knife to show them my weapon and dropped it. By the time they got out of their vehicles, I was already sprawled out on the concrete, arms outstretched, face down.

You know, you can't take any risk as a black man in this world when it comes to dealing with the police. All I remember after that was being cuffed, asked questions, being loaded into the squad car and seeing ol' boy's body being rushed to an awaiting ambulance on a stretcher. For the rest of his life, whenever his dick got hard, his ass would be scared of pussy." He stopped right there. As a human, I thought to myself that he did what any of us would do and go the hell off. As a therapist, however, I had to decipher my words carefully and concentrate on helping this man recover from his situation. In my head, I silently prayed for the right words to release.

"Ok, first off, I can never relate to this, yet I empathize with the feelings you have harnessed. With the anger from your sights in the war, combined with the anger that is seething through your blood with an adulterous wife, I can totally feel your pain. My main purpose in this evolution is to help you harness that anger into relief, so that you may continue on as normal as possible."

We talked for another good thirty minutes as I constantly watched the tears beat down his face. I found out that he only served six months in a military prison, due to the judge taking in the account of his mindset at the time. Whoever his lawyer was, he darn sure was a good one. We wrapped up our session and I escorted him out of my office. Immediately, I went back to my desk, took off my glasses and just leaned back in the chair, closing my eyes. I knew what it was like to be at a low point in your life like this gentleman was. From watching Dontae murder my mother, to watching him take my innocence, there was an even bigger incident that forever haunted me. It haunted me more than any physical abuse could ever do. The bad thing is that while it happened, I was completely immune to any emotion. It was something that I highly regretted to this day.

At fifteen years old, what do any of us really know about life? For most, that is the age where we first enter into high school. It's when we really start to think that we are grown and run shit. In reality, we really don't know shit and we don't run a damn thing. I was the same way. The only difference is that I firmly believed I ran my own life, seeing that the foster system really didn't give you much of one. There I was, rebellious, drifting off into my own world and doing my own thing. The night started off pretty chill. It was a Saturday night and my foster peeps had no idea where I was at. They weren't going to know either. It was myself, Tiera and Tiana, two runaways who I had befriended, which was rare for me. I had known them for a good two months. They didn't care about life and neither did I, so it made it easy for us to get along. We went joyriding with a couple of brothers from Topeka who were in town. They were both nineteen, so we really thought that we were doing something big. We told them we were all eighteen when they scooped us up at a local park. We certainly looked the part, so we felt that we should play it.

We ended up at a simple looking house. They said it was their home boy's place. They crashed here whenever they came to Wichita to kick it, smoke and drink. That was cool with us, especially me. Anything that distracted me from what I was going through in my screwed up life was ok in my book. We smoked weed and took shots of Crown and Henny, laughing hysterically at any and everything that we talked about. This for me was fun, as it was for Tiera and Tiana. "A I'll be back. I gotta go pis." That's what one of them said as he took off up the stairs. Meanwhile, Tiera started doing her best version of a stripper dance in the corner for the friend who stayed downstairs. All was good in my book, as I took another puff of the blunt. By the time ol boy came back downstairs, Tiera was almost naked grinding on ol boy.

"A so shorty," the other guy asked Tiana. "We gone get this shit cracking or what?" Tiana, higher than giraffe pussy just laughed.

"Nigga we ain't doing shit." I was almost gone myself, zoned out in another world. That's when he struck Tiana, knocking her out on sight.

"**WHAT THE FUCK!!!**," I yelled. That's when the gun came out and got pointed directly in my face.

"Shut yo ass up bitch before I treat you like I did this bitch." I was transfixed. My body locked up. It was like any energy that I had inside of me quickly vanished. Tiera was screaming, as the other guy grabbed her and started punching her, telling her to shutup at the same time. The other guy went to grab Tiana, gun in hand. He then looked at me. "A bitch. You just sit down, shut up and watch how we treat this bitch. Say something and you'll be next. I like you, cause you just been chillin and smoking with a nigga. These hoes though gone set something out."

I sat down and literally watched as they beat and raped them both. They did all kinds of outrageous shit to both of them. The worst part about it was that in my sick little world, I was sort of enjoying it. I was watching somebody else take the punishment that I had been so used to receiving in my life. I kept hitting the blunt as they continued on, moving from Tiera to Tiana.

"Keep taxin them hoes," I told em. I even began to laugh as one of them came over and hit the blunt before they continued their madness. After all was said and done, neither one of them nutted. Being high as hell and enjoying what I had just saw, I willingly got on my knees. I sucked them both off until they released in my mouth. We then left the house, leaving Tiera and Tiana in a bloodied and battered mess inside of the living room. We drove around, smoking and laughing into the wee hours of the morning. High out of our minds, we pulled up in the parking lot of a park. I let em both fuck me willingly outside on the hood of the whip. Satisfied and with a stomach full of cum, they dropped me off at a house I requested around 2:30 in the morning. It was like I was immune to someone else's pain because of the pain I had suffered.

That house they dropped me off in front of was a few blocks outside of downtown. I didn't know whose house it was. I just didn't want them seeing where I stayed. Here it was, cold as ever and I was a fifteen year old rebellious girl who thought she was a woman, walking through the outskirts of downtown Wichita.

My home was not a home, so I figured I would learn what it was like to literally live on the streets. I ran into all kinds of strange people during my journey. Tweakers, mentally disturbed, heroin addicts, handicapped men, pregnant women, children, all of that.

Eventually, I stole a blanket and a dirty pillow out of a sleeping winos buggy and headed for a dilapidated building that was covered in vines. It looked like something out of a Jason horror flick. Inside, there was a steel garbage can, full of old wood, paper and anything else that you could imagine. This place stunk, and I know bugs and shit were crawling all around here. I didn't trip though. I lit some old newspaper with my lighter and ignited the barrel. It became good and warm too as I watched my shadow come to life on the walls with the illumination.

With a bunch of old linens I found lying around, I made a small pallet for myself and laid it down next to the flaming barrel. Homelessness wasn't so bad in my mind. That was until I noticed something out of the norm. I was the only one in this place. I thought that I was surely going to end up in a place where hoards of people lay their head at. It kind of seemed like that I was meant to be here by myself for a bigger purpose.

After ten or so minutes, I began to cry. I didn't want this life. Lord knows that it was much better for me inside of that house than out here in the world. However, at this point, I felt like I had nothing left to give. It was literally me against the world like Pac had once said. I was lonely inside and out. That feeling of being needed had worn off as it hit me once again that I was nothing more than a quick fuck to the two men who dropped me off. To sum it all up, I was dead. No life resided inside of me, much like this building.

I eventually drifted off to sleep. Truth be told, I didn't sleep very well, as my emotions were scrambled everywhere inside of my cranial. It seemed like the more that I concentrated on sleep, the more bad memories started to arise. When I arose in the morning from my broken sleep, I was met with the sun beams blinding me through the broken windows.

The smell of my body was atrocious, but the odor from this dreadful life was just sickening. I dusted myself off, leaving the pillow, dusty linens and blanket there. I headed out back to the streets. I didn't have a watch on me, so I didn't know what time it was.

I knew it couldn't have been past six or seven in the morning, seeing that no one was really on the roads yet. I walked through all the outskirts and made it into the heart of downtown, looking at things in a way that I never had. My foster peoples probably didn't even notice that I was gone, nor did they probably care. After a good thirty or so minutes of walking, I stumbled across a church. It was an eerily huge building. It literally looked like The Vatican had come to the Midwest. I stopped in front of it and just stared at the huge cross sitting atop of the building.

I wasn't deeply religious, nor did I care much about God at the time. I did however wonder one thing. Why did Christian churches put crosses at the top of their buildings? I mean, really think about this. If you were Jesus, and you got beat up, tortured, mangled and died on a cross, would you want to see a cross everywhere you went? It's like having your mom killed on a stake, yet every restaurant you went to, there had a statue of a huge stake sitting in the window. It boggled me, along with a lot of other things that I had read in the Bible.

How could Adam and Eve be the first two people on Earth, have two sons, but then they had children? Where were the women at if it was just them? How could God create evil and be against evil when he said everything that he created was good? These were just some of the questions that I pondered in my mind.

"Morning young lady?" I looked over to see a middle aged black man standing at the doors of the church. I just looked and didn't say anything.

"Do you need some help? You look like you had a rough night." I walked up to him slow and distraught.

"Why doesn't Jesus love me sir?"

"But Miss Lady," as he put his hand on my shoulder. "Jesus does love you. Come inside so I can help you?" I froze up, got scared and started to back away slowly.

"No, No," I kept saying, shaking my head and crying at the same time.

"It's okay young lady. That's why we're God's people. We are here to uplift, not judge." I kept back peddling, shaking my head, yelling no, until I eventually turned around and went into a full fledged sprint. I heard the man steady screaming for me to come back, but I wanted no parts of that. I knew he was there to help, but deep down, I felt like taking the steps to be healed would do me more harm than good. I continued running for about four blocks, until I stopped inside of an open lot. I keeled over at the waist, tired and damn near out of breath. I took my time to regain myself while looking around to make sure the man from the church didn't follow me. Finally, I rose up and observed where I was at. The bricks were decorated with graffiti of all sorts. The grass was growing through the concrete, showing that Pac wasn't a dummy when he said a rose can grow in concrete. There was old port potties, littered hats, bottles and even your typical broke down couch set. I just walked around, nervous and alone. At the same time, I was wondering why had I not discovered this place before in all my years of going all over the city?

I saw the remnants of an old stage. I assumed that old DJ battles and outdoor singing contests used to go on down here. Maybe, even a few freestyle sessions between local hip hop artists. Whatever the case, this area was much like my life. Old and abandoned. I made it over to an old splintered bench, hoping that no stray pieces of wood would poke me in the ass. I buried my face in my hands and just started to really hope for a better beginning one day. I wanted life. I wanted to be somebody who people could rely on. I didn't want to be known as just another girl who was shared by the masses. Nor did I want anyone to look at me and say *"That's her. That's the crazy girl you stay away from."* I truly was out of my mind. I had no friends, no family, no anything. I missed my mom. She was gone. I had nothing but the clothes on my back and a house that was far from a home.

I sat on that bench for about two hours, thinking about the atrocities of life, until extreme hunger started to kick in. I was starving, funky and just down and out. Finally, after what seemed like forever, I got up and walked out of the lot and to the corner, where a bus stop sign was.

I patiently waited for the number 9 as seen on the sign. 40 minutes later, it was here. I boarded the bus, joining a crowd of people who looked like they had hit the lowest point of their lives. I sat quietly in a middle seat, discreetly looking around and analyzing my environment. As we hit one stop, a man arose from the back. He had to be middle aged 30's. I would give him no more than 34 years old. As he began to walk past me, we made eye contact. Then, he stopped directly in front of me.

"God told me to tell you that breakthrough is coming." I just followed him with my eyes as he walked off, not even turning back. I looked out of the window as the bus pulled off, seeing him adjust his headphones and not even give two cares to the world. The rest of the ride home, my mind was totally boggled. I got back to that lowly house in which I called home.

Just as I figured, the moment I walked in, nothing was said. Not from my foster caretakers, nor my makeshift brothers or sisters. My father just looked at me, as he sipped some drink in a styrofoam cup and gave me a look that said "Fuck. You still alive." I went down to the basement and found an old dusty notebook and some pens. I plopped down on that beat up blue couch that was probably infested with spiders. I could care less at this point. I just needed somewhere to relax and put my mind at ease. Right then and there, I began to write a future letter to myself.

Dear Star,

You have literally been through hell fire and brimstone since you came out of your mother's womb. He never loved you or her. Matter fact, he killed her just so he could hurt you even more. I know you remember all of those times that he molested you and made you feel less of a person. Well, that was the old you. Look at how you have matured and blossomed into a beautiful woman. You met a great man damn near on the other side of the world and you two blossomed to have three kids. He helped you heal from your past and became the best friend that you always wanted, but you thought you would never have. The job you have helping others heal from the same thing you went through is amazing. You meet so many interesting people and touch so many lives. The smile you have is very impressive and you truly found out how beautiful of a woman you are. You once thought your beauty lie within the eyes of other men. Then, you grew up and realized that your true beauty lies within the eyes of God and the man you allowed to capture your heart. It's amazing what we can do with our lives when we put our mind to things. I hope you continue on the path that you are on and leave footprints across the globe, where others will follow. Remember, when you think it's over, realize that it may only be the beginning of something that you thought you would never accomplish. Take these words to heart and strive on. Never come back to see me.

Sincerely,

Your past.

I folded that letter back up and placed it in my purse. Never did I think something that I wrote at fifteen would have so much meaning today almost ten years later. Here I was married, pregnant when no one thought I would be and a totally different person. I was indeed blessed. Yet, at the same time, I was still in utter shock that I had made it through what I had made it through.

Never in a million years would anyone have thought that Star Jennings would ever make it out of Wichita alive. However, here I was, ever so enjoying life to the fullest. The only thing I cared about was Carl making it back home and having a healthy baby. I looked at our wedding picture that was on my desk and just got misty eyed. Two months prior to that, we were in a terrible accident. Then, we were there, married, happy as can be. I loved my husband and I owed everything to him to be the best wife possible, in and out of the sheets. I finished out my day a little bit later than everyone else. When five o'clock rolled around, I put all my files away and locked up the office building for the night. As I sat in my car, I just let out a sigh of relief. Everything was still surreal to me. My true life was here and I was just getting started.

3 JULY

I was now three months and some change pregnant. I wasn't the size of a butterball turkey yet, but the small bump was surely telling me that I was on my way. Those heavy food cravings that pregnant women get were getting on my nerves. Truthfully, I didn't know if it was the pregnancy or just my inner fat girl that wanted me to snack on everything I saw.

Either way, I was eating for two now. I had to keep the fried foods and sugary sweets to a bare minimum. I didn't want to harm my little one in any way, shape or form. No matter what I had, I would be happy. If you asked me what I wanted, however, I'd tell you straight out. I wanted a boy. I figured boys would be so much easier. Boys, from my observation, were simple creatures. Give them something to play with, keep them busy and they were good. Girls, oh my damn God. They were a handful. Plus, I really didn't want to deal with a little girl who would have the same snobby attitude that I had, the same foul mouth and a head full of hair that I would have to do every darn day. And if a daughter was anything like me when I used to get my hair done by my mom, she would be a mental patient at the psych ward bouncing off walls.

Carl called me on this Friday evening, which was a relief because I was truly bored and needed someone to talk to. He was in The Persian Gulf over in Dubai. I told him to bring me something back or that was his ass. Furthermore, I asked him about the man who was claiming to be my dad. He say they hadn't spoken much since the last time, but he could tell he was concerned about me through the way he looked at him whenever he went to the gym. Our conversation lasted about a good thirty minutes and he went back to starting his day off over there. I had finished cleaning the house and was now relaxing on my couch watching TV. 7:00 p.m. was the time to be exact and it was great to just sit back with no worries. I poured myself a glass of almond milk and watched House Party 3. Usually, I would have a glass of wine during my me time, but I didn't want to put my child at risk. I swear on my life this movie never got old. Just as it was getting to the dinner table scene, my phone rang. I looked at the screen to see RESTRICTED.

I didn't answer any RESTRICTED calls or numbers that I didn't recognize. I let it go and continued watching the movie until my phone buzzed, signaling that I had a voicemail. I didn't think much of it and was really too busy laughing my ass off to this classic to even give it consideration. I headed back to the kitchen to pour me another glass. I hit the voicemail on my phone to see who this was.

*"Hey Mrs. Jackson? How would you like…***Click!** I swear I didn't have time for telemarketers or anyone offering me free trips to God knows where.

"Now I remember. I even remember ya name. THEY USED TO CALL YOU JAWBONE!!" I damn near fell out in the kitchen listening to Bernie Mac's crazy ass. As I took a gulp of this blessing in a glass, I suddenly felt a sharp pain in my side. I jolted back against the kitchen counter, clutching the area of pain in the process. I didn't think much of it after a minute as the pain disappeared. It was probably nothing but a random cramp that I had caught. As soon a I took another gulp, I just dropped the glass.

"FUCK!!!" I was now thriving in pain, balled up on the floor. That's when I saw the blood and felt it running down my leg. I started to freak out. I didn't know what was happening to me. I pulled myself up with the strength that I did have. Then, I fell back down.

I began to crawl on the floor, heading for the living room to get to my phone. It was crazy how the simplest things became complicated when your life was on the line. This reminded me of the opening scene of Saw 7 when the doctor was crawling across the ground with blood everywhere. I made it to my living room table and reached for my phone. Dialing 9-1-1, I was begging and pleading with them to hurry up. It felt like someone was stabbing me over and over again. I sprawled over the floor, screaming and cursing with every other word as this had become the second most painful thing I had ever endured. Looking back at the trail of blood I left, and it looked like the St. Valentine's Day Massacre. I felt like I was back on Pacific Highway on that fateful Halloween night. It wasn't a great feeling as death seemed to be creeping back up on me once again. Despite my painful struggle, I managed to make it to my front door and crawl out, yelling for help.

"**STAR!!!**" I made eye contact with my neighbor David and he knew without me saying a word that this situation was dire. I heard him call back to his wife for a blanket. I was soon covered, but I felt little warmth. My body started to feel extremely cold. I felt the life being sucked out of me. I don't know how much time had passed, but I was starting to fade out. The blood loss was tremendous. As I heard the sounds of the sirens from the approaching ambulance, I literally blacked out.

I woke up groggy and sore with tubes going all throughout my body. I was completely out of it. No one was in here with me, but I wasn't freaking out. I was so drugged up that I really couldn't go crazy if I wanted to.

"Mrs. Jackson," a voice strung out from across the room. I looked over and saw a doctor with his white lab coat and a clipboard. I still didn't comprehend anything. I thought he was an angel to be quite honest. He walked over next to my bedside.

"How do you feel?" I looked over one way and then looked back his way. I seen a second doctor had joined him.

"What happened?," I whispered.

"Well, ma'am." Here we go I thought. "I am sad to report that you had a miscarriage."

"What do you mean I had a miscarriage?"

"You had a miscarriage. I'm sorry." I just plopped my head back on the pillow and began to cry.

"Nurse, could you give us a minute?" She left the room and doc raised my bed up about 30 degrees.

"Are you a little bit more comfortable?"

"No. I'm not. How did this happen?" He took his glasses off and let out a big sigh.

"Mrs. Jackson, first off, I humbly apologize that this happened to you. This is not something that is easy to deal with or live with, no matter how long I've been doing this. Hell, I was having a damn good day until this happened. I am however grateful that you are still alive." I heard the sadness in his voice as he lowered his head. I reached out to grab his forearm, signaling to him that I was trying to be there for him like he was being here for me now. He lifted his head back up with tears in his eyes.

"A few years ago, there was a college student who was big into community projects. Her name was Karey. She was as bright and vibrant as you could ever imagine. She met a man named Terelle, who became a bestselling author. Eventually, they got together and she became pregnant. When she was rushed in a few years ago, bleeding the same way you did, I thought I could save her. As a matter of fact, I took an even extra sense of urgency with her, seeing that I knew her personally. Unfortunately, in the end, Karey didn't make it. I remember when I had to go break the news to Terelle and everyone that was with him. As crazy as it may sound, it pained me more than him. That was the worst night of my life. I went back to my office that night and cried. I mean, I cried like a baby who didn't have his bottle. I told myself that if this situation ever occurred again, it wouldn't be any way in hell that I would lose my patient. If I did, I would retire from this life and never deal with any patients ever again.

I just couldn't live with myself. Not to mention that I felt her people's pain directly, seeing that my wife had two miscarriages, only to die on the delivery table after delivering our son three years later. After the funeral was over and I was leaving, Terelle stopped me to thank me for putting all of my efforts into saving her. He gave me a free copy of his smash book "The Writer's Block" and also ensured that I always held onto it. Karey loved the story that was written and he felt it was a great way to remember her. As a man, I felt more than honored. Now, with saving your life, I feel as if I have achieved a feat that no medical school could have ever prepared me for." We just stared at each other for what seemed like forever. I never wanted to be looked at as anyone else. However, being looked on as Karey right now was a great thing. I really don't know how close I was to losing my life, but I was forever grateful that this man did what he had to do in order for me to live. I didn't know Karey and would never know her. Maybe, just maybe, though, her spirit was watching over me on this day.

"My husband. Doc. My husband."

"The red cross message has been sent through to his ship. Once he gets it, he should be on his way home." That was music to my ears as all I wanted to do right now was rest easy and see my husband. The night continued on with me and doc becoming better acquainted with each other. I learned he was also a product of the foster system. His mother left him abandoned after birth in a dumpster in Calumet City, Illinois, right outside of Chicago. Adopted by some folks in nearby Hammond, Indiana, he found himself lost in the shuffle of the back and forth wars that happened on both sides of the border. However, with persistence, and a family who wanted to see him do well, he made it out to the tune of a scholarship to Florida A&M University. His success there transferred into being selected as a Rhodes Scholar later down the line. Now, he was a top of the line surgeon in the quote on quote World's Finest City. It was good to see black men doing great things in this world.

Once our conversation ended, he went on his way. It was late night and the lights had been turned out for the night. I was alone and it was an uneasy feeling. I drifted off to sleep eventually, but I arose at approximately one in the morning out of sheer fear. I woke up seeing nothing but the city lights outside of my window. I was starting to relapse. I know that I overcame my past, but my past is what caused the mess that I was in right now.

I cried throughout the early wee hours of the morning, trying not to lose my faith or my sanity. I swore I had become a different woman, but now I was questioning my mere existence on this earth. Was I deserving to live? Why did a man choose to marry a ho? I started to ask myself these questions and many more. Simply put, I was lost yet again. Two and a half days passed by. Monday morning was here and I was feeling better physically, but not mentally. There was a knock on my room door.

"Mrs. Jackson. You have a visitor." Through the doorway came Carl. My heart started to skip a beat as he stared at me and gave me a look of relief. Just as I began to cry, he hurried over to the bed and embraced me in a hug that said more than any "I love you's" from any lips could ever say. I swear we hugged for at least seven to eight minutes before we let go of each other.

"Baby. Before you say anything, let me tell you something. I don't want to hear anything about your past causing this. I don't want to hear about you felt like you ruined my life because you can't give me children. All I want right now is your love and warmth, because the best gift I have right now is seeing my wife alive and well. That's it. You blaming yourself is not an option." Those words made me fall in love with him even more. To have a man like that was something that a woman could only dream of. I was being released today to go home and having my husband here made everything better. That is except for the guilt that I felt deep down in the pit of my stomach. After a few hours of final tests to ensure I was good, I was finally given the green light from the doctors. I was released with some meds and I was on my way home.

"Just talk to me babe. Tell me everything you feeling right now?"

"I don't want to talk Carl. I just want to get home."

"What did I tell you in the hospital woman?"

"Look. I know you just trying to do your job. But let me have a moment to myself."

"I'm just trying to let you vent."

"SHUT THE FUCK UP CARL!!! DAMN!!! JUST SHUT THE FUCK UP!!!" I punched the dash as I screamed those words to him. From the shocked look in his eyes at the stoplight, I must've been looking real evil. The rest of the car ride home was a mum one. I felt terrible and I knew he was hurt. I didn't mean to do that. Once again, I let my emotions get the better of me instead of conscious thinking. "Carl?," I said as soon as we parked. He just exited the car without saying a word. I took a deep breath, kicking myself in the ass for ruining everything. I got out and followed him to the door.

"Carl?" Again, no response as he unlocked the door. As we entered the house, the amount of blood

I saw was perplexing. It literally looked like a cow slaughter inside of our home. Carl walked slowly through the house not saying a word. He went over to the kitchen, gazing at the blood stained floor. He then came back and walked into the living room. He knelt down, looking at the blood stains that were embedded in the fabric. He started to touch the carpet, rubbing his hand across it briskly, as if he was expecting the blood to tell him a story.

He got up and walked back to the kitchen. He continued to walk back and forth between those spots. I was scared shitless, as I knew he would blow up into a fit of rage from losing the child he had always wanted any minute. I watched him walk down the hallway to our bedroom and shut the door. I was waiting on the sounds of broken glass and overturned furniture. To my surprise, I heard nothing. He had been in there for ten minutes. I stood by the front door just in case I had to make a quick escape. Fear wasn't the word. We loved each other, yes. However, this was one of those times that I just knew he was going to put his hands on me.

The bedroom door opened up and I placed my hand on the doorknob to the front door, ready to make my escape. He simply came out, walked back to the living room where I was at and stared at me. I seen a range of emotion in his eyes from hurt to anger. We were about two feet apart. I noticed his fists clench up and his eyes began to water. I took my hand off the doorknob, wanting to brace for when his hand struck my face. I honestly hoped he knocked my lights out. I deserved it.

"Why us beautiful?" He took two steps and collapsed. I tried to catch him, but I was too weak. We both fell to the floor, lying in my dried up blood. I grabbed him as he was face down in the floor, balling his eyes out. We both were crying at this point. It pained me that my husband was hurting, and I could do nothing but blame my damn self. He came up slowly after he finished letting all of his emotions out.

"C'mon beautiful. Let's go get you something to eat." All I really felt like doing was letting him bash my face in. It was me. I was the cause of all this madness. How could he continually love me at this point? I grabbed and held him, with all these thoughts in my head. I should've jumped off the boardwalk when I had the chance.

"WHY DO YOU STILL LOVE ME???!!! WHY CARL???!!!" WHY???!!!"

"WHAT ARE YOU DOING STAR???!!! STOP!!!" I was bashing his face, body, wherever my hands were landing in the process. I didn't see my husband at this moment. I saw my dad.

"STOP LOVING ME!!!," as we were now halfway down the hall with my hands still connecting.

"**WOMAN STOP!!!**"

"**FUCK YOU NIGGA!!!**" And with that last fuck you and connection to his right eye, there it came.

"**BITCH!!!,**" he yelled, as he grabbed me and threw me through the bedroom door. "**FUCK!!!,**" I heard him scream in what was a literal echo. My life went back to the days of listening to music with my mother on Saturdays when my dad wasn't there. We were in the kitchen, laughing and singing while she let me butter up the fresh biscuits she had pulled out of the oven.

"Star? Star?" I was hearing my name and seeing Carl, but I was totally out of it. It was like I was Ronnie from The Players Club after Diamond had just beat her ass.

"Get up babe." He helped me up to the bed as I was still groggy from that Incredible Hulk type throw.

"I'm sorry babe. I'm so sorry"

"Huh?"

"Here lay down. I'm a go get you a towel." He darted to the bathroom as I lie on the bed. I put my hand to my forehead. I had a headache that was bigger than the Khalifa tower in Dubai. I sat up, rubbing my head gingerly. I got my ass cold clocked.

"Babe lay back and relax."

"I'm fine Carl," as I shooed away the cold towel in his hand. "I'm sorry. I spazzed out. I didn't expect you to love me anymore for losing the baby. So I hit you. I was mad you still loved me. Okay." He lowered his head and shook it.

"Babe ain't nothing on this earth gone make me stop being in love with you. I done told you. Stop blaming yourself." He grabbed me and I began to sob like I was accustomed to doing by now. I was happy he was still here, but I felt empty inside. At this moment, however, I wasn't going to deny myself any time with this man. Even if I was feeling lower than dirt. It was already difficult for him flying over 20 hours and some change just to get back to me. I didn't need to, and shouldn't have made things harder than what they already were.

The positive in all of this is that he didn't have to go back to the ship for the rest of deployment, so we would have time to build us again. He took me to SouPlantation to calm my nerves and explained everything to me. His Commanding Officer would allow him to stay home with me. He got him TAD orders with another command so that he could take care of our situation. Years before he became a full bird Captain, he went through the same thing with his wife. He had to fly home in the middle of a deployment because she had a miscarriage and almost perished. I was beyond grateful, but still hurting. Carl couldn't even see it as I hid it well at this point. Usually, he was dead on, as he would see through my façade and ask what's wrong. Not this time. I had ruined his life enough and I didn't want to ruin anymore.

To say that I put on the act of acts since we had left the house was an understatement. We got home later that evening and just rounded out our night with Netflix until we both drifted off to sleep. It was about 12:30 in the morning when I got up to go use the bathroom. I cut on the lights, squinting my eyes like a vampire who had seen the sun. As I walked past the bathroom mirror, I stopped and gazed at myself.

I didn't like the person that I was looking at in the mirror. I wasn't who I wanted to be, all because of one incident. It's crazy how they say the past always catches up to you. I was looking at it face to face. I used the bathroom, but didn't flush, not wanting to wake Carl. I cut the light off and creaked open the bathroom door. There he was, knocked out, snoring, gone to the world. I shut it and walked through our second bathroom, and into the living room where my shoes were. I grabbed my keys off the table next to the door and slowly crept out the front door. Once out, I ran to my car, put the key in the ignition and jetted out towards the streets.

Here it was, the middle of a summer night, in some basketball shorts and a tshirt, and I was flying down the 5 freeway, teary eyed with no sense of what I was doing. Not to mention that there was the rare summer rain dropping all over San Diego, thanks to El Nino or whoever they decided to name the storm after.

My purpose was to just drive until I couldn't drive anymore. By the time I was near H street exit in Chula Vista, my phone was blowing up, as Carl kept calling and calling. I refused to answer. I was a terrible wife and a terrible friend for letting such as travesty happen. Regardless of what he said, it was my fault. Taking the gift of life away from him was something that I could not bare on my soul any longer. Finally, I arrived at my random destination. It was the spot that haunted me some ways back. The sign was as clear as day and illuminated like the pyramids in Kemet.

I parked the car, got out the car and stood right in front of it. THE BOARDWALK. I was back. Again. This time, it was my turn. Only now I would be taking the plunge and not just testing my faith. I braced the now downpour of rain as I walked towards the middle of the pier.

Flashbacks of me running to save Carl immediately popped in my head as I contemplated the worst. I made it to the center of the pier and knelt down to feel the cold hard wood, just to see if it could feel what I felt. I got up and looked down to the end of the pier. Besides the lone restaurant, there was nothing. I looked back towards the beginning of the pier. It was much of the same. The wind had kicked up now. Combined with the rain, it was the perfect setting that seemed to tell me to jump. With tears in my eyes, I looked up towards the heavens one last time.

"Mom, save me a spot next to you," I whispered. I took both shoes off and walked over towards the old wood railings along the side.

"**STAR!!!**" I looked down to see Carl standing on the pier in the blinding rain.

"**STAR!!! WHAT THE FUCK ARE YOU DOING???!!!**" I looked back between him and the side of the pier.

"**STAR!!! WHAT THE FUCK!!!**" I slowly stepped towards the middle of the pier. Carl was now frantically walking towards me. As he got within ten steps of me, I backed back towards the side and he stopped. We locked eyes with each other. He look pissed, but scared at the same time.

"Star. You remember the last time we were here? You remember the pain you felt when I felt like ending it all. Now I feel your pain. Baby. Don't do this. I'm not leaving. I'm not your father, your foster parents, those men in your past, none of that. I'm Carl, the man you fell in love with." As he inched closer, I became nervous and scared as if he were a stranger. I backed up some more as I was now touching the rail. He stopped once again.

"Look at your left hand," he said. I gazed down and saw nothing. As I looked up, he reached in his pocket and tossed me a box. I was surprised that I caught it in the rain.

"You remember the day we got married? We had nothing but each other. Now you have something to symbolize our forever. Put it on, but don't leave me." I opened the box to see the most amazing sight of my life. I don't know how expensive this rock was, but it was the most beautiful thing I had ever seen. If I had to guess, I would say it was at least 1 ½ carats with about 9 stones. As I was distracted by it, he rushed over and grabbed me.

I dropped the box and started to fight him. I knew he was my husband, but all I could see was my father grabbing me once again, trying to rape and abuse me once again. I swung on Carl repeatedly as he tried to gain control of me. The punches to his face were connecting. It was a repeat of earlier in the day. He slung me off of him.

"**STAR STOP!!!**" As I got up and ran back over to him, **SLAP!!!** I dropped instantly.

"**I'M NOT HIM!!! I'M NOT FUCKING HIM!!!**" I looked up at him still feeling the jolt that his hand left throughout my face. He was breathing deep, tired and full of anger. I know he didn't wanna do that, but I had really left him no choice. I was acting like a man so he treated me like one.

"Star," he said softly, wiping the blood from a cut I gave him above the eye. "I'm not him. I never will be." He picked me up and I immediately began to sob hard on his chest. I never felt this much pain and joy at once in my life. I don't remember how long we stayed out there holding one another in the rain. I really don't remember much to be honest. What I did see was that when I arose in the morning, there was a blanket over me as I arose in the passenger seat of the car. I don't remember even going back to the car, but it felt warm to know that I was loved and waking up next to him. I had never seen a sunrise over the ocean and I know that I missed this one. When I looked at him, however, all I saw was light.

"Carl, Carl," I shook him until he woke up.

"Why didn't we go home?" Groggy and clearly blinded by the sun, he rolled over to look at me completely.

"Last night, home reminded you of pain. So the only way to heal pain is to confront it. You felt pain when I tried to hurt myself. So I kept us in the same place so you could face it head on. Shivering my ass off last night was crazy. But I'll do it again in a heartbeat to make sure that you are well. You're my wife and I love you." He reached up to give me a kiss that felt like it put me on cloud nine. "Now, let's go home. I swear my balls turned into icicles last night." He always knew how to be funny in the strangest of times. As I raised the seat up and got readjusted in my seat, I went into immediate shock.

"CARL. THE RING!!! WHERE DID IT GO???!!!"

"That shit gone. Fuck it. They can make another ring. They can print more money. They can't make another us." I knew he was pissed, but he just didn't want to show it. He wanted to take the high road. Although it was a material loss, I needed to make up for it. That ring cost at the least $3000 from the looks of it. He started up the car and we began our trip home.

Two weeks passed by and life was still far from normal. We started meeting with a therapist to help me combat my inner demons that were inside of me. Carl didn't start work until the beginning of August, so he took care of the house for the most part to allow me to rest up. Today, we were headed to a follow up at the doctor's office to see how my body had healed from everything. That would be my next hurdle. Entering a hospital and staying in it. I never feared hospitals until that miscarriage. True, I hated them when I watched my dad die inside of one. The hate however was something else. They instantly became places of evil in my eyes. The smell of the hallways, the looks of sick people, the building in itself, it all affected me. It struck fear inside of me.

We drove up this Thursday morning as usual and instantly my heart began to palpitate. Seeing the ambulances and EMT's shook me to my core. Carl grabbed my hand as we entered into the parking garage, letting me know that he was there. As comforting as it was, I knew that someday I would have to learn to face fear without him, because one day he wouldn't be here. It's something we all have to do. Dependency can cause us to become comfortable and fall into a zone. It's sort of like a child growing up in their parents' home. They get complacent and comfortable with the notion that someone is taking care of them 24 hours a day, seven days a week, 365 days a year. Then, that time hits when they become 18 and they have to start learning how to fend for themselves. Momma and daddy can't be there forever. If they're coddled, then they will never learn what it's like to be independent and make it on their own. That's when you end up with 30 plus year old men still living in the house with their parents. I was lucky for now. It may not be that way in the future.

"Mr., Mrs. Jackson, how are you doing?" That was the doc greeting us as we entered into his office. Amazing how he saved my life just mere weeks ago and now he wasn't even looking like a doctor. His doctor's gown was off and he was just himself in his regular civilian attire.

"So Mr. Jackson as you know, your wife unfortunately had a miscarriage and I am sorry for the loss of your child. From the looks of her history, she was very fortunate to get pregnant. However, we will have to remove her egg. Her previous abortions from her teenage years caused major damage to her system, therefore making her risk of bearing a child critical. My suggestion is that you either try a surrogate mother option, or adoption, if children are what you want."

"I can't bare to see another woman carry my child sir. And it would be hard for me to adopt, knowing that I didn't make that child. I don't know doc. This one is going to be difficult for me."

"Well sir," as doc wiped his glasses. "All I am doing is offering suggestions. I understand that this is a difficult predicament for you both, but these are the only options that will not put your wife in danger of losing her life. I figure this is a matter that you two would like to discuss in private, so I will step out for a few minutes before we finish up and schedule another follow up." Doc shut the door and we just sat there quietly, grasping each other's hands.

"Babe I'm sorry," I told him. "I'm sorry." He looked at me and didn't say anything. I figured this was the straw that broke the camel's back. He said he was cool all this time, but now, things had finally taken a turn for the worst.

"Gary," he said.

"Huh?," I responded back to him.

"Gary, Indiana beautiful. I got some demons I need to heal from."

"When Carl?" With a deep look in my eyes and a grasping of my hand as if his life depended on it, he answered.

"Tonight. Three days. Back home Sunday night. Trust, I need to be truthful to you about my whole life. Okay love?" We kissed, telling each other a story through our lips that not even the greatest of author's could write up.

"Let's do this then. Team Jackson."

"This is the only way that I can heal love. I don't know any other way. I need you right now. More than ever."

"I'm here Carl. I'm here." I would pack up as soon as I got home, preparing for my first trip to Gary, Indiana, where my husband was born and raised. I already knew about the murder, his mom's death, dad's death and the hardships that plagued him as a child growing up there. I just had to prepare myself for what was next in the storyline. This was his Wichita. The roles were now reversed.

We landed at Chicago Midway shortly before eight o'clock in the evening Central Standard Time. I had never been to the Windy City besides when I flew in to go to boot camp years ago. Just looking at the lights out of the window when we were descending had me perplexed. This place was a far cry from Wichita. We got to baggage claim to get our stuff and headed out towards the greyhound bus service to Northwest Indiana.

"Who's gonna be waiting for us?"

"My nigga Dee. He a good dude who bettered his life. We gone stay with him for the time that we're out here." I was good with that, as I trusted my husband with his judgments and the people he accepted as his family. The bus was scheduled to leave at 8:35 p.m. and arrive at the Highland, Indiana bus terminal in an hour. Hubby was upbeat to say the least. This was his first time coming back home since everything had went down with his mother.

"Northwest Indiana Highland Station bus has arrived."

"That's our cue beautiful. Let's roll."

"Well damn Flash. Can you at least take your bags?" The fool was so happy that he took off without his bags or me.

"Oh sorry babe," as he ran back, grabbed his bags and completely ignored me. As upset as I was at him, I just shook my head and smiled. I knew this was a major moment in his life. When adrenaline and excitement takes over, there is nothing you can do to control it. We talked the whole bus trip as he told me stories about J&J's

Chicken, Sharky's, Da Link Bar and everything else Gary, Indiana was offering up.

He loved his city to the core from the way he was talking on it. I just wanted to experience everything with him. We arrived at the bus station in Highland sometime after 9:40. It was a cool, chill summer night. Our bags were unloaded and I followed him as he made his way towards a Red Buick. A man in similar height with cornrows got out of the car.

"**BRUH!!!**," he holla'd at my husband. Carl dropped his bag and they dapped up with a huge embrace. You could tell these two were very close.

"Dee, this my wife Star. Star, Dee."

"So you the one who locked my mans down huh? Gotta be something special for him to do that." He was very gentleman like in his greeting and it was comforting to see that men like that were still around.

"Y'all hungry man?"

"Bruh. Purple Steer my nigga. I need my fix like a muthafucka."

"The Steer it is then. As for you Star, let me get those bags of yours." They loaded all the bags into the trunk and we headed out towards the restaurant.

"Dave what city is this?"

"We in Highland. Don't worry. You safe out here." They let out a chuckle as to tell me that this wasn't the hood and that I didn't have to worry. I didn't mind, nor did I trip. I hadn't seen G.I. yet, but a hood is a hood no matter where you go. Some may look worst than others, have different gangs than others and just all out have a different lifestyle. The point is that all of us who are from the hood, we got the same goal. That's to get out of the hood. It saddened me sometimes how people would try to bang their city as being harder than the other. 20 story projects don't make that area tougher than the one with sunshine and palm trees.

The blocks with the cracked streets didn't make it harder than the ones with the brownish green grass. Poverty doesn't care about race, creed, color, gender or location in the world. It does not discriminate. I for damn sure seen it first hand, along with a lot of other black folks. Hell, traveling around the world in the Navy, you'd be surprised to learn just how poor some people are.

They would literally give an arm just to live in the projects here in America. We arrived to a nearly empty restaurant. All that meant for me is that our food would come out quick and fresh. We walked in and to me, it didn't look like anything extraordinary. The moment we sat down, that's when those two started their madness.

"So you getting your usual man?" My husband started laughing.

"Yea man. Ain't nothing changed. Ham and cheese omelet for me. Baby, you gotta get one of these too. They the bomb."

"Aight babe. Order up two." The waitress came and we placed our order. Dee and my hubby got to chopping it up some more about old high school basketball games, classic parties and some dude named "The Great Pooh." Everything was gravy, but the conversation went left field real quick as they started to rap about life.

"When you gone make that move to California man?" Dee sipped his water, as if he were going into a deep thought process.

"Man, I want too. Believe me my nigga I do. It's hard to just up and leave, though. Especially when you're so used to something. Plus my little ones here bruh. I gotta have them straight before I do anything. Pops can't just up and leave. I ain't trying to be labeled a deadbeat."

"I can respect that mane. I definitely can. However mane, I know what you done been through the last few years. Leaving the streets ain't the easiest. Let's face it. Jobs out here just don't cut it. I ain't trying to sound Hollywood or nothing like that, but you damn sure better than the steel mills or the riverboat my dude. True, everyone gotta do what they gotta do to feed their family and it's all gravy. That's what a man does. I just hate to see a lot of folks all gravitating towards the same thing, when it's so much more out there my dude. Remember, you ain't too good to work any job. But you know you are too good to be working at some places." "But that shit we say we better than is what's paying the bills for folks round here man."

"Can I chime in guys?," raising my hand as if I were back in elementary school.

"Sure thing Star. What's up?"

"Dee, I don't think Carl was saying that you are literally too good for the steel mill. What I think he was trying to say is that you have too much talent to be working there. It's like that kid that everyone knew in school who could hoop and shoot the lights out, but he only did it on the court in the projects. That's fine and dandy, but what if he took that talent to the high school courts? Now, he can ball his way into college, a free education and possibly further. That's all I think he was trying to say." They both looked at me and looked back at each other. Finally, Dee turned back toward me. He stuck his hand over the table towards me.

"I appreciate that sis," as he dapped me up.

"Maybe one day. Until then, I'm just gonna keep grinding. But enough about me, talent and jobs or what not. Tell me the story behind you and this man. How did y'all meet?"

As our food came out, we all engaged in a conversation that was hilarious as ever. Me and Carl were both lying when we were telling our story. He tried to make it seem like I chased him and I made it seem like he was drooling over me upon first sight. No matter what we exaggerated about, one thing was common with both of our stories. We both fell in love and needed each other to make it in this world.

"Bruh, I hope I find that one day man. That's some cool stuff," Dee said. It was always a blessing to give motivation to someone else looking for what we had, because there was once a time that I was wishing for the same thing. I now had it and it felt lovely. We finished up our late night shenanigans at The Purple Steer and headed out towards the house. We got to the house a little bit after 12 midnight.

Dee stayed over in Merrillville, which was right outside of Gary. He said people around here considered the 'Ville the come up. It didn't look bad from what I saw. It looked like a place where you could raise your family without a care in the world. We got set up in the guest bedroom and I was immediately calling it a night after I took a hot shower. As for Carl, he was down in the basement with his bruh, choppin' it up and drinking some of that White Hennessey that you could only get from overseas. I showered up and plopped in the bed, staring a hole through the ceiling. Here I was in the reverse role. Carl came home with me over a year and a half ago to help me heal from my past demons. Now, I was here with him in Northwest

Indiana doing the same exact thing. If part of his healing was being alone with his family, then I gave him that courtesy. That was my job as a wife. Support him in any way possible, even if it didn't directly involve me. As my mind went in a million directions, I thought back to a time when I waited in a bed for another man.

"I'll be back Shorty." Me and this guy named Jarrell had just finished having sex. I was sixteen and he was my supposed boyfriend at the time. Later, I would find out he just gave me that title to get in my draws on a regular. I lie there naked under the bed sheets. Feeling like I was loved, I thought I had found it all once again. I was so gullible back then because of the lack of love I received growing up. It was unbelievable and quite embarrassing to tell you the truth. I waited and I waited for him, but he still didn't come back in the room. 20 minutes had elapsed and I started to grow anxious. I needed comfort and I needed it now. Frustrated, I got up, wrapped the sex juice stained bed sheet around myself and walked towards the bedroom door. As I got there I stopped and placed my ear to the wood. I heard his voice going on and on. I couldn't make out what he was saying, but I could tell he was talking to someone.

"Man hell yeah!!! I hit this dumb bitch from all sides nigga. She suck, swallow, liked getting slapped, all that shit. My nigga this shit is like taking a fat kid to the cheesecake factory."

I just turned around and sat against the door, crying my eyes out. I had thought once again that I was in love. However, once again, I ended up being the fool and disappointed. As he continued on, laughing at me to whomever he was talking too on the phone,

I put on my clothes and exited out of his first story window. It led right out to his backyard. I made the fifteen block journey home that day and just sobbed my eyes out the entire way. My heart was hurt, my soul was hurt, my entire being was crushed and I just hated everything about life. I had nothing or nobody to blame but myself. Back then, I didn't want to tell myself that. Once I got home, I simply walked towards the basement, hoping to get down there before my foster dad said anything.

"Why you in a hurry?," I heard him ask from the stairs.

"Just want to be left alone dad."

"You probably got fucked and he left you. I hope yo' ass hurry the fuck up and get out of here." I rolled my eyes and slammed the basement door behind me. I went down to that dusty blue couch and just cried my eyes out. Around 1 in the morning, not even six hours after I made it home, I awoke to a text from another wild child I knew named Sheila. It was early Sunday morning, and her and a few buddies were in a house sniffing lines, or doing coke for those who don't know what that means. I figured what the hell did I have to lose. I was already looked on as a nobody. I had just gotten fucked and thrown away like I was nothing mere hours ago. Why not destroy myself even more since I was already a nobody? Fuck it. Why not just kill myself? I didn't have any use left in the world, so why not go out with the high of highs. That's the true reason that I went to that house that night. It was crazy as I walked eight blocks in the wee hours of the morning to a raggedy ass house. I arrived at exactly 1:58 in the morning. I stood at the front of the house and took two deep breaths, preparing myself for my last ride. I walked in through the busted screen door to a dimly lit home. I saw that the action had already commenced.

"**HEY GIRL!!!**," Sheila blurted out. "**C'MON OVER HERE AND JOIN THE FUN!!!**" She immediately turned back around and grabbed a bottle of liquor from some boy and took a long swig. At that moment, I felt complete. For the first time in my life, I was about to sniff coke and do it with people who gave two shits about their families as well. I dropped my jacket to the floor and went to join in on the madness.

"Hey you. What's your name?"

"Star. What's yours?"

"Brandon. Here, take a hit of this. This some of that Cali Kush. Get you good and fucked up." Brandon passed me the blunt and I inhaled hard. That shit was hitting hard. I inhaled once again and passed it back to Brandon. All over the living room, much of the same was going on between everyone. Me and Brandon went back smoking and kissing for the next 20 minutes. I was going to be his slut for the night and I didn't care. The next 30 minutes saw me drinking Olde English, smoking and being fondled.

"**GO, GO, GO, GO, GO!!!**" The nine or so people in that house were egging Sheila on as she snorted the white powder on the glass table. I was scared shitless, but at the same time, I was stoked. I went next as I pressed one nostril closed and sniffed everything with the other one. It felt like someone had taken a lit cigarette and stuffed it up my nose. My shit was on fire and I started tripping out something serious.

"It's cool, it's cool," one of the boys said as they grabbed a hold of me. After a good minute, I started laughing along with everyone else in there. It was a high like I had never felt in my life. Weed, ecstasy, nothing could compare to the high that cocaine gives you. I couldn't tell you whether it was pure, cut or what. All I knew is that I started seeing some of everything. Moons, stars, circles, squares, quasars, nebulae and eclipsed suns were just some of the things floating in my existence. I was gone to the world. When I looked at the corner of the house as I leaned back against the couch, I swore that I seen a leprechaun standing next to a miniaturized rainbow.

"ONE MORE STAR!!! ONE MORE!!!," the same crazy dude from before shouted. I said screw it and took another hit. I hit the floor because I was done. At this point, I was literally feeling like I was floating on clouds. I was expecting to see angels any minute now.

When I woke up the next morning, we were all butt naked on the floor. Five girls and four guys. I don't remember what happened, but from my guess, we had one big orgy in there. I arose while everyone else was still passed out. I felt like less of a human once the high wore off.

I walked to the upstairs bathroom and looked in the mirror. All I could do was shake my head as I wet a towel to clean up the dried semen that sat on my face and my breasts. A little bit over a month later, I missed my period. I went to the school nurse and found out that I was pregnant. Do you know how it feels to have someone ask you do you know who the father is and you can only answer with the phrase

"I have no idea?"

That is more than embarrassing. That two and a half month pregnancy ended up being my second abortion, to compliment the one I had at fourteen. When I told my foster caretakers about it, they laughed at me.

"You ain't gone be shit and never have been shit. If it wasn't for this money we were getting from the state, we would've been got rid of your funky ass. If a muthafucka marry you when he get older, he gotta have literal shit for brains." That was my so called foster mom saying this. It was the worst shit that I had ever heard in my life. There were words that can cut you. Those words right there made surgical wounds. From that point on, me and her rarely spoke.

My foster pops wasn't shit either, but damn, he never said any fucked up shit like that. That taught me right there that you have to be careful who you place your care in, because not everyone has your best interest at heart. We all arose the next morning and Dee took us down I-65 South to a joint called Cracker Barrel. I had never been there ever in life, but it definitely was something that I wanted to experience. It was like the old country meets a down home southern restaurant. Upon entering, it definitely felt like I was on a farm instead of a restaurant.

I ended up smashing the chicken fried steak and mashed potatoes with the home style country white gravy. It probably was to that point the best meal that I had ever eaten. As Dee and the hubby continued eating, I lounged around in the country store of theirs looking at everything they had to offer. I saw that they had the 8 ball that you ask a question to, shake up and it gives you an answer. I loved these things as my mom gave me one when I was three. Of course I didn't ask about anything back then, but shaking it as a three year old and seeing magical words appear was the most entertaining thing in my eyes.

"Will my husband find his peace while here?" I shook it up and waited for the answer to float up to the glass opening.

"Yes," it read. I know that a material thing didn't have any spiritual powers, but I firmly believed that Carl was going to get what he came for.

"You ready beautiful?," as he snuck up and grabbed me from behind.

"Yep. I'm following you." Dee was generous enough to let us use the car while he was busy at his 9 to 5. We dropped him off at work and headed towards Gary. It was right next door, so it was a quick drive down Broadway. I could tell we got there. It changed from a decent looking area to dusty buildings, broken roads and just sheer emptiness. He was quiet as ever. I wanted to say something to him, but I didn't want to mess up his focus.

Sometimes, the best thing you could do is stay silent. It speaks more volumes than words sometimes. All of a sudden, we made a turn off on a side street and he parked the car. We sat there next to an open lot. He placed his hand on his forehead.

"This is it beautiful. This is where my life changed."

"What happened here Carl?"

"Get out the car. I'll show you." We got out and slowly walked over to a spot on the concrete. I leaned against a brick building while he walked around in a circle numerous times. He was scanning the concrete, inspecting the ground as if it were gonna talk back to him. He looked up at me with a distraught look.

"It was right here where my partner shot the dude we chased. I-I-I really don't know what I was doing that night. I knew I was wrong. Hell, we were all wrong. But I was so about the hood that I didn't want to disappoint the hood. I was too stupid to realize back then that the hood couldn't and would not save me. We started way down the street," as he pointed back towards Broadway.

"We saw him and chased him up this street in the car. When we bent the corner, we jumped out the whip and robbed him. He was unconscious after we beat him. As I turned around to go back to the car, that's when I heard the pop. It was right then and there that I knew my life was over." All I could do was give him my attention and try to learn.

"This is one of my wounds babe and I needed to come here to put my bandage on. Thank you." I just hugged him and held him as close as possible. He was hurting inside and my comfort was necessary. They say cracks in the concrete are caused from rain, snow, and wear and tear from uncontrollable weather. Today, I saw that the cracks in the concrete were caused by human error.

"You ready?," I asked him.

"Yeah. Just give me a minute to myself." I went back to the car and just sat there, observing him as he stood in that spot by himself for the next five minutes. Finally, after picking up a rock and launching it into some nearby brush, he came back to the car and we were on our way to the next destination. Carl cut on the radio to the local Power 92.3 station as if to say that he was trying to make things normal again. We headed about two miles north down Broadway. After crossing 5th Avenue and cutting through some side streets, we ended up parked on a desolate block. It looked like this whole area had got hit with the atomic bomb. Hell, two or three of them to be quite honest with you.

"Are we getting out?"

"Nah," he said. "You see that house?," pointing to the two story brick building with trees climbing all over it.

"This was Dant's house. This is where we hid out after we did what we did. All four of us thought we were jimmy scott free. That was until the next morning when the feds came busting through the door. I remember particularly my black ass in a state of shock while the others did their damndest to try and run. They didn't get far. Hell, they didn't even make it three steps before a knee was in their necks." The house was abandoned, but the spirits of the men who once dwelled in it were still here.

"I want you to show me Carl."

"What the hell you mean? You looking at the muthafucka right here."

"I want you to show me. Like, really. It's one thing to sit here and ponder on what occurred. Show me face to face so I can understand it." He sat there for a good two minutes, not saying anything.

"C'mon love," as he got out of the car. He looked frustrated, and I know he was. But, he needed to face his fears head on. Wasn't shit ever accomplished from a distance. If you want to deep fry bacon, you stand up close and drop the bacon in the grease. You don't throw the shit in there from five feet away and risk catching your house on fire from splashing grease. I followed him out as we walked through the gate and the knee high weeds that had grown here. Carl led me to the back of the house to a small window that stuck up above the ground.

"Let me see if it still opens." With barely any energy, he pulled at it and the entire frame came off. The weakened glass that was left just disintegrated, symbolizing the broken friendship of four young men if you asked me. Carl swept away the few shards of glass left and double checked the way in for spiders. If it's one thing that he hated, it was spiders. He looked back at me as if to say he really didn't wanna do this.

"You got this babe," I told him. He turned around and slithered his body in. I followed behind him. We were met with dust, trash and probably a bunch of roaches that hadn't showed themselves yet. I walked around analyzing the basement while Carl stood in the middle of the room dusting himself off and coughing. As he handled himself, my eyes wandered around the entire basement. Ripped up posters, including one of a naked woman littered the wooden walls. There was an old bubble tv on the floor, old clothes and just out right junk. I caught something in the corner of the room and walked over to it.

"What CD is that babe?"

"Master P. The Last Don." As I picked it up, blowing the dust off of it, I saw something else that was lying underneath it. It was a picture. In it were him, another man and a woman.

"Babe what's this?" He turned around as I handed him the picture. The smile that came across his face was refreshing.

"This is me baby in the good ol days. This is me, Dant and my mother on my graduation day from West Side. If you look closer, you can see Tez and J.J. running up in the background, trying to get in the picture. Those were the other two who were with me that night when that madness went down. These were the simple days, where life wasn't so complicated. I always thought this was it. I would move on from this point, go to Michigan for school and graduate as a Wayne State alumni in four years. But unfortunately, things didn't work out for me."

I just listened and watched him. I seen resentment and anger slowly build up until he just balled the picture up and tossed it.

"**FUCK!!!**" He plopped down on the couch, sending up three tons of dust with him. I sat next to him and just placed my arm around him, trying to console him as much as possible.

"**YOU DON'T UNDERSTAND STAR!!! I RUINED MY LIFE. I RUINED MY FUCKING LIFE!!!**" Immediately, I backhanded the shit out of him with a wrath of anger I hadn't felt in a long time. He was shocked and pissed all in one. I was on my feet and he jumped to his. We stood face to face and there wasn't an ounce of fear in my body.

"YOU DIDN'T RUIN YOUR FUCKING LIFE!!! THIS SHIT DON'T HAPPEN, YOU DON'T GO TO JAIL. YOU DON'T GO TO JAIL, YOU DON'T MAKE IT OUT!!! YOU DON'T MAKE IT OUT, YOU NEVER FUCKING MEET ME!!! AND IF WE DON'T FUCKING MEET EACH OTHER, NEITHER ONE OF US ARE HERE FOR EACH OTHER, TRYING TO HEAL EACH OTHER!!! TRYING TO LOVE EACH OTHER!!! TRYING TO BE EVERY FUCKING THING WE THOUGHT WE WOULD NEVER HAVE!!! SO GO 'HEAD AND HIT ME BACK. THIS AIN'T THE PIER WHERE I DESERVED IT!!! I HIT BACK NIGGA!!!"

I was pissed beyond belief. My heart beat was on a hundred thousand trillion. My breathing was intense and my spirit had the fury of 10,000 slaves that never made it free in it. We stared each other down for what seemed like forever until he turned around, pacing back and forth with his hands on top of his head.

"You're right," he said, turning around to look back at me.

"I'm sorry. I didn't ruin my life." The tears started to roll down his face.

"I never would've thought in a million years that my dreams could come true without the aid of a textbook. I was so up on making it out, getting degrees, living a wealthy life and running the world without a care in the world. I was so hell bent on all that, that I failed to realize that I became rich the day I met you. I fucked up with what I said. I can't take it back. But I was stupid, and I'm sorry." I wanted to stay mad at him, but I couldn't. I remember when I was the same way with him, thinking that my life was trash, yet not realizing that I had everything with him. I ran up on him and hugged him. For once, he cried on my shoulder. I wasn't use to this role reversal, but nonetheless, I accepted it.

We stayed there for the next thirty minutes, laying on the couch with his head in my lap. In that moment of absolute silence, we bonded more than we had ever done in our life. When we finally left the house, it felt as if a huge burden was left off of Carl's shoulders. We got in the car and headed out towards the West Side of the city where he grew up. As we got to the Tarrytown liquor store, I started to get a sad feeling in the pit of my stomach.

We walked in past a man who was outside talking to himself with a Wild Irish Rose bottle at his side. I got me some pork skins, while Carl grabbed some skittles and a green tea. We made our way back out towards the car. Only this time, we didn't have to be worried about being followed and gun down because we had skittles and some green tea. It's funny how America operates doesn't it?

"Hey youngsta?" We both turned around.

"What's up old man?"

"I once had a pretty thang like you. I was the muthafucking man."

"Whoa bruh. You ain't gotta stagger over towards me. Just stay right there and speak what you gone speak mane."

"Muthafucka I can't whoop yo ass. I'm a drunk, I'm fucked up and I got one foot in the fucking ground already. Just remember this. Even a crab go without a shell in its life for a little while." The old man dropped and hit the concrete right after he said that.

"Let's go babe," I told Carl.

"I'm way ahead of you beautiful." We drove through the streets of Tarrytown. There were a few kids out walking in groups. For the most part, however, it was dead out here. Looking for life out here was like looking for a needle in a haystack. It was rare to see and rare to find. I hadn't seen too many people out and about since we entered the city a few hours ago. I wondered was it because of the lack of things to do, or did everyone out here consider themselves dead? Finally, we got to a boarded up house. He parked the car in front and just sat there, looking at it in disdain. His head was kicked back against the seat with his eyes never losing focus on that sight for sore eyes.

I grabbed his hand to let him know that I was here. I wasn't going to even tell him to get out of the car because I know where we were. He stayed transfixed, zoning out into whatever world he was zoned out in.

"This is where I grew up babe. This is where the shit all started. Moms, my brothers, we all laid our hats here." Again, I just sat there, trying to listen and understand his situation.

"I lost everything and everybody. One by one, they all slowly disappeared until it was me left. Over there," as he pointed out of the window. "That's where my mother's body lay. That's where she met her demise. I remember seeing patches of blood on the street leading to her final resting spot. So whoever killed her, she crawled, ran, did whatever she had to do in trying to get away with all the strength she had remaining. They didn't have to do my mom's like that. More importantly, I didn't have to do my mom's like that."

"It wasn't your fault Carl."

"Why not love? It was my actions that sent people after her. That's something that I have to live with for the rest of my days. As they said on a thin line. A night full of passion can lead to a lifetime of pain. That one night, where our passion was robbing, turned into a nightmare for the rest of my life. I try to blank it out of my head, but I simply can't. If I could've taken those bullets for her, I would have in a heartbeat. That was my mother babe. The woman who gave me birth. The woman who worked multiple jobs so that me and my brothers could have clothes on our backs. A roof over our heads. I just don't know why I'm still here and she's not."

The car was silenced. I didn't know what to say to help him. I know what it felt like to lose a parent, but not under his circumstances. True, both of our mothers were murdered. However, my actions didn't result in my mama's demise.

"Who's that in that black car on the corner babe? It looks like someone watching us."

"Some niggas Dee called up. I texted him before we left the house. Ain't nobody fucking with us while we out here. Especially with you being here. Dee ain't playing that shit. I guarantee it's about 15 guns in that car alone."

He started up the car and as we began to pull off, the occupants of the black car flashed their lights at us. Carl chucked up the deuces at them and took back off down the street. I didn't even ask where we were going. I just took the ride for what it was. A ride. I made more analysis of Gary as it was quiet as a mouse in this car. Being here at the light on Broadway and fifth, I could see the remnants of a city that used to be. It looked like things were popping back in the day. Now, it just looked popped.

The only thing that looked like it still had somewhat of a life was The Genesis Convention Center. There was an old Sheraton Hotel across the street from it, but its best days were far behind it. We turned right and continued on our journey. After a good amount of driving, we were deep in the city.

"Where we at Carl?"

"Miller," he said. "Someone who's like a sister to me stays over here. I want you to meet her." To my surprise, it looked a lot nicer over here. It wasn't a sparkling gem, but compared to the rest of the city, it wasn't bad.

"That's Wirt High school over there. They shut it down and moved the performing arts school over here. My cousin J.J. used to play wide receiver for 'em. I remember one night they played East Chicago, the neighboring city next to us. I was at that game. They lost 44-6, but cuz had a grip of receiving yards. They had some linebacker trying to cover him and he was torching his ass. If the rest of the team didn't suck so bad, he would've probably had a good 6 or 7 touchdowns. Dude guarding him wore number 37. He must've been praying hard that night because God was shole looking out for him."

"Where he at now?"

"He graduated from Alabama State and made it to the NFL to play for the Vikings. It was good to see not just my family, but someone out the G make the league." It was good to see Carl was much calmer than what I had seen not even 45 minutes ago. Old sights do that to us sometimes. We all have that one place that we see or go to that can automatically bring us down to our senses.

For some it's the beach. For others, it's simply the four walls that they reside in when they come home from a long day of hard work. For me, it was him. When I saw him, I saw life. I saw my life. To me, that's all that matters at the end of the day. As long as you are sustaining yourself and the ones who you are responsible for, then why let anything else in this world matter? I went through my years in the navy dealing with assholes and those who thought they were better than you because some of their skills outshined yours.

Truth be told, we all have unique skills and everyone functions as a unit. The person who is a great technician may not be a great speaker. The great speaker may not be a great writer. That junior guy at the bottom of the totem pole who they have reduced to sweeping duty all day may be a five star financial guy. What I'm saying is that everyone has a skill and there is no one person who is better than the other. It's simply a bunch of humans who need each other in different ways. We pulled up in front of a red house. I could easily see the relaxation on his face as he put the car in park.

"Feel better?," I asked him. He turned and smiled at me, leaning over to give me a kiss.

"Sure do love. Thank you." We exited the car and walked up to the door, irritated by the next door neighbor's dog barking in the yard. I swear I never got why the smallest dogs always barked the loudest as if they would kick your ass.

"Well I'll be damned." Those were the words exhausted by this woman who opened the door.

"COMMERE AND GIVE YO' BIG SIS A HUG!!!" Now, I saw something that I had rarely ever saw. Carl was acting like a big kid. He was a fun person, yes. But, acting like a five year old? Unless I was surprising him with some workout gear, I didn't see this often. He was overly ecstatic like he had gotten the last piece of candy out of the jar.

"Darni, Star. Star, this my sister Darni." I stuck out my hand to greet her, but she wasn't having that.

"HELL NAH!!! WE HUG OVER HERE!!!" I laughed as I embraced my sister in law and was brought inside the house.

"Y'all sit down so we can rap for a minute." This was another observation I made. This place was a home. Carl felt comfortable. I felt comfortable. It was a family atmosphere.

"So I'm not gone even ask about you. Cause one thing I know about my baby brother is that he knows how to pick 'em cause his big sis taught him well."

"Here we go," Carl said as he started shaking his head with a smirk on his face.

"Oh you know I'm gone get you. Look here, this boy done had some ones back in the day. **LAWD I SWEAR I WANTED TO CHOKE SOME OF THESE THANGS!!!** Lemme tell you about this one he took to a dance."

"Ahh shit, I'm gone to get a drink. She ain't gone never let this shit die." We laughed as Carl got up and waltzed into the kitchen, not wanting to hear what I assumed was another round of this story about to be told.

"I GOT HIM FRESH!!! YOU HERE ME!!! FRESH!!! From head to toe. Bought him some glasses to match that tie with that suit. My little brother was ecstatic over this girl. And do you know she had the nerve to make this boy's night a living hell. Man he came and told me what happened, and the bullshit that followed it afterwards. Child, I had never seen him so hurt and down in his life. I was mad girl. I mean mad. Like I wanted to go out and kick her ass mad. **OOOOOOO!!!"** The story continued, as Carl was in the doorway of the kitchen looking at us, sipping some orange juice.

"She will never live that down baby. Never."

"**HELL NAH!!!**," she responded. I enjoyed the stories that flew around and the comfort that resided between them. Their relationship wasn't of blood, but they were brother and sister nonetheless. Darni and Carl crossed paths when he was a youth, going to the Boys and Girls Club in Gary. She drove the bus that took him home and on field trips. Well, she had three daughters. She also had two more boys Carl's age which she looked on as little brothers. Mo and Dee, the latter was the guy that we were crashing with while we were here. They were like uncles to her kids.

Every time they went on a trip to Chicago or wherever, each one of them had their favorite daughter. In Carl's case, it was Apree. That was his baby. Whatever 'Pree wanted, Carl got it for her. If 'Pree said she wanted Mars, somehow, someway, he was gonna get to outer space and get that girl Mars, along with the entire ET population. They kept a relationship that flourished well throughout their adult years and it never died down.

I knew how much it meant to him, seeing that he lost both of his parents and all of his brothers to either death or the jail cells. We all needed family. Even if they weren't blood, family is still family. We kicked it over there for a few hours until five o'clock hit. We had to start making our way back towards Merrillville to go pick Dee up from work.

As we were leaving, Darni pulled me aside and asked me something very straightforward and direct.

"Star, stay by my baby brother side please? One thing I know about that boy is when he loves, he loves. And he loves you. And I love you."

"I love you too Darni." I hugged her tight. I already had set in my head that I would do anything in the world to make this man happy. Now, I had even more of a reason to ensure that I would never go back on my word. We took to the road and headed back towards Merrillville. We picked Dee up a little bit after six and the man was pooped.

"What y'all trying to do tonight?," he asked.

"Man bruh, all we want is to kick it with you fam bam and just chill. I know wifey cool with it." Indeed I was. All I wanted was to help my man heal and nothing more. If we were here on the side of the road in a cardboard box and that helped him, then I was down. That's what true love does to you. It puts a spell on you. We got back to the house after a trip to the liquor store to pick up some goods for the night. Pork skins, Hennessy, Apple Crown, more dark liquor and some Vanilla Coke. It was going to be one of those nights that all of our livers hated us. Dee started making some calls, we all showered up and around 10 o'clock, it was on and poppin' for a Friday night. Dee called over his cousin B.G. and some more cats from around the way. They were all mad cool to say the least. They all treated me like family.

You know how you get around some new people and they kind of don't gravitate to you instantly? This wasn't the case. They conversed with me as if we were kinfolk all of our lives. It made me think back to when Carl came with me to Wichita. It was sad that I couldn't give him a similar experience. I really wished that I could have.

Things don't fall how you want them too sometimes. But that's okay. Life will not always do that. You simply have to live your life off of the P.E.E.R.S. system. The P is the planning. As we know, our plans are subject to never go how we want them to, but we still need a blueprint or a basis for the things that we plan on doing. It gives you a clear picture of what you want to accomplish. The first E is for execution. You execute that plan to the best of your ability. Take it like construction. After the blueprint, your execution is to build that building so that people can reside in it. The second E is for Evaluation. Or, for those who may have a knack for writing, Editing. Whether your plan went good or bad, you evaluate to get better the next time.

Let's take Michael Jordan for instance, who many assume to be the greatest player to ever play the game of professional basketball. Even though being from Kansas, I'm going to always say the great Wilt Chamberlain. They changed the rules of the game because of him. Any who, Jordan was steady getting his ass kicked by the Bad Boys Pistons.

Let's face it, Bill Laimbeer was probably the last great tough white boy the league has ever seen. Not saying that other great white men haven't came through the game, but Bill struck fear into those who came in the lane. The same with Isiah, Vinnie, Spider Salley, Rick Mahorn, Rodman and the rest of those nuts in D Town. Each ass kicking was a way to get better. He got beat up, he got stronger. He got stronger physically, but then he had to get stronger mentally. He got stronger in both, and then had to exhume that strength to the rest of his team. The result? Well, I think we all know what happened. Even when he lost in 1995 to a young Shaq and Penny led Orlando Magic squad, he had to evaluate his game.

Ok, he was getting older, as they all were on the Bulls. He needed additional help. He helps bring in Rodman and Ron Harper, and three titles later, his legacy is cemented. The cycle never changes. Only the people do. The R stands for redo, repeat, replay or retry. We all learn lessons from our mistakes or our shortcomings.

So once we experience an entire situation, we redo the entire process, only we get smarter about it. The S stands for success. Once you do all the steps that proceed the S, you have finally achieved the success. However, just remember, success never stops. Once you reach one milestone, then another has to be accomplished. That way, you will never get comfortable or complacent. The night was going great. There was boxing on the screen, a few of us shot pool on the other side of the basement and this Hennessey was starting to get me hornier than a TCU horned frog.

I hadn't had any since the miscarriage and I know Carl's nuts were as bout as blue as the ocean. He didn't say much cause he figured that he would let my spirit heal and bring up sex when I was ready again to comprehend it. Not to mention that it was recommended I wait six weeks even after all of the bleeding stopped. I understood and was grateful for such a caring husband. However, I needed him and he needed me. If only he knew how I was going to make his shit disappear in the back of my throat tonight, he wouldn't have even been focused on getting some drank. My goal was to suck his shit like I was dehydrated.

"**HEY B.G., GONE GET THOSE CHOPPERS OUT THE TRUNK NIGGA!!!** I need a few flicks for the gram." One of his cousins bellowed that out and all of a sudden, all of these crazy fools in the house went disappearing outside. When they all came back in, I swear to goodness it looked like we were in the middle of Iraq and the hunt for Saddam Hussein was on. It was AR's, 38's, joints with the extended clips and every other gun you could imagine in life.

These niggas rolled hard and carried more metal than the steel mill. I couldn't blame 'em though. You grow up between Gary and Chicago, two former murder capitals, and you'd stay strapped up all the time yourself. We got to flickin' pics holding them joints. I had never in my life held an AR with the banana clip, so I felt like gangsta chick 101. The female Al Capone. The female John Gotti, or any other mobster that you could think of.

"Cuz Carl. I know you Vice Lord, but this here is what I call my 5 star chopper. Cause it chop up anything I see riding 5 nigga."

"WELL GOT DAMMIT NIGGA YOU AIN'T CHOPPIN ME UP!!!"

"I KNOW NIGGA!!! CAUSE WE FAMILY!!! If ya ass wasn't kin though, we'd have problems."

"Darryl, shut yo ass up," one of the cousins holla'd out. Yea we were all good and drunk now, and the fun did nothing but continue. Around three in the morning, everyone started to filter out, until it was just us and Dee.

"A I'm going to sleep y'all," Dee said.

"Y'all got it." We all walked upstairs as we were right behind him in hitting the bed. At least that's what Carl thought. I walked into our bedroom first. As he came through the door, I put my finger on his mouth and shut the door softly behind him. Dee had one of those light switches that dimmed instead of instantly cutting off.

Carl was pressed against the door as I dimmed the room just enough to make it feel like candles were lit instead. Right there in front of that door, I started to kiss his neck, whispering for him to be quiet. I slowly stripped his shirt off, letting my tongue travel down those pecks and that four pack of his that got me wet on sight.

I came back up and grabbed his face. We tongue wrestled in each other's mouths for a little bit. Finally, I got down to what I wanted. I didn't play with him, rub him or nothing. I was on my knees and just yanked his pants down. I went to work. I couldn't moan as loud as I usually did, seeing that I was in the company of someone else's house. However, it turned me on being sneaky. I could hear Carl trying not to be loud when he was breathing. This was like heaven for me. It had seemed like eternity since I had my husband and this moment was fucking awesome.

I licked all around his shaft, had drool dripping all down on my shirt and my pussy was wetter than the Splash Brothers jump shot. I backed my mouth off his dick and just began to look up at him. *"Watch this,"* I whispered. I backed back on my knees as I told him to step away from the door. He took a step or two up. I took off my shirt, exposing the baby blue lace bra that I had on. I grasped that football player booty of his and slowly inserted him back in my mouth until his dick was completely in my throat.

I held it there, moving my head around, being freaky with it, licking his balls at the same time. I had no gag reflex. I heard this nigga smack his hands against his head, not believing that I was capable of this. I pulled back and started to laugh.

"I hate you," he whispered, all while chuckling. Hey, if you couldn't laugh with your partner while being intimate with them, your sex life was boring and unexciting straight up. I did it again, holding it there as he ran his fingers through my hair. I came back off it and he grabbed my face, kissing me ever so passionately and pulling me up.

He started to strip me of the clothes I had on ever so gracefully. He did it in such a way that I wish I could get dressed and have him do it again. He grabbed my ass and hoisted me in the air, kissing me like only he could kiss me. I loved the way our tongues danced in each other's mouths. I was hot as a fucking furnace. He kept kissing me as he dropped me to the bed.

With no hesitation, he slid his body down with a handful of my breasts and put that mouth of his that I loved so much to work. I was laid back, clutching the sheets, head whipping every which way. I swore he drove me crazy when he went down on me. Ladies, you know how a blender motor is? You know. You plug it in and it goes to warp speed? Doing all kinds of things to the food? Puree, beat, chop, mix, stir. He had all the settings going. That's what my husband's mouth was like. It was a motor that once it got to going, it didn't stop unless you pressed the button to stop. I was losing my fucking mind.

Carl was licking and sucking the soul out of me. I swore that I would see my spirit leave my body any minute. I grabbed a pillow, put it over my face and just screamed into it. I couldn't take it much longer. I swear if pussy eating was a sport, this man would be the Michael Phelps of it. After what seemed like not long enough, I was bustin'. I was bustin' hard. It was the orgasm of orgasms. The fucker kept fucking going as I was trying to push his head off of me.

He finally stopped after a vicious right open hand connected. I heard him laughing, but I didn't know if he was looking at me or not. I was still clenching the sheets, looking up at the ceiling, trying to catch my breath. He came up to kiss me while I was still trying to let my soul enter back into my body. I tasted good and took care of myself so it was all good. Once I got my breath back and she wasn't so sensitive, he slid inside of me and it was like the doors of the church had opened. It wasn't the sex that felt good. It was the man that I loved inside of me feeling good. It was quiet, hot, passionate, dirty sex. The quiet aspect is what made it worthwhile. We had to keep everything to small moans and whispers, but it invigorated both of us.

We flipped to every imaginable position and had a good thirty minute fuck session before he let off inside of me. It felt good to have him again. It felt good that he could do his body in whatever way he liked. When I said his body, I meant mine. That's marriage. His body becomes yours and your body becomes his. Whatever he wanted, I did.

There was no if, ands or buts. Our limits were cut off with anal and all that R. Kelly shit that those crazy ass Chicago niggas are known for. Besides that, it was on. If he wanted to nut on my face, I granted him that. If he wanted it swallowed, I granted him that. Fucked rough, slow, fast, whatever, I granted him that. He did me the same way. Being a therapist, I have dealt with some couples who talked to me about sex. A lot of the times, it was either the man wasn't fulfilling the woman's desires or vice versa. Either way, whoever was the dissatisfied party ended up cheating, or thinking about someone else while they had sex.

To me, the latter was the worse. If your partner had to think about someone else while they were with you, then you already lost the battle. Some of y'all need to stop being so *"I'm too good for that,"* or

"I'm not that type of person" bullshit. And a lot of times it's my fellow ladies. They get raised in a church and think sex is some nasty sport or something. Then they wanna cry to me when the husband is entertaining the side piece. Just remember in life, and this is not just about sex. What one person won't do, another one will.

Y'all complain about Mexicans taking all the jobs in America? Well guess who are the ones out there busting their humps, willing to do whatever to make a better life for themselves and their families? Yea, just like I thought. Hush that mouth.

Saturday morning was here. Rather shall I say Saturday morning was here for me. I was an early riser period. I looked over at the clock to see that it was 8:03 in the morning. It wasn't a lot of hours of sleep, but I felt good. Carl ass was passed out, snoring so loud that alien life heard him in the next galaxy.

I usually hated it. This time, I know I was the cause of that snoring in a major way, so I dealt with it. I knew Dee wasn't up because he was more than likely hungover. I didn't hear anyone walking around the house. Hell, these two probably weren't gonna be up until mid afternoon. I wasn't hung over, seeing that I didn't drink on their level, so I was good. I went to the connecting bathroom, brushed my teeth and took a shower. I came back out and this man was still sleep. Damn, I fucked him good. I relaxed for a minute, indulging in a book I was reading called

"Sleeping with the Lights On." It was an interesting story to say the least, and it kept me well entertained and on edge. I liked books like this. A good fiction novel that not only told you a story, but also at the same time taught you a lesson. The lesson I learned from reading that was that sometimes, you have to step back and analyze a situation. I was once told that by an elder mentor of mine and I seen that it applied in this book. I truly knew that writing was a gift, but everyone didn't have it.

Actually, the writing wasn't the gift. It was the quality of words that were written. I read on until ten o'clock rolled around. Carl was still knocked out, so I threw on some sweats and a t-shirt, grabbed the keys and headed out the door to go get me something to eat. I was pretty good with directions. Plus, I had GPS in case a sister got lost. I made the quick trip down 1-65 South, headed towards Southlake Mall.

That was my first mistake. Heading down to the mall. I said screw it. Why not go ahead and see what was up in there? When I arrived and walked around, I came to realize that it was three stories of really nothing much. I mean, it was cool for what it was, but it didn't have anything that I was looking for. I did however find something for the hubby.

He had always liked the KD's that came out, but he could never find them in his size. It was hard finding size 15's anywhere, but Foot Locker had one pair. I dropped the $160 and concluded this mall trip. It was the small things like this that I enjoyed doing for him. They always say happy wife, happy life. Well, I also say happy dick, happy day. Keep the dick that resides with you happy and all of your days will be the same.

I was starving now as I hit the road back towards the freeway. I put in my GPS the location to the nearest White Castles. I always knew about these mini burgers, but I never had them even though they were all over Wichita. Now was my chance to actually taste the real thing. I found one not too far from the mall.

"Can I take your Order?"

"Yeah, lemme get a ten sack, two orders of nine piece chicken rings, six chicken with cheeses and three large cokes." If that wasn't the most gangsta order ever, I don't know what was. I made sure to get all of this so I could feed the two hungry bears who were at home still hibernating in their caves. When I got around to the window, I seen it was some salty ass chick taking my money. The fact that I was in a nice car and looking good without makeup probably pissed her off some more, but I didn't care. I handed her my money.

"Why you ordering all that for yourself?" I wanted to really go in on her ass, but I kept it calm. It was too early for the bullshit.

"Well, I have a husband to feed and I make sure he eats well if you must know." As she handed me back my change and my order, her response amazed me.

"Shit, you wouldn't catch me feeding no man." I just looked at her like "bitch," because it amazed me how petty she was.

"Well, enjoy ya dildo, cause I got in house dick. A pretty, long, phat one at that." I chucked the deuces and peeled off on her. I swear I hated these rats. I couldn't believe that I used to have that low self esteem and funky attitude about myself. Thank God for growth and opening up to bigger and better things in life. I turned up the music as I got on the freeway for the short ride back to the house. I don't know who this was in the CD deck, but the music was hitting. Dude who was rapping spit some sick shit.

"*We 'liminate muthafuckas/talkin bold when y'all know y'all some bustas/soft muthafuckas/I apologize type niggas/freeze up on they homeboy type niggas/type of niggas that get they ass kicked in they own club…*" He kept on. "*Ment niggas/get down and dirty for they shit nigga/man y'all represent Dubb 2 C in this bitch nigga/callin our studio/playing on our phone like broads/sound like bitches that try to talk hard/now look here we already know niggas is hatin/waitin' for the Grind to fade/that's why we bout to invade and terminate/niggas with this rap shit/we already told y'all* **WE AIN'T BULLSHITTIN**"...

Just as he finished up, another cat came in and slaughtered the last verse, ending it with: "*It ain't no harm in it/for yo' birthday get you a cake with a bomb in it/and tell em Vietnam sent it/Grind Fam syndicate.*"

I ain't know who a Grind Family was or where they were from. All I knew is that I was an instant fan. I got back to the house at exactly 12:30. As I got out, there was a young girl riding her bike who was passing the house.

"Excuse me miss?"

"Yes pretty lady."

"Do you know my Uncle Jr.?"

"Why no I don't. Does he stay around here?"

"No, he lives in California, but this is his friend's house he comes to when he visits home."

"Okay. Do you want me to deliver a message to your Uncle Jr.?" That's when she got sassy.

"Yea, tell him his niece Amaya still waiting on her Jordan's and I ain't approve of him to get married." All I could do was laugh.

"Will do sweetheart."

"**THANK YOU!!!**," she shouted as she rode off, going to do whatever she was going to do. I walked in the house to see both of these fools up in the kitchen.

"And what time did y'all finally raise from the dead?"

"Just now," they both said in unison. All I could do was shake my head.

"Well, look. I got y'all some White Castles to soak up that liquor from last night." As soon as I put the bag down on the table, those two grizzly bears literally ripped the bag open, stuffing their faces. I mean they didn't even take the time to breathe. Thank God I ate an order of the chicken rings before I got here, because I wouldn't have had anything if I had tried to compete with those two knuckleheads. I let them be and went back in the room to continue reading my book. Carl came in about fifteen minutes later.

"Baby? Today, I need you." I closed my book.

"I always got you. What do you need?" He came and sat on the edge of the bed.

"Ever since my mother died, I never had the chance to go look at her grave site. I'm not haunted at the thought of seeing her resting place. I'm haunted at the thought that my heart won't be able to bare it." I threw the book on the dresser and put my arm around him, kissing him on the cheek.

"We'll pull through this together. She's my mother too. Just let me know when you're ready. Okay?"

"Okay." He got up to shower and I immediately began to pray. That's all we can do sometimes is just that. Some things are beyond our control. This was our last day here and this would indeed be the biggest hurdle out of all of them. Finally, Carl came out clean as a whistle. He got fully dressed, putting extra care on the shoes I just got him.

"It's time babe."

"You want me to come with you cuz? You know. Case them niggas out there trying to start some shit."

"I appreciate it cuz, but I gotta do this on my own."

"I respect it dawg. Do what you gotta do." They dapped up and we bounced out, headed to what perhaps was the last bandage he needed. That bandage was a mother's love. We got to the cemetery about 15 minutes after leaving the house.

As we drove slowly through the graveyard, he started pointing out everyone who he knew was buried here. It was almost sad that it seemed like he had a family reunion right here. He showed where his dad was buried, his great granddaddy, his great grandma, one of his brothers, his cousin Keida, his cousin Hoodoo (pronounced who-do), friends and even the old lady who lived across the street from him as a youngin. It was truly a sad scene to watch.

"Right there love. That's my cousin Snook. The most gangsta old lady with a cane. She was the only Crip in a hood full of GD's."

"Really?"

"Naw love," he said laughing. "We called her Crip because of that cane she had, but you didn't fuck with Snook. Her grandaughter, my cousin Shayna, we went to school together. That's my favorite cuzzo that I hope to introduce you too one day. If you needed to know where the party was, she had the answers. I hope like hell she never get married. I don't like any of her boyfriends. Never have and never will."

All I could do was laugh. We kept going until we got all the way to the end of the gravel road and stopped. He sat there for a minute, quiet and to himself.

"Is that her all the way in the back?" He looked over at that headstone teary eyed. "Yea," he whimpered out.

"C'mon. I got you." I got out and walked over to the driver side. I opened the door and Carl wouldn't budge.

"I can't babe. I can't." He kept saying that. In a positive way, I gave him the words he needed so that he was able to face his fears. Rule #96798 of being a wife. Know when to turn it on and turn it off. Believe it or not, there are some wives out there who would've probably just said "Just get it over with." You can't always be blunt, brash and straight to the point. In situations like this, you have to comfort, heal, let the individual know that you are with them, and that they have all the time in the world to complete the task at hand.

I definitely understood his situation, because I lost my mother and looking at her grave was always painful. I waited patiently until he was ready. Taking one step out of the car, he broke down. I caressed his head, kissing him repeatedly, letting him know that I was here, wasn't going anywhere and that he could do this. As his second foot planted on the ground, he stood up, his face in the palms of my hands. He looked up as if to ask God to please let him make it through this trial. He gathered himself. We locked arms and slowly made our way to her headstone. Once there, it was like time stopped. Carl kept trying to catch himself, but it was to no avail. He dropped to the dirt and so did I. He lied there, face first in the dirt, sobbing to his mother. I was right there on the ground with him, doing what I had to do to keep his soul intact. I heard him whisper *"It's my fault"* over and over. After the fourth or fifth time, I couldn't take it anymore. That's when I turned him around on his back and sat on top of him.

"Look at me Carl. Look at me."

"No I can't. I can't" He didn't want to, so I grabbed his face and forced him too.

"Listen to me Carl," I told him in the softest, yet firmest voice possible. "This is not the time to feel guilty. This is a time to say goodbye to your mom. She wouldn't want you like this and neither do I. I know it hurts. Look at me," as I snatched his head back towards my direction.

"It's okay to cry. It's okay to be hurt. It's okay to grieve. However, it's not okay to beat yourself up for something you can't control. I love you. Been in love with you since the day you saw through my bullshit and opened your soul up to help heal mine. Now, I need my man to stand tall. I need my man to face his fears. I need my man to be a man."

I stood up and backed away from him, as he wiped the tears from his face. He stayed there planted on the ground for about another minute until he got up, dusted himself off and faced his mother's headstone. Sniffling and trying to control his remaining emotions, he placed one hand on her headstone. I was about five steps back, knowing that this was a moment that he needed to be solo.

"I love you mom. Your son is now a man. I can't bring you back. All I can do is make sure that I keep our families name alive. He bent down to kiss her headstone and pulled something from his pocket.

"What's that babe?," I asked him. He looked down, juggling whatever it was.

"Come here Star?" I walked over to him and watched him open his hand. In it was a pair of small earrings.

"At seventeen, before the start of my senior year, I got a young lady pregnant. My mother never knew. My daughter was a stillborn that March day in 2010. I never have been the same since. I apologize for never telling you about that portion of my life. It has haunted me for years." I wasn't upset as most people would have thought I would be. I empathized instead.

"Did you name her at least?"

"Yea." That's when he turned around to me, looked me dead in the eye and said something to me that would forever change my life. "I named her Star. Star Jackson. I was a science geek on the low, and she was the most beautiful creation that I have ever seen in my life. Even in death, she was beautiful. I told doc that I wanted her name to be Star, seeing that stars are beautiful when you look at them in the night sky. Also, stars live and die. Doc was a very religious dude, and he pulled me out of the room after a while. He told me. He said. I don't know why I'm about to say this. God placed it on my heart. What you just named that baby. That is your future. I don't know when, where, how. All I know is that a Star will come into your life and shine so brightly and live forever." I was in complete and utter shock.

"When I first met you, and I seen the attitude you had, I thought about a star. How they are big balls of gases, and gases are unpredictable. That day you introduced yourself as Star, I didn't say nothing, or make assumptions. I simply went back to my rack on the ship that night and asked God is this what doc meant. All this time later, I see my star is you."

Tears were an understatement for both of us as we gripped each other's spirits in a hug so tight that it threatened to cut off the circulation of the both of us. I never wanted to let him go from this point on. I don't know what God looks like. I don't know if God was manifested into one of these trees out here or what. All I knew is that I felt his presence today as not only was my husband's wound healed, but a bandage I never knew existed came off of his body. At the same time, a bandage was placed over my heart. He cut deep into it with those words. When we put a bandage on, it usually is to keep out infection and other impurities, therefore making the healing process quicker. However, in this case, the words he cut me with, I didn't want them to bleed out of my heart. I placed this bandage on my cardiac, hoping that I would go into an eternal state of cardiac arrest, because what he said I never wanted to let go of. We must've stayed hugged up for at least twenty minutes at her gravesite.

I realized we were healed in a major way. There were still a lot of unanswered questions in both of our lives. For right now, though, this by far was the greatest day of my life. We buried those earrings right there by the headstone. We got back to the car and left back towards the house.

Dee was working a double shift, so we celebrated our love by making love all throughout the night. Cemeteries usually represented death. In our case, it represented life. Gary, Indiana had been good to me. I was forever grateful for it. So to the residents of this great city, from Delaney, to the Bronx, Miller, Oak Knoll, Tarrytown and everywhere else, I give you my gratitude. Thank you Gary, Indiana. Thank you much.

4 AUGUST

Being back home in San Diego was refreshing. During the first week of August, me and the hubby got readjusted to our work schedules. He was working at the Naval Hospital Balboa from 10-6, Monday through Thursday, and 12:30-6 on Friday.

Even with the chance to sleep in every morning, he made it his duty to make me breakfast every morning. It was refreshing to have such a great man. It's not always easy leaving the house at seven something in the morning and fighting traffic to be on time at eight. Having a good meal to start your day and your lunch prepared made things much, much easier. I even rewarded him some mornings with a quick blow job, just to show him my appreciation. I was catching back up on my clients today and I saw I had yet another session with Mr.

Pierce, the former Marine who nearly stabbed a man to death after he caught him sleeping with his wife. It was scheduled for 10, so I had a chance to get some things in order before he came in.

My co-workers were great, as my office was littered with flowers, cards and well wishes. My boss even came in and gave me a donation pot that everyone in the office put in on. Once I counted it up, it came out to a total of $967.25. Kudos to whoever put the quarter in there. I was grateful for everything, even the money that jingled. Ten o'clock came around and Mr. Pierce was a no show.

I asked the desk clerk Carla had he come to check in and she said no. He didn't call or anything. My next appointment wasn't until one in the afternoon, but it was concerning to me when a client of mines didn't show up. Mental health was a serious issue in this country that often got overlooked. We see the guys on the corner talking to themselves, or the vets who can't even bare the noise of a firecracker because it reminds them of a gunfight. Even if a simple talk with them provided healing, then that's what needed to occur.

By 10:30, I had called Mr. Pierce's phone several times, but he didn't pick up. I finally just chalked it up as a loss and started to concentrate on my 1:00 appointment, a lieutenant who was getting over an abusive relationship with her now confined husband.

"Star, come quick to the break room. Look what's on the news." That was Carla screaming as I got up to see what the fuss was all about. I got to the break room, trying to get a glimpse of the TV that all these tall ass men were hovering in front of. Once I got a clear view, I got the shock of my life.

"As we reported earlier on KUSI, a man is on the Coronado Bridge threatening to jump. Police have now identified the man as 32 year old former Marine James Pierce. We will keep our cameras rolling and follow this story as it progresses." I didn't say anything, nor did I know if anyone in the office knew he was my client or not except for Carla. She looked over at me and we kind of gave each other that look where we knew something bad was about to happen.

"I swear it's some crazy fuckers in this world." That was one of my jackass co-workers being completely immune to the situation as he walked out with a coffee in his hand. In a way, I understood where he was coming from. People jumped off this bridge all the time. It was as normal out here as seeing the beach when you drove by.

When you are closely connected to someone, however, the situation is a totally different one. The room started to file out, but me and Carla stood there, hoping and praying for good news.

"My gosh I hope this young man doesn't go," said Carla. Me and her both. He was literally backed up on the ledge. All he had to do was flip backwards and it was a wrap. Suddenly, as the negotiator inched within maybe 5 steps of him, James threw his hands up. I thought to myself good, this will all be over soon. He is giving up and will receive the proper treatment he needs. Just when I thought that, he flipped backwards. The news crews were silenced and they cut their feed right before he hit the water. Immediately, Carla started to cry. I was in a severe state of shock as I tried to tell myself that what I had just witnessed wasn't real. Unfortunately, it was. I consoled Carla. She knew firsthand what this was like. Her brother had served two tours over in Afghanistan. On his second tour, his humvee convoy was struck by an improvised explosive device. Everyone inside died or was seriously hurt except for him.

How do you even live with yourself after that, knowing that everyone was gone except for you? One night, as Carla arrived home from work last year, she found her brother Daniel in the backyard, hanging from a tree. He had hung himself from some chains that he had found inside of her garage. I couldn't even imagine what I would've done if I walked in and found one of my family member's dead in that manner. They say there is no pain like a mother's pain. That is indeed true. But, I'm pretty sure a sister's pain is also a tough pill to swallow, especially when it's your only brother. I walked back in my office, forgoing lunch. Hell, I really didn't care about my next appointment, but I had to keep moving forward. It was officially one of those days that I just wanted to get home to Carl and vent. I simply took an hour nap. My phone alarm went off at 12:30 and I arose feeling a little bit better.

As one o'clock approached, I began prepping myself for my next client. I truthfully was worn down from the events of today, but I couldn't back out on the people who needed me. They depended on me. I shut my office door and indulged in a Pepsi. I stayed away from pop, but this was my form of cigarettes when stressed.

"Star, your one o'clock is here."

"Thanks Carla." I took a deep breath and said a real quick "Jesus take the wheel" prayer. Hell, I was just hoping that he would carjack me at this point and hold me hostage for ransom. "Diana Stevens," I yelled out as I entered the lobby. She rose up. All five foot two of her. I knew this would be an interesting one. A pit bull in a skirt is what I thought of. Actually, I thought of the typical hoodrat. Three colors in her hair, overly long press on nails and some ghetto heels that she was struggling in. You know I wanted to hear this story. Not just how she overcame the abusive son of a bitch who was locked up now, probably playing the jailhouse bunny. I wanted to hear the way she was going to tell me. All I could think of was Jamie Foxx's Wanda character from In Living Color.

"Go ahead and have a seat Ms. Stevens."

"Mmmhmmm," she responded. "That's the last words that nigga told me before those hot grits got thrown on his ass." Oh yea, I could tell that this was going to be a good one.

"So first things first. Why don't you tell me how we got to this point?" She readjusted herself as if to say get ready for the ride.

"Whelp. I met his ass two years ago. Ahhh girl, he was fine. Fine and clean. I mean he was so damn clean he could wipe his ass with his hand after shitting and wouldn't have nothing on it." I really didn't need to hear that, but I kept the emotion in as she continued.

"Yeah I approached him in that lounge, thinking that I met the right one. You know that lounge girl. Phantom Lounge, where all of them San Diego niggas go. I was just hoping his mental matched his physical. We started out cool on the first date. By the second one I asked him, If the goal ain't marriage, then why are we talking? You know this nigga responded with Maybe cause it's the second damn date and I still don't know you. The hell you think you suppose to get a ring because you made it to Olive Garden status? I ain't even tested the draws and you want a ceremony. Girl bye. I was like hell nah girl. This nigga trippin'."

I wouldn't have even given this crazy heffa Jack in the Box status. She continued.

"So this nigga wasn't going anywhere. I let him think he was winning, so I played along. For the next six months, we were actually gravy. It was the honeymoon stages of the calls, texts, all that. I was in the service. He was in the service. I was an officer. He was an officer. Hell, I figured we were a.j. squared away. At our one year mark, we went to the courthouse and got hitched. Then, it all went to shit four months later. I was on sea duty and his ass went to shore duty. I leave on sea trials, bitch in my house. I have duty in port, bitch in my house. I would find all kinds of evidence, throw it in his face, yet he'd deny it to the fullest. I was a stupid ass for staying, but one incident made me leave for good. One night, I lied and said they switched me duty sections. Oh you could tell that he was happier than a sissy with a bag full of dicks." Her metaphors were priceless.

"I went home late since he said he wasn't doing anything for the evening but watching TV. I walked in. Nothing. I searched all around the house. Nothing. It was a Tuesday night, so there was only one place he could be in San Diego on a Tuesday night."

"Neo Soul Tuesdays."

"HELL YEA GIRL!!!" Yea, I could tell this broad was nuttier than a fruitcake.

"Any who, I strolled up in there, listening to them on the mic thinking they were Love Jones or some shit. As I scanned the crowd, there I saw him. He was up front by the stage with another bitch. Oh girl. I lost it. In the middle of somebody's performance, I ran up and started giving him the business. I ain't even see how the bitch looked cause I was so focused on whoopin his ass. You would've thought I was Floyd Mayweather in that muthafucka." By this time, I was tired of listening, cause it all seemed like a real life episode of Love and Hip Hop. Then came the part that got me going.

"He came home," she said. "He walked in the house, with the bitch. Lo and behold. It was my own damn sister." My focus was back, because I wanted to hear how this went down.

"So how did it all end up? How did he end up in jail?" I struck a chord right there as she went dead silent.

"Ma'am?," I asked her. She was ballin' heavy at this point. The hood shit disappeared and out came a broken woman.

"He beat my sister to death in front of me." My heart dropped. I wasn't trying to believe what I had just heard.

"He asked me, do you wanna feel pain? I stood there, angry as hell that my own sister was banging my husband. Then, he hit her so hard out of nowhere and she dropped. I ran up on him with the intent to kill him, but with one solid blow, I was out. I was dazed when I opened my eyes, seeing his fist fly up and down. I didn't even know who he was hitting to be quite honest. My memory lapsed that bad. The last thing I remember was a kick to the face and darkness."

Once again, she lost it. Inside, I lost it. These males hitting females was too much. Ain't no room for that. If they try to act like a man, then yeah, I understand. Just to hit a woman though for sheer joy, that shit wasn't cool. That's not a man. That's a pure bred bitch. Words weren't going to do me any good right now, so I just hugged her. I held her as she rocked back and forth in that seat, trying to release the pain of what once was. In that time, I thought about everything she told me about that relationship. Lust on first sight. Few months and falling in love. Married in one year. That fairy tale may work in the movies and with very few people in reality. For the majority of the population, that is not the case. True, me and Carl were married in just under two years. For most, that still isn't enough time. The phases of love have to occur. There was the learning of each other. The mental battles with one another. The healing that occurred. The falling out. The anger. All of that.

We met each other in hell before we even decided to try and reach heaven. And before we reached heaven, we almost reached heaven, literally. Would we be married right now if it wasn't for that fateful Halloween night accident?

The honest to God truth is that I couldn't answer yes or no. We were at that lovers point, though, and it wasn't one regret behind it because we knew each other inside and out. Ladies, this is my honest to goodness advice. Stop falling for what you think the size of the dick is. Trust, a dick can be attached to a pussy in more ways than one. In this young lady's case, it was a man. I got home that night wore out and exhausted. Carl seen me come in with bitchy and stress written all over my face.

"Sit down babe." I heard him, but I was getting out of these shoes and clothes first.

I was irritated beyond belief because of that last session I had. I plopped on the couch next to him in my comfy clothes of sweats and a beater.

"Tell me what happened love?" And with that question being asked, I rambled on for a good thirty minutes. All Carl did was shake his head on occasion and play the interested role. Whether or not he was listening, that was another question. However, when you need to vent, you need to vent.

Like Chris Rock once said. When a woman is in her mood, sometimes you just gotta shut the fuck up and let her have it. No matter if it's a horny mood where she wanna screw your brains out or a pissed off mood where she just wants to yell at the top of her lungs. Let her have it. Life becomes so much simpler when you allow that. Mid August came around and things were flowing smoothly. My mans was a Leo, so you know it was time to turn up for him. We mobbed up to Athens Park in L.A. one weekend. When I first told him where we were going, he was trippin' hard.

"Baby what the hell kind of birthday shin dig is in Athens Park? **AIN'T NOTHING BUT KILLAS OUT THERE!!!**"

I mean, he was right. Athens Park was Blood central in L.A. Plus, it was an odd ball place to throw a party. I let him know that it was cool though. Since he let me decide the festivities, I figured we go to a hole in the wall line dancing spot where we could just groove across the floor all night. I told him that a bunch of people that I knew would be there and he was gravy after that.

When we pulled up to The Family Room that night, I realized that this shit was the size of a living room. Hole in the wall was an understatement. A crack in the concrete was more suitable. The joint was decorated in Leo this and Leo that. All the letters were in red of course. We got us a table and just started mingling. Carl was gravy now, especially when they brought him an order of twelve wings. Oh this foolio was in heaven then.

"Baby, you go dance and I'll finish smashing this." He was so nasty for talking with his mouth open, but I let him have it seeing that it was his turn up session. I ended up dancing most of the night by myself because he was too busy getting full off of wings and liquor. I stepped and I stepped, enjoying the groove. My husband was having a good time. I was having a good time. Dancing was my getaway from a lot. As I scanned the room, watching grown folks enjoy life, there it came. Memories of what once was.

"Ok Star. Now twirl." I twirled and I twirled and I twirled. My mom had so much fun watching me enjoy my youth. I was four and I swear I was a princess ballerina.

"Mommy, mommy, I'm queen Zaviah."

"And where does the name Zaviah come from may I ask?" I smiled and started jumping around.

"Because it just sounds pretty mommy." I had the wildest imagination in the world. As my mom was teaching me how to twirl and dance, I was completely immune to the bruise marks and scars that were so easily visible. I wondered why there was peace whenever my daddy wasn't around. I was too young to understand it, but I could comprehend it. Me and my mom did this whenever we were alone. She was a dancer when she was in high school. She belonged to a group called "The Platinum Steppers." I don't know if it was anything like the stepping you see nowadays, but from the pictures I used to see of her and her friends in their shiny outfits and puffed out afros, I knew she was having fun with her life.

When I twirled out here, that's what it reminded me of. Her. I danced for my mom and not necessarily for myself. It brought me more than joy and happiness. It brought me an inner peace that I had desired for so long. By 1:45 in the morning, I was good and wore out. A lot of people had filed out of the joint already and it was time for us to follow suit. Carl was good and toasty. The amount of Crown Royal that he drank should've been illegal. We had us a hotel about an hour West in Anaheim near Disneyland so we wouldn't have to drive all the way back to San Diego. I figured I wouldn't get any sleep tonight, since I know the alcohol had woken up the horn dogs inside of him.

"Baby I'm hungry," he told me in his slurred speech state.

"I'll get something for you when we get closer." By the time I said that, he was K.O.'ed. I made the drive to Anaheim with no music except the sound of his snoring. Actually, being irritated by that freight train seemed to make me put my foot to the pedal harder than ever. The end result was me getting to the city pretty damn fast.

Once I hit Brookhurst, we were scott free. He was hungry though, so I had to get him something. I headed some ways down the street away from the amusement park and ordered some Jack in the Box for him. He arose at the smell of the supreme croissant. It was like a zombie waking from the dead. I handed it to him and he instantly started murdering it.

"Well you're welcome."

"Oh I'm sorry. Thank you beautiful." What more could you expect from men though? We headed back to our hotel near Disneyland. I was sleepy as all get out and ready to call it a night. We were at the light on Euclid and Ball. 3:37 in the morning was the exact time. I never got how lights could change so slow when there is no one on the road but you. I saw the car coming up next to us, but I didn't think anything of it. It was a Brown Chevy Impala, with tinted out windows. I saw the opposite lights turn yellow, signaling that it was almost time to go. Then, the window of the Impala came creeping down. *POP! POP! POP! POP! POP! POP!* The glass flew everywhere as the sounds of bullets hitting the metal were petrifying. Six shots had been put into the whip. I peeled off as fast as I could, but I was in pain and disoriented.

"**CARL!!! CARL!!!**" I wasn't garnering any response from him. "**CARL!!!**" As I tried to keep my focus and drive, I called his name yet again. When I didn't hear his name after a third time, I looked over to find him slumped over the seat belt.

"**CARL WAKE UP!!! BABY WAKE UP!!!**" I was shaking him and screaming so hard that I was crying. That's when I felt the pain in my side. I looked down and saw blood.

"**AAH SHIT!!!**" I started to freak out. The next thing I saw was the light pole and everything went dark.

"**BABE!!! BABE!!!**" I woke up screaming and swinging.

"**LOVE!!!,**" Carl shouted as he grabbed a hold of me, trying to calm me down. I couldn't catch my breath and I felt like I was having a panic attack. Sweat poured from my forehead like a rainstorm in the amazon. I was too freaked out to comprehend anything.

"Beautiful, shhh. Shhh." I slowly but surely got brought back down to Earth.

"You're okay babe. We're safe."

"Where we at? How we get back in the room?"

"Love, we been in the bed for over an hour." I didn't know what was going on. I eased back down in the bed with Carl's arms wrapped around me. I looked around to make sure we were in a hotel room. I looked over at the clock. 3:37 a.m. on the dot.

"What happened babe?" I sat up, trying to get my thoughts together.

"I had a dream. We were on Ball and Euclid. Someone shot us up. We came from Jack in the Box and someone shot us up." I don't know what Carl was thinking, but when I looked over and saw that empty bag of Jack in the Box laying next to the bed it gave me chills. Why did God give me this dream? I have no idea. I was just blessed to see this in a dream and not in my reality. We eventually fell back asleep and I arose sometime after nine o'clock. The sun gave enough light through the slits in the curtains to illuminate the room. My phone had been blown up with missed calls from Carla. What in the hell could she want this early on a weekend morning? I called her back expecting an apology from a drunken call spree she made.

"Oh my God are you okay?" She was ecstatic on the phone.

"Yeah I am. Why are you so hyped up right now?"

"Well I know you said you and the hubby would be staying in Anaheim for the weekend. So when I cut on the news and heard about the big shootout that took place up there last night, I immediately got worried."

"What shootout are you talking about?"

"If you're near a television, cut it on and watch the news."

My energy immediately came up on ten thousand. I sat up, reaching for the remote lying on the table next to the bed. I cut on the hotel television and there it was.

"*Shootout on Euclid and Ball leaves a young couple dead*" were the words that were flashed across the bottom of the screen. They had just left Jack in the Box and were headed home. Subjects in a Brown Chevy Impala with tinted windows opened fire on the vehicle. The couple fled the scene but crashed a few blocks down.

"Carl, Carl? Wake up?" His groggy tail was moaning and not budging.

"CARL!!!"

"WHAT DO YOU WANT WOMAN???!!!" I grabbed his face. "Look negro." That what the hell look turned into one of shock and awe as the same feeling that was going through my body was now going through his.

"How we were that lucky? We did the exact same thing this couple did, yet not catch bullets."

"I don't know Carl. I don't know." Immediately, one would think that I would automatically say God did this. God prevented me from being in the wrong place at the wrong time. God got me out of there in time and safely back to my hotel.

I thought of none of that. As Carl was still transfixed on the television, I thought about one person and one person only. My mother. It was always one thing she used to say when it came to dancing.

"Make your greatest step off the stage." Indeed, it was true. Maybe I did make the greatest exit off stage no performer had ever seen. Maybe mom was driving my steps towards the right place and the right time. Nevertheless, I was more than grateful. Dance mom. Dance on the clouds for eternity. We got back to San Diego later that day, still enjoying the time we had left in the weekend.

"What we doing tonight babe?" I thought about it. I really didn't want to do much of anything but lounge around the house on this chill day. I was tired and Lord knows that I needed to rest up. However, he was amped for his Leo season, so I did what I had to do. We started off as big kids. We went indoor rock climbing near the Old Town section of the city. Now, this was all new for me.

He was the one who was overly adventurous, talking bout he wanted to go to Africa and ride in a truck looking for Lions and shit. You would've swore he was white sometimes with his wildness for nature. I locked up my harness next to him as he was strapping up laughing at me.

"You ready to do this? Or, is that big ass of yours gone weigh you down?"

"Nigga please. You ain't complained about this ass now have you?" We just both started laughing. He moved over to the big wall while I stayed my tail on the medium sized, almost straight one. It shouldn't be too hard I imagined. We both began to climb. I was cool until I grabbed maybe the sixth or seventh rock. I looked over my shoulder and just freaked out.

"GET ME DOWN!!!"

"Just be easy ma'am and lean back off the rocks."

"I AIN'T LEANING SHIT!!! I'M NOT BOUT TO BUST MY ASS!!!" I saw Carl out of my side vision on the other wall laughing hysterically as he completely stopped in mid climb to make fun of my misfortune.

"THE FUCK YOU LAUGHING AT???!!!"

"GIRL YO ASS IS BARELY TEN FEET OFF THE GROUND!!! LEAN THAT PLUMP, BUMP RUMP ASS BACK IF YOU WANNA GET OFF!!!"

"SHUT THE FUCK UP CARL!!!" He was laughing so hard now that I thought he was gonna fall off. I pondered for about five seconds, then I let go. I thought I was gonna die upon release, not realizing that I didn't even make it 15 feet off the ground. I was now on solid ground telling the observer to hurry up and get this thing off of me. He was laughing, a bunch of others were laughing and Carl was climbing with the biggest grin imaginable. He finally made it to the top and came back down.

"Baby," as he kept laughing hysterically. "What the hell?"

"Shut up Carl. I'm scared of heights. You know that."

"You don't say nothing when I lift you in the air now do you?"

"Well you can lift ya shit with ya hand tonight."

That famous smirk came across his face as I side eyed his ass. He was tryna be funny, but I was going to get the last laugh on his ass if he kept fucking with me. After that quick adventure and me cussin his ass out, we headed back to the car to head off to whatever else we could think of.

"You wanna hit the zoo beautiful? See some of yo family members." I swear he was asking for a kick in his nuts. I obliged, seeing that I hadn't been to the zoo one time since I got to San Diego. It was a cool experience to say the least. It was a little late, but definitely a good experience.

We saw the ever so famous pandas which weren't doing anything but sleeping. Hell, every other animal except for the sea life looked to be on screw it mode because they were laying down, not doing a damn thing. We stayed for a little under two hours and I regretted it much. Those damn hills in that zoo were made by the devil I swear. My legs were worn and walking anywhere else wasn't an option.

"Babe," I asked him wore out in the parking lot. "Can we go somewhere, get some eats and sit in the car?"

"Damn girl. That big ol ass too much to carry through the zoo?" I gave him a quick, swift tap to his nuts. He keeled over at his waist in an instant, looking up at me like what the hell.

"Bet you won't talk no more shit now will you?" I smiled as I got in the car. He came in, trying to look mad, but he wasn't. He couldn't hold it in as that silly grin came across his face.

"I'm a fuck you up woman."

"You try that on a regular. You ain't good." Oh the way to get a man going. Talk about his sex game and watch him get humbled real quick. He knew I was lying, but I knew how to get him going for later. As we left and hit the light on Washington, I told him to drive towards the freeway.

"I thought you wanted some food? HIllcrest right up the street."

"Just drive Carl. We gone eat. Trust me." Waiting for the long ass light to change, I had time on my side.

"Whip it out."

"Huh?"

"Pull ya dick out?" Now, here was the funny thing. He started to unbuckle his pants, all while giving me a lost look. He knew what was about to go down, but he was trying to play it cool. Or, maybe he didn't. I had never done this before with him, or any man. The light turned green. We had tinted windows, the sun had started to make its descent and I wasn't worried about anyone seeing us. I unbuckled my seatbelt, leaned over, kissed it and gripped it.

"Drive normal nigga," I told him. I had never done this, but it was something else to add to my bucket list. I didn't look up at him, but from the noises he was making, I could tell that his concentration level was fading. I fucked with his mindset something serious. When I felt us coming on the on ramp, I kept it slow and steady. I didn't want this nigga veering off the highway and have us fall to our deaths. When I felt we were on that open road, I went to town on his ass. I sucked like I was trying to get the cure for cancer out of him. By the time I rose up, we were at the 52 freeway exit, almost to La Jolla, going the complete opposite way from our house. I pulled back up in my seat and he took that exit all the way to the Clairemont Mesa exit, and just stopped the car on the side of the road.

"What's wrong Carl?," I chuckled. He couldn't do anything but look at me. He shook his head a few times, laughed and pointed to the sky. This dude was wild. He got back on the road and stopped at some Chinese Restaurant over there in the area. I don't think any of us were in the mood for Chinese food, but we just made the best out of it. In that moment, it hit me that I was beyond blessed. I may have lost a baby, but I still had him. I still had my life. I still had another chance and another day to make things better than what they once were.

We capped off the rest of the night with beach hopping and the movies. Once we got home, even though it was extremely late, I gave him what was his and that was me. All night, we didn't stop. He fucked me. He didn't make love to me. He fucked me. Like, real good. Truthfully, that's what all women desire and needed sometimes. It was cool to be in love. It was cool to do the soft music, candles, massages and all that other sweet and sensual stuff. However, every few sessions, we desire our man to just take the pussy and own it. Let us know who the fuck is running shit in the house. Treat us like the dirty girls we love to be sometimes.

Everyone always says you can't turn a ho into a housewife. However, they fail to realize that you can't spell housewife without ho. Ho's do it all, and it was cool to be a ho for your man. That was the great thing about being married. You didn't have to call up any random person. You didn't have to sneak around because you didn't wanna be seen with someone.

It was just me and him, exactly the way I wanted. I already knew that come tomorrow morning, I was going to be up early cooking grits, eggs, bacon, sausage, pancakes and toast with two types of jams. As I was up early cooking this Sunday morning, still feeling like my entire body was a spaghetti noodle, the doorbell rang. I looked over at the oven clock to see that it was just 8:03 in the damn morning. I don't care who you were or where you lived in America. No one was supposed to be coming to your door this early on a Sunday morning. It had better be Publishers Clearing House or someone of very high importance to be coming over this damn early. It rang again.

"**OKAY!!!**" I opened the door to see a police officer and a lawyer.

"Yes. Can I help you gentlemen?"

"Ma'am, I am a lawyer for your father, Mr. Donald Thurman."

"That's impossible because my father is dead and I don't know any Mr. Thurman."

"May we come in?"

"Let me go get my husband and I'll be right back." I woke Carl up for two reasons. One, this was some stuff he knew about. Two, in case they were some frauds, trying to get in our house to do harm, my husband was here to defend us. He left the room in some jeans shorts and a long black tee, with a 9mm Beretta concealed in his waistband. I went back to the door and let them in. Carl was sitting in the living room just waiting for some shit to pop off.

"Ma'am," the lawyer stated as he ruffled through a folder. "Your father died on a Navy ship as a civilian employee two weeks ago. In this box I have his will, in which he leaves everything to you to include bank accounts, a home and a vehicle."

I looked at Carl not knowing what to do.

"But he isn't him. He is dead."

"We can do a DNA test ma'am to confirm if you will allow us," said the officer. I looked at Carl once again, confused and not knowing what to do.

"What do you have to lose babe? If it leads to a truth that you must know, then let it lead you to it." He placed his arm around me as all eyes in the house were on me. In my mind, I only had Dontae, but he was dead. I hated being stuck between a rock and a hard place. It was difficult to ponder.

"Okay. I'll do it." The officer took a swab from inside my mouth. The lawyer's contact info was left with us and now I had to wait until the DNA tests confirmed that this guy was my actual father. Carl hugged me as I just burst out into tears. This was pain to the next extent. What if he really was my daddy? That would've meant that all those years, I was just getting raped by someone who played a daddy role in my mama's house. One million thoughts started to creep through my head.

"Let's go for a ride babe?" I didn't want a car ride, ice cream, any of that. I just shoved Carl off of me and went back to the bedroom to cry. He followed me into the room and rubbed my back as he sat on the edge of the bed. It's good to have a spouse that is always there for you. However, there are just some things as an individual that you have to fight through yourself. Confusion and anxiety was an understatement. Another wound had been open. The wound of uncertainty. I cringed at the notion of the words that were spoken to me. It was something that I would not be able to get out of my mind very easily.

A few days passed by towards the last ten days of the month. The phone rang on a calm, Wednesday evening.

Me: "Hello?"

Technician: "Hi. I'm looking for Mrs. Jackson?"

Me: "This is she."

Technician: "Hi. I'm calling from the DNA testing facility in San Diego. You have a case pending of matching your DNA to that of a Mr. Donald Thurman. Your test came back a positive match."

Silence was there on my end as I just hung up. I don't know how to describe the feeling that I had, but it was not full of grace and joy. My worst fears had been confirmed and it sucked. Carl was not yet home from the gym, so I had no one to talk with. It would've been easy to call him and tell him that I needed him urgently. I didn't want to interrupt what he was doing. At least if he was going to hear all of my grief tonight, I could at least give him the courtesy of letting him get a full workout in.

Time ticked by slow as ever as the television began to watch me instead of me watching it. My biggest focus was on how I would deal with my feelings. Yes, we are emotional creatures as women. That shit is still no excuse to let it dictate everything. The worst thing you could do in life is attach emotion to everything. You'll always be in a fucked up situation if you do that.

"Hey beautiful. Wassup?" I didn't even say a word when he came through the door.

"Babe what?" I didn't wanna tell him, but I didn't wanna hide anything from my husband.

"It's true," I told him in a somber voice.

"So now what do we do?" We, I thought. Why is he asking we? It upset me to my core. He didn't have to deal with this shit.

"**WE CARL!!! WE???!!!** We ain't worried bout a daddy. We ain't stressing over lies throughout the past. We ain't going through shit. **IT'S ME!!! YOU ARE SO SELFISH!!! I FUCKING HATE YOU RIGHT NOW!!!**" I thought I did something. I thought I made him feel my pain. He stood there for a minute staring at me with a look of disdain. Then, he started to laugh.

"What the fuck is so funny? **HOW IS THIS SHIT FUNNY???!!!**"

"You know Star," in the calmest voice possible he said. "It's one thing you fail to realize right now. When you become married, the I's, the me's, they get replaced with we. They get replaced with us. If you mess up financially, we mess up financially. If I start a fire in here, I don't lose the house. **WE!!!** We lose the house. Right now, I'm upset, but I'm calm, because I've learned that raising your voice all the time won't get you anywhere in life. Not even a minute ago, you said the most selfish shit you could possibly ever say.

You are very selfish to think that when you go through something, that I don't go through it. Hell, even when your friend comes into town to visit for a few days a month, I gotta suffer sexually. So, keep thinking that what you go through is just by your lonesome. You thought the same shit when you decided to give me a chance until you saw that I was different than what you imagine. So I tell you what I am going to do. I am going to go in this kitchen. Fix me a whey protein drink. Then, I'm going to drink me a monster ass glass of almond milk. You know out of the big ass cups that we never use. Then, I'm gonna go take a shower. Follow that with some of the leftover spaghetti we got in the fridge. And then, I'll go to the bedroom and watch television. Hell, seeing how you in a fucked up mood tonight, I may just cut on pornhub and beat my dick graciously. I'll give you time to think about what your definition of we is."

He gave me a smirk and walked away into the bathroom, completely ignoring the fixing of his post workout protein drink. I couldn't say anything. I felt like the scum of the earth for what I had told him. He indeed set me straight. His mood right now was one of hurt and pain.

I knew my husband and one thing I have learned about him is that he is loyal. I heard the shower water cut on and him singing. I definitely knew he was upset now because he was acting like he wasn't caring. That was his tell tale sign. Once finished, he did exactly what he said he was going to do, and that was pour a huge cup of almond milk, walk to the bedroom and watch television. It was now 8:00 and we both had work in the morning. I felt terrible for my words and didn't even feel worthy of laying next to him tonight. I cut off all the lights in the living room and just let the TV illuminate everything. The tube was on mute while I became entrenched in deep thought. He was in the back laughing at whatever he was watching.

By 10, I was under the blanket with the fan on, reclined back on the sectional, crying my eyes out. They say sometimes we want to make a person feel what we feel. That shit can backfire, though, as we unnecessarily take out our anger on the ones who don't deserve it. As I finally became indulged in a deep sleep, I felt shaking.

"Baby, scoot over?" It was Carl. I didn't say anything. I just happily obliged. He kissed my forehead and held me as we both went back to sleep. This showed me not only the type of husband he was, but the type of man as well. Not even a few hours ago, I made him feel worthless. In spite of all that, in one instance, he made my life feel worthwhile again. I learned a valuable lesson about marriage and life that night. I knew the mistake I made would never happen again. The next morning rolled around and Carl had taken off to the gym. He left me a note along with some cherry pop tarts on the counter. It was the little things like this that kept me in love with him. Other than that, I prepped for work, but still had the news I was given the day prior on my mind.

I usually left the house at 7:00 to hit the gig in 30 minutes, which gave me time to review my cases for the day. Today, I was intrigued by the folder I found on the dock the night I was gonna jump. Something told me to go look at it again, even though I pulled everything out of it the first time. I walked back to my bedroom and opened the closet door. There it was, lying in the middle of the floor, looking full as ever. Ironically, I wasn't weirded out like last time, because I had come to expect the unexpected.

I grabbed it and took it back to the living room. I rummaged through it, finding old letters that my dad used to write to me, but never sent off because he couldn't get in contact with me. I found all types of newspaper clippings of my mom in her high school track days. Yea, this was deeper than I had ever imagined. As I was about to put the folder aside and head off, another pic caught the corner of my eye. I grabbed it and was left speechless. In it was him and my mother. Her belly was big with me inside of it. I tried to close my eyes and act like it was a huge dream, but it wasn't. Attached to that picture was an envelope. I opened it up and was lead on the journey of my life through words.

Anita,

Look, I know we haven't seen eye to eye since the pregnancy, but I would want to put all these differences aside so that I can be there for you and my future daughter. You don't understand how important this is for me. When you said it was a baby girl, I was more than excited, but you won't let your stubbornness see that this child will need both of us in her life. Right now, you're thinkin of me as just a quick nut, but this other nigga you seeing has your mind whipped in a way that you really don't realize the mistake that you are making. Now, I am committed to being a father, unlike what you think. You're letting all of your friends get in your ear and tell you different things, so therefore I have been feeling the brunt of something that I should not be feeling in the first place. I'm telling you, the worst thing you can do is listen to a bunch of no good having ass bitches with multiple baby fathers. They don't know shit. If they did, they would know who their child's dad is. I am humbly asking you to think about what you are doing before you do it. If you take this child out of my life, you are depriving her of more than you are depriving me. And that knight in shining armor that you are so in love with right now, he will end up being the one to give you the worst nights of your life. I am sincerely asking you to think about your actions before they kill us all, mentally and literally..

Donald

That was indeed powerful and it struck a chord with me. My sole mission after work was to find out everything. I needed to know for my own good and inner peace. The next phase in my life would be a mission critical to my happiness as a person. I went to work that day and handled my business as usual. When I got home that night, me and Carl went to work on that happiness that I so desperately needed. All had been forgiven from my actions the other night as I made sure to solidify that by cooking his favorite meal of mackerels and grits. Not to mention that I took the time to type him a 5,000 word letter as to why I loved him. I know it sounded high schoolish, but you sometimes had to show a person you love them by doing childish things. We read every letter in the folder over and over again. It led to a bunch of nothing. Letter upon letter, picture upon picture, newspaper clipping upon newspaper clipping. This would possibly be an all night process.

"**BABE!!!**," Carl yelled. "Look at this shit." He handed me a clip from a newspaper article. *"Local man charged with battery and assault."* It was an article on Dontae, that man who I thought was my daddy all along. In the story, it said he battered his girlfriend and her four year old son. Further along, it said he had some defenders, saying that the Dontae they knew was a charming, savvy and a great guy.

I see why my dad wrote her what he wrote. He knew what was up and he did not want me being a part of that. Everything was starting to add up. Dude must have had a serious first impression. Once he was in, his true colors showed. Now, I was even more hurt due to the fact that I was tortured by a literal stranger.

"I can't look at this no more Carl. I need a drink." He got up and poured me up some Crown Royal, and I took the meanest of shots. It didn't make me feel any better, but it certainly took some of the tension off of me. As he rubbed my back on the couch, I asked him one question.

"Carl? What would you do if your whole entire world just shattered around you?" He continued massaging me ever so gently while responding.

"I'd marry you again. Plain and simple." My over emotional self once again began to cry. I was lucky even in the midst of one of my biggest storms. Who? What? Where? When? Why? How? Who else should've had my husband besides me? What was I ever thinking giving him the grief that I gave him from the jump? Where were we going from here? When would I ever become everything that he ever wanted? Why did I ever doubt this man? How could I become better for him? He took my focus off the task at hand.

"Let's save this talk for a different time," I told him. "I just want to be with you right now." He smiled as we ended the night with our usual Netflix and cuddling. By God, I was the luckiest woman alive.

The last weekend of the month was here. This Saturday morning, we were meeting with my dad's lawyer for the entire financial turnover. As we entered the office building, I just had this feeling of shock and awe as I felt that I wouldn't leave the same way that I came in. Eight o'clock in the morning was more than early, but I wanted to get this over and done with.

As we got into the heart of the meeting, finding out the inheritance that he left me had me stunned. In it, his whole retirement, which was totaled well into the hundreds of thousands of dollars. A home in Manhattan, Kansas, fully paid off. He also owned the land that it was built on. Lastly, we were left behind a special box with a key, but was strictly said to not open it until September 5th of whatever year he became deceased. I found out that was his birthday. We decided that we would sell the home in Manhattan, and use that money for some of our future endeavors. However, we would keep the land so that we could make money off of any future development.

The almost $780,000 in retirement would well suit any future college needs for the children we may adopt further down the line. This box ,though, was simply a mystery. It was a pretty decent size and had some weight on it. All I know is that in the matter of some days, the contents would possibly change my life. Until then, I just wanted to de-stress from this situation now that it was over.

We stopped at IHOP before we went home. Pancakes could always cure my woes and Carl's bottomless pit of a stomach was able to smash omelets at a shrews pace. Anyone who knows how shrews eat knows that they eat a lot and fast as hell. We got back home around eleven in the afternoon. Carl in his usual fashion went to the gym, while I stayed home and cleaned up. My cleaning took a different turn this afternoon, as my mind was in a million places at the same time. I thought back to when I had nothing. Walking through the projects in Wichita and going to the candy store with only a dollar. The projects are special I tell you.

If you're from there, you can walk through virtually untouched. No one would bother you. I used to walk past gangsters of all sizes with no problems. When you are a part of a project family, that's what you are, literally. FAMILY. Those were the early days before things started to take a turn for the worse. The abuse became very major after that. I saw my mom starting to get beat, have bruises, black eyes and any other injury that you could imagine.

I still can never forget when I used to lay snuggled up under her, and he would give me a look from across the room. I caught it, but she didn't. He was plotting on me in his sick mind. All that led me to believe that I was indeed nothing more than a piece of meat for any and every man that I encountered after that. My mind was so messed up that sex was the only way that I truly felt loved. I never told Carl how many partners I had in my past, because I am still scared that if he knew, he would leave me where I stand today. The number? Well, it's high. I mean very, very high. I am almost embarrassed to tell anyone. Have I changed? Yes. However, the past is something that always seems to stick with you. It's the place that people go when they want to make you feel at your lowest. It is definitely something I am not proud of.

I can only imagine the damage that would occur with me internally if I ever had a daughter and someone did to her what happened to me. It's a cruel and unjust world. Even though I didn't want to think about things like that, I unfortunately had too. I looked at myself many of nights when I was in the navy. The mirror can tell so many stories. I remember vividly the night where things began to shift for me. I bumped into Carl, causing him to drop his pop.

Earlier that evening, he cleaned cursed me out and basically told me I was ugly as shit. As a human being, the man was right. He shut me down and kept it moving like it was nothing. I honestly became scared at that moment. I had never had a man affect me the way he did. Only this time, it was in a positive light. I walked down the port side p-way towards my berthing all screwed up. Then, I stopped. I can't remember where we were in the world, but in my world, I was lost. I turned around and went back to the forward mess decks looking for him. He was nowhere in sight. I continued searching for him everywhere throughout the ship. I couldn't find him to save my life.

I must've searched for a good hour from the 2nd deck all the way up to the O-10 level. He had lit a fuse inside of me and it was a scary feeling. As I ended my search for Carl, I took a trip back down to the flight deck. It was dark as hell out here with the airplanes looking like dead remnants of what once was. I could hear the noise coming from the pier, so I made sure to walk on the opposite side of the flight deck where no one would see me.

I got to the starboard side edge and just looked down at the water. It would be a long way down from here. The reason for my suicidal thoughts that night were unlike anything I could ever tell. I wanted to jump all because someone called me beautiful. I clearly remember his words. *"You are beautiful, but ugly as shit."* That is what he told me. No one had ever called me beautiful. I for sure thought I was ugly inside and out. I wasn't even worthy to be on this earth. That's what happened with all of the years of mental pain that I endured. I didn't realize how great of a person I was until his words sparked something inside of me to search for myself.

I backed away from the edge that night and said to God "That will be my husband one day." I really don't know why I said it. Maybe it was to give myself hope for something that I had been searching for my whole life. Now that those words came true, I was more than grateful. All I wanted to do now is give him children, because I had given him everything else, including grief, which I deeply regretted.

I stopped cleaning and started to hit Google search on my laptop. I looked up the whole adoption process. I wanted to honestly see how he felt about it. It's one thing to say you're cool with giving someone else life. It's another to actually give them life, knowing that you didn't help create them. I knew he was a man and that he had a huge heart. How huge his heart was, that was the question that I needed the answer too. I took a ride out the house around noon time when I was finished with everything. I had the taste for a surf-n-turf burrito. Those joints were like crack out here. Where was the best joint to get one from? Well, you can take your pick. You had "The Barrel" on 69th and Imperial. El Cilantro was down on 13th in Imperial Beach. Cotixan was everywhere, but the one in Point Loma was beyond fire. El Patron in Mira Mesa, Roberto's, Alberto's, I could go on. And to keep it 100, any place in this city was a win win when it came to Mexican Food.

I shot on over to the Old Town area to hit up Lucha Libre, which was arguably the best burrito in town. When I pulled up, I considered myself lucky because the line wasn't out the door like it was on a usual. I bolted out of the car and waited in line. While looking at the menu, I observed an old couple sitting by the window. They had to be at least in their late 60's, if not early 70's. Any who, he was feeding her nacho chips as if they were still young and in love. I didn't know if they still had their teeth or if the dentures they purchased were holding on for dear life. I did see that they were still having fun at an old age. I finally got my food and went looking for a seat.

"Come sit," the old man bellowed at me. I pointed to myself because I wasn't sure that he was talking to me.

"Yes, you. " I just smiled and pulled up a chair at their table.

"I'm Herb. This is my wife Peaches." They extended their hands as I thought this was the funniest thing in the world. A couple named Peaches and Herb.

"Is that you guys real names?"

"Oh hell yea," the old man bellowed out. "I call her Peaches, because after 37 years, she still is sweet to me and ripe like some good fruit. She'd kick my ass if I said her real name. Ain't that right Melina?" I looked over at her to see her just smile.

"I don't see a ring on your finger. Why not?"

"I'm married. Almost two years sir." The smile that came over his face was as big as the Eiffel tower.

"Well shit got dammit. Peaches, you've made me buy you four rings over our time together. She's happily married and ain't asked for shit."

"Herb shut yo' crazy ass up."

"Anyways, let this old timer give you advice. If you wanna stay together as long as we have, there are three things you must remember. One, make each other laugh every day. Two, give each other the kind of sex each other wants. And three, most importantly. Three. Keep doing the same things you did to get them for life. When I first met my wife, I was on another date. She was a waitress at an Italian restaurant I frequented. She was new and I knew this because I had never seen her, and I was there at least once a week for lunch. Any who, I was with this one girl and Peaches served us. I thought in my head, how in the good hell am I going to get rid of this one and get that one. Well. Long story short. Me and that other woman didn't last long and I went back to the restaurant every week until she agreed to go on a date with me. That ended up being nine weeks in a row because she didn't want to give me the time of day. Finally, and I mean finally, she opened up her heart to me. Now, many dates, 40 years together, 37 years married and four kids later. We are still very much in love. That's the key. I treat her like a queen. She treats me as her king. And I still kiss her forehead every day before I go on my morning jog."

"Oh Herb, stop telling her all our secrets."

"**THEY WORKED ON YOU WOMAN!!!**" It was amazing to see the humor in these two. After all these years, they still had that fire and desire for each other. It was definitely an inspiration to see. That's what I wanted. To make it 40 years was great. However, I had to keep my focus. Before I could make it to 40 years with Carl, I had to make it through the next day with him. That was rare nowadays, as the invention of reality television had people not wanting to get married, or just thinking that it was a joke.

I wanted that forever love. I honestly needed that. I looked up my family's history one time and found out that my great grandparents were together an astounding 72 ½ years. There were some good people that I knew in San Diego that were together 35, 40 and even 50 years. By the time we were finished eating and talking, I saw that two hours had elapsed and this place was now packed wall to wall. I headed out towards the car and my phone rang.

"Babe, hurry up home. I got something for you." That was a sign that he was up to something crazy. The last time his nutty tail said that, I sped home from work. I walked in the house to candles lit and soft music playing.

"Baby, welcome home. Gone head and sit yo fine ass down." I was intrigued to see what this man had planned. He pulled out my chair at the kitchen table, which was covered in an Ivory sheet, so I wouldn't see the contents of what was underneath.

"Baby, as he pulled out a glass of sparkling Apple Juice (which was also the first sign that I knew this was gonna be something nutty), I love you and only you. And tonight, I give you my all through cooking. Now, after we toast this marvelous cider, I want you to rip the sheet off this table as you will my clothes later." I could do nothing but laugh. I couldn't even take him serious. He was my husband, though, so I went along. He handed me my glass.

"Toast." I toasted with him and sipped it. It actually had a little kick to it for being some cider.

"Now babe. Go ahead and take that sheet off and remember this night for the rest of your life."

I gave him that negro you gone get FUCKED THOROUGHLY tonight look. He actually melted my heart with this one. I took off the sheet and literally hit the floor laughing my ass off. I heard him cracking up as well as I hit the floor.

"Baby," I said laughing hysterically, pulling myself back up to the chair.

"What the hell is this?"

"It's your favorite." Do y'all know this negro had under the sheets two big, red bowls, two spoons and a box of Peanut Butter Cap'n Crunch, which just happened to be my favorite cereal. I couldn't believe this man had gotten all dressed up to serve me some cereal. I was expecting some lobster, steak and broccoli. You know, some food like that. This negro here though? He was just crazy and that proved it. In the end, we actually ate the whole box together, laughing the whole time while doing it. It was so funny and hilarious that I had no choice but to give him some. Hell, we couldn't even make it through the sex session that night without laughing, because the thought of Cap'n Crunch kept popping up in our heads. It was a memory that would last a lifetime and one that I would surely never forget. I got to the house, anxious to see what he had for me.

"**STOP RIGHT THERE BABE!!!**," he yelled from the window. There I was in the middle of the parking lot, when he came out with the most innocent and precious creature I had ever seen. He sat him down and the dog came running over to me. I was in complete awe. It was a cute baby Jack Russell Terrier. I scooped it up in my arms. She looked so innocent and happy. Carl came over with us.

"Thank you babe," as I planted a kiss on his lips.

"What you gone name him beautiful?" I thought about it for a quick sec.

"Oggi. I'm a name her Oggi." He looked at me weird.

"Why in the hell would you want to name a dog Oggi?"

"Simple. Because that's what I feel like eating tonight. Some Oggi's pizza."

"I mean that's cool. We can eat that. But shit, you can't name the little nigga 2Chainz?"

"Why the hell would I name my dog 2Chainz?"

"I mean I don't want him to be a punk. People come up asking me what your dog named after, and I tell them pizza."

"Well, it's Oggi. Not no damn 2Chainz." He shook his head as I turned around and walked towards the house. We both entered the house joyful as ever. We ordered that pizza and played with our new baby. Well, let me rephrase that. I played with my new baby. He didn't even get to hold her ever since he had come over to me.

August was indeed a trying, yet good month. I learned my true past. It may not have been the exact circumstances that I wanted them to be, but that's life. We don't always get the gifts we want packaged up in a nice blue ribbon. You just have to take what you can get at times. The month of August. Wow. That's all that I could say about it. The end of summer was now the end to one of my wounds. I could finally tear this bandage off because I was healed.

5 SEPTEMBER

Labor Day weekend was here and we were enjoying our days off from the gigs. We thought what the hell and took an impromptu trip up to Seattle. The Emerald City is what they called it and it was indeed a gem. The Space Needle awed us and The Pike Place Market was truly a sight to see.

The 12th man was in full effect as CenturyLink Stadium was just a gem against the water at night. You could almost hear the roar of the Seahawks crowd as if Russell Wilson threw that pass to Jermaine Kearse again, sending them to the Super Bowl. Had only Pete been smart enough to run the damn ball with Marshawn Lynch and he'd have another one. However, you can't fix stupid. As Sunday rolled around and we headed back to the airport, I all of a sudden developed that gut feeling that something bad was about to happen. We were at our gate and I was off into my own zone.

"Babe you okay?," Carl asked.

"Yea. It's just I feel like something isn't right."

"What?"

"That's the thing Carl. I don't know." I know I sometimes was an emotional wreck, but this really felt like a bad feeling in the pit of my stomach. We boarded our flight and took off. The flight was smooth as I expected. However, I couldn't really sleep thinking about this feeling. Carl on the other hand was knocked the hell out. About two hours into the three hour and some change flight, I was messing around on my laptop. My e-mail clicker buzzed. It was a notification from my deceased father's lawyer.

"Star. I am so glad we got a chance to settle things so that you and your family can move on and your father can rest his soul peacefully. However, I was recently contacted by his father, Donald Thurman Sr. He is 81 and living out of a retirement home in the Los Angeles area. When you are available, please email or call me so that we can discuss this matter. I believe that what he needs to disclose to you is very urgent."

I closed my laptop and just sat there in my thoughts for a good minute. This couldn't be real. I thought I had all the unanswered questions answered. Just when I thought that, a new twist had emerged. I swear my life was turning into a James Bond movie. I wanted to wake Carl up and let him know what was going on, but I was starting to really feel bad for dragging him through the mud with this drama of mine. He didn't need to be involved in any more mysteries or drama involving his wife. Marriage was a unit, yes. Sometimes, you just wanted to let your problems be solo. We landed back in San Diego at 12:30 in the afternoon. Carl was upbeat and I didn't wanna disturb that mood of his.

"Let's go to Crab Hut beautiful?," he asked me. I nodded in agreement, but the look on my face told another story.

"What's wrong Star?"

"Nothing babe. I'm fine."

"Don't bullshit me babe."

"I'm good Carl, damn." That's when he grabbed my face at baggage claim, looking at me with that I know you're lying look.

"Beautiful? What's wrong?"

"I'm tired Carl. You got your rest. I need mine. Sorry I'm grumpy."

"Aight, well we'll go home so you can sleep. I'll go to Crab Hut." That was actually cool with me as it would give me an ample amount of time to think on how to break the news to him. I say ample time because when that Negro gets a platter of seafood in front of him, it's a wrap.

He was going to be at least an hour and some change. I called Carla to see what she thought about the situation that I was now facing. She thought that I should go up there and see my grandfather. He was elderly and we never know when our last breath will be taken. The key words in that phone conversation was "He may have the last answer you need to close the final chapter in your life." She was exactly right. When Carl came home almost two hours later, smelling like he was swimming in crab juice, I sat him down and explained everything.

"Why even ask me beautiful? You know what you have to do?"

"Will you go with me?" He turned away for a minute. I was unsure of how he was feeling on this.

"Look. We are married. Marriage is a team. Sometimes, though, beautiful, the test is meant to be taken solo. Now I've went back to Wichita with you. You've went back to Gary with me. We answered a lot of questions and healed a lot of wounds. But this time around, I feel it in my heart that you should go see this man dolo. Call your pops lawyer up, find out all the information he has and make that trip. Just remember that I'm in your corner always."

I was honestly scared because I felt like I needed him in this moment. But, he was right. All battles weren't meant to be fought with a team. Sometimes, you had to run into a battle with your guns blazing, dolo as ever. You had to tell yourself that if they kill you, that you are taking 100 people to hell with you. That was the mindset I had as I gave my father's lawyer a call. I wanted to meet my Grandfather, Donald Thurman Sr. It was something that I had to do. A week went by as I set up a visit to go see him at his retirement home located In Burbank.

Once the moment came, I had a drive like you wouldn't believe up the 5 North. It was definitely a pulsating and nervous ride to say the least. I played no music during the entire two hour plus ride there. I swear Los Angeles traffic was the worst in the country. It was already bad enough that California people couldn't drive, but how in the good hell do you have traffic jams on the weekend? I thought that was just for rush hour during the workweek.

Not here, however. And then, they have the nerve to call this place the City of Angels. Well, from my perspective, no one here was an angel. They were all devils with attitudes that literally came from hell. Finally, I arrived and just sat in the car. One, so I could prepare my mind for what I was about to encounter. Two, so I could lean the seat back and relax from sitting up for over two hours. I took a good fifteen minutes to myself and then I exited the car. I indulged in the surroundings. This place looked like a resort for old folks. There were palm trees everywhere, a well cut lawn and it just gave you the sense of peace. I would hope to die next to my family one day.

However, If I couldn't, I definitely wouldn't mind dying in style like this. I walked in to the smell of potpourri. For a quick second I thought that I was in a flower shop. Looking at the desk clerk as I walked up to the reception desk, it looked like she was waiting for Mr. Right to come up, seeing that she looked like she was here to go on a date rather than assist old folks.

"Hello ma'am. Are you here to see someone?"

"Donald Thurman please."

"Ahhh yes. You must be Mrs. Jackson. The lawyer to Mr. Thurman's deceased son called and informed us that you would be here. May I take you too him?"

"Sure." The walk was indeed a long one, as this place was huge. Passing through the halls, I saw the opposite of what I thought I would see. I saw old people playing chess and checkers. There was a group huddled around a television watching old westerns. There were the old people who had met while here and fell in love, gazing into each other's eyes, trying to relive their youthful days. In a place where many people feel that others come to die, I saw nothing but life.

This was very therapeutic for me. It taught me that if me and Carl ever reached the ripe old ages, we would continue to have fun and indulge in each other, never falling out of love. Life doesn't stop because you gain a few wrinkles or because your hair turns a little bit grey. Life is meant to be lived and you live it until the day you clock out. Even then, you never die. One, because we are nothing but huge balls of energy, and energy only transfers. Two, because your memory, name and legacy live on.

Legacy, it is so underestimated in our world. People are too busy trying to put legacy tabs on athletes, yet they can't define their own legacy for themselves. Trust, it doesn't come from dribbling a basketball or throwing a football. It comes by how you lived your life and the people you impacted throughout that journey.

"Mr. Thurman, you have a guest." Here I was on the third floor. What I saw was exactly what I thought I would see the whole time. My grandfather was sick with tubes in his nose. He looked a little bit frail as well.

"Mr. Thurman," the nurse said again, as she went over to check him.

"Huh?" He popped his eyes open. "Who here you say?"

"Your granddaughter Star is here." His head whipped around so fast that I thought he was 21 instead of 81. He was pretty stealthy for an old guy to say the least.

"Is this what I have been waiting all these years for?" The nurse walked back over towards me with a smile.

"He's all yours granddaughter," she whispered as she exited the room.

"Don't just stand there. Sit down next to me." I walked over so nervous with help me Jesus written on my face. I sat down in the chair and just stared at him.

"Don't be nervous," he said. "I've been around a long time and that's the look as if you seen a ghost. As you can see, I ain't dead. So don't treat me like I am." I didn't know what to say back. Here it was, all these years later and I finally met family that I didn't even know existed.

"I'm just humbled right now to be meeting you." The smile that came across his face at that moment was indeed priceless.

"Girl. I love you. But you're my granddaughter. You honored to meet Malcolm, like I did back in 59. You honored to meet Huey, like I did in 81. You ain't gotta be honored to see me. Just be happy. But you look beautiful. Just like your mother. Yea, ol Anita. She was pretty as a penny, but cutthroat like a pirate."

I stayed quiet. I didn't want to jump the gun too fast. Maybe there was a method to his madness and his words, so I decided to be patient.

"I never thought that I would see the day that my son would find his long lost daughter. It makes me even more appreciative that I'm looking at my granddaughter right now. Don't mind the tubes and the raspy voice of mine. It's just old age and the things that come along with it. When I had Donald way back yonder in Manhattan, it was the greatest thing that ever happened to me. He was my first and only born. I worked my skin, nails and toes to the bone with odd job after odd job just to make ends meet. I had the support of his beautiful mother, who is now gone. God rest her soul. Any who, the boy was always a responsible and respectable young man. There wasn't much that I ever had to discipline him for as he learned his discipline through observation.

I remember the day he met your mother Anita. They were in high school together. I mean, the boy would always come home everyday talking about Anita. Anita this and Anita that. After a while, I wanted to tell him shut up with the Anita talk, but I was happy to see my boy infatuated over a woman. I once was the same way with your grandmother.

He called the house sometimes after they rekindled, happier than a gopher who found a fresh hole. He was saying how beautiful she was and how great of a person she was. I told him that day. Son, don't shoot off your gun too soon. The bullets you waste now on your target may be needed later down the line when you have to shoot at someone for real. What I meant was that I didn't want him to get too happy too quick with your mother. That's not being disrespectful to her, but we all can go crazy when we have infatuation for someone. And infatuation can be mistaken for love very easily.

I did the same thing with your grandmother. It was kind of different back in my day, as we didn't do the flowers and candy stuff. We simply walked to the woman's house and met the daddy to see if he would allow us to even take his daughter out. If he didn't, then we would have to sneak. Over the nine months that Anita carried you, things took a terrible turn for the worse. He found out she had messed around on him, around the same time she got pregnant with you.

It came out when they were having one of their usual verbal spats. That was about two months into her pregnancy. They would go off and on saying they were in love, but I knew my son was unhappy and your mother really didn't care for him. Around the five month mark, she met a fast bit hustler named Dontae. Oh man, from the outside, this brother had it all. He had a Cadillac that was smoother than a baby's ass. He was clean cut and dressed sharp. Yo' daddy didn't find out about him until he went home one day and Anita was in his living room, with this brother sitting on his couch. A scuffle ensued from what he told me and he ended up getting wounded. I can't remember what the weapon was or anything. I just know that I still had my son and I was grateful. Ironically, we both got wounds. I got mines right here. Right here, see?" He slowly with the little strength he had pulled up his right pants leg to reveal a grizzly scar.

"How'd you get that granddaddy?"

"Granddaddy. That's a blessing to hear that word. I fought for my wife when the Klan tried to move us out of a neighborhood in Manhattan. I refused to leave, because I had the same right to raise my family in a good area like they did. Donald was only three years old when that occurred. It was only five of them, but it seemed like a 100 of those sorry bitches came to the house. I'm from Mississippi and how I was raised is that you fight with your hands. These punks nowadays can't take being a man, so they shoot. Got they gang bang with a hat this way, hat that way. My rag this color. Yo' rag this color. Ah hell, they all punks. And now they feminine punks with the skinny jeans and tight ass clothes. Coming up, we were one man gangs. Your gang was self. You didn't need any affiliation, because being black in itself brought you more trouble than these punks could ever bring to you today. Sorry, I got caught up in a moment.

But any who, they came to my porch and I told them if any one of you sons of bitches step up, you getting dropped. One by one they came up. One by one, they started to fall. Then, that's when one of them pulled a knife. I fought him and all the others off. I wasn't no easy win. In the end, I caught a stab wound to my lower right leg. What they caught was a stab wound to their pride. I dealt with many graffiti marks and GO HOME NIGGER remarks for a long time, but I never left. That's what made me who I am and that's where your daddy got it from. I'm not here to bash your mama. We all got mamas and we love them dearly. Hell, mines been gone for over 35 years now. Anita had you. Yep, she had you. She told a bogus story to the police that your daddy put his hands on her. The thing is that it wasn't bogus. It was just about the wrong man. Dontae beat yo' mama on a regular, but your daddy was the scapegoat. By the time she realized what she had gotten herself into, it was too late. Your daddy's father rights were stripped. No visitation. No contact to be made. It was like they made him nonexistent on Earth. Oh there were many nights that he cried on the phone to me, asking what he was gonna do. As a matter of fact, I want you to see this." He reached for a photo album next to his bed with the little strength that he had.

"Here, take this and open it up until you see a huge 8x10 black and white photo." I flipped through the photo album. Lo and behold, there it was.

"Where was this at granddaddy?"

"You know I have been waiting 81 years to hear that." I knew he was near the end of his days because he didn't even remember the first time I called him grandaddy.

"That right there, it's a beach in San Diego. You were about four years old and your daddy called me from a pay phone. I said where in the good hell you at boy? He said he was in San Diego. I said what in the John Henry you doing in San Diego? He told me he caught a bus, not knowing where it was going.

He just wanted to disappear away from Manhattan, Kansas. The boy was saying that he was gonna take his life that night by jumping in the water. He couldn't take it anymore being away from you and knowing that you were in harm's way. He felt he exhausted every resource that he could, but it was to no avail. I begged and pleaded with him not to do it, but after numerous failed attempts, he hung up the phone on me.

I thought I had lost my son. I didn't hear anything from him for the next two weeks. When he called me back, I was stunned. I asked him what happened. He told me that he stood on the wooden railing of a pier and outstretched his arms, as if to say goodbye to the world. It was the middle of the night. Just before he was about to lean over and fall, he looked towards the beginning of the pier and seen a young man walking towards him. He immediately came down, seeing that he wanted no one to see him jump. As the young man got closer, he started to walk his way until they were almost a few feet apart. What's going on young man he said he asked him. He said the young man responded back to him. Said his name was Carl.

He asked him what he was doing around here at this time of night. Instead of asking your daddy the same question back, he told him some words that neither he, nor I will ever forget. *I'm looking for my wife. Star. Have you seen her?* Donald said he couldn't believe what he had heard. You know how you shake your head and close your eyes. Well, he did that. He said when he reopened them, the young man was gone. He was gone as if he had vanished into thin air or something. He looked up and down the pier for that young man, but he just couldn't find him. All he found was an open box on the ground. In it, a wedding ring and some sand. Inside the lid, the exact date of that day, September 5th, was etched into it. That's also his birthday. He was so freaked out about it that he ran to his car and said he would never go back to that beach again. He said if he did, it would be his spirit and not his soul. But, he did go back days later he said. And that box was still there. He took it and kept it for some reason. I don't know what that means, but it's in the grave with him. My boy. My son. Your father." In that moment, my mind was in awe at what I was just told.

The words perplexed and stunned were understatements. I had completely forgot about the box that was left for me.

"I see you have a look in your eyes saying you need someone. Who's the unlucky man?," he asked while laughing as only old folks could laugh. A lump popped up in my throat. All of a sudden it was hard to speak. "Who is it? I know my granddaughter got someone special in her life." I started to cry.

"Granddad, his name. His. His name is Carl." The look in his eyes was one of shock.

"Carl. The same young man who saved my son?"

"Yes," I responded, tears streaming down my face. "And I got the box too at home. It's not gone. I have it. And now I know what's in it." Just then, my granddaddy leaned back on his bed, smiled one last time and looked at me.

"You know. I always prayed to God that he made sure my wife kept the house clean until I came up there with her. I said **GOD**. Don't take me until I know for a fact that my granddaughter is found and that she has a protector over her. I now know, that the young man my son seen that night, was destined to be your protector." He smiled and reached his left hand out. I grabbed it and immediately felt a spiritual energy within me that I couldn't explain.

"One last thing Star, because I'm about to go to sleep. I want you to remember this. You a Thurman. Lord forgive me, but you don't let a muthafucking thing break you ever. I love you sweetheart." With those last words, he lied back on his bed, closed his eyes and smiled. I watched his chest heave up and down for the next 12 minutes. By the thirteenth, it stopped. I didn't freak out. I didn't go crazy, looney, none of that. I simply watched my granddaddy go in peace and transition into another realm, happy that his prayer was finally answered. I calmly got up to place a kiss on his forehead, tell him one last I love you and walked out of the room.

I informed the nurse in the hall that he had just passed and I stayed at the nursing home all the way until they came and wheeled his body out on the gurney. As I saw him driven off one last time, I stood outside that home and looked directly across the street. Carl's Jr. was over there. It wasn't just a burger joint sign to me anymore. It was something more than special.

It was something that I couldn't explain. It was a sign of things to come. I got back on the road for the journey back home. Between being misty eyed and relieved at the same time, I realized my inner peace had started to come. All my life, I wanted a family. All my life, I just wanted to feel a part of a family. From my foster brother Dorian, to Carl, to my now deceased dad and granddad. I had finally found it. Four may seem like a small number, but the biggest impacts can come from the smallest things. At the end of the day, I could live at night knowing that I had four genuine people who loved me. It was better than having 1,000 family members who you were uncertain of. It was all about the people who you knew loved you. And never would I be one of those all I need is God people.

Let God take everyone away from you and see how you function. I had been through it. I lived it. I know that all too well. Those folks are the ones that I don't wanna be around. They get so spiritual that they literally forget that they are human. I'm pretty sure Jesus played hide and go seek as a kid and watches a basketball game on top of a cloud every now and then. Yes, God may bring us through, but he doesn't want you to be scared to live.

If my husband is in the mood for sex, he don't wanna hear bible verses. If me and some friends are at a football game, I won't hit them with the story of David and Goliath when the Colts are running in for the touchdown. Learning how to live was the best thing that happened for me. Loving God isn't being afraid of what's out there. It's the same things that were out there before. We just started using that thing inside of our head called a brain. The only difference is that you just started to use it more and handle things in a better way.

Thinking about the transformation I made in my life, I all of a sudden had an urge. About 30 minutes north of San Diego, in Oceanside, I jumped off a random exit and drove until I found a tattoo parlor. This must've been my lucky day cause in no more than five minutes of jumping off the freeway, I found one. Frontline Tattoos was the name of the joint.

I pulled up in front and thought to myself why in the good hell was I in front of a tattoo parlor? Carl's body was inked up to the core and it did turn me on. I can't tell you what it was, but tattoos just did something to me. I figured that if I was going to get one, then I might as well get something meaningful while out here to symbolize everything that I had been through. I walked in and the smell itself got to me. It was just pure ink. The pictures on the wall of all these folks who were tatted up were somewhat intimidating to say the least. My skin was bare. I felt like the Chihuahua who was in the middle of the pitbull kennel.

"Can I help you?," the young man at the desk asked so politely, inked up all over himself.

"It's my first one, so I want something meaningful."

"Confident," he said. "I like that. You don't see too many people, man or woman come in like that. Most of them are shaking in their boots at the thought of a needle. You know where you want it?" It was only one place I could think of.

"My stomach," I told him.

"You like pain I see?" With those words, I responded the only way I knew how.

"I am pain. Pain wrapped up into the soul of the alpha bitch." I could tell he dug me. For him, this was the shit he liked. A woman who was bold with her words and not nervous about anything.

"Wait here. Let me go talk to the owner Jason. See if he has a slot. He's the best out West, so you won't be disappointed at all." As he went to the back, I really thought about what pain was. There I was, standing by the front counter, going into meditation mode. I looked at my skin on my arms. There was nothing there. I looked at my hands. There was nothing there. I took a look in the mirror they had. There on my right cheek, was a scar. It wasn't just any scar. It was something that reminded me of what true pain really was.

I was 12 years old, only a few years removed from the torture of seeing my mother killed with my own eyes and suffering with foster folks who could give two shits about me or anyone else who lived in their house. At that age, I was only beginning my journey down pit road.

I hadn't experienced the hardcore drugs, the wild nights of uncontrollable, emotionless sex, the hard liquor or anything of that nature yet. I was still in the basic phase of morphing into an almost teenager. Weed was the plant of choice as I blazed that every chance I got. Simple beer, Miller Genuine Draft to be exact, cooled my insides, making me feel like one of the boys. Then, there was my introductory sexcapades. Age 12 was when I first gave head. It was in the basement of my foster home. I snuck a 16 year old boy in that night who was a local track star at one of the high schools. Looking back at it, he was the pervert for dealing with a twelve year old. I didn't have rational thinking back then. The only thought I had was do what eases the pain.

I had become so used to this over the years doing it by force that when I had my own free will to do it, it wasn't nothing. He sat on the couch while I went to work. I really didn't know what I was doing. All I knew was that the painful memories processed in my head as it was going on. As crazy as it may sound, that is what actually motivated me to try and do it good. I wanted in my head to show him that yeah, I am good, and it's with a guy who ain't supposed to be my daddy. I just sucked and sucked until he exploded right in my mouth. It was a weird feeling, but I swallowed and didn't think twice about it at all.

"Damn girl. You did a good job," he told me. At twelve years old and going through what I had gone through, that sounded like a million bucks. I made doing that for him a regular thing for the next couple of weeks. How fucked up was I you ask? I let him cum on my face once and thought to myself that *"He's happy and he loves me."* Once that shit took place, it was a downward spiral from there. He would come around every so often after a while. Our meetings started to dwindle dramatically.

It all concluded when one time, I tried to pull him towards me as he was walking away. He turned around and slapped me beyond hard. Seeing that he had nails like an iguana, he opened up a good slice of skin on my jaw. Then, I met the next guy. I had turned thirteen. He fucked my head up so much that I let him take my virginity. I enjoyed choosing a sex partner at my free will.

It went from simple intercourse with one guy to having two on ones to eventually just going all out slutty. It wasn't something that I was proud of as a now refined woman, but I couldn't run from my past. I think the most painful part of it looking back was that I actually thought these gentlemen loved me. Since I had the power of choice, it cured everything in my eyes. I was simply just fooling myself.

"Hey how you doing? I'm Jason." He came from the back and shocked me. I thought he would look like the typical punk rocker guys that you see. Naw, not at all. He was what I'd say simple looking. Sure, he was tatted up all over, as I could tell from his forearm tats that disappeared all the way up in his sleeve. He, however, looked quite normal.

"So you lucked up. I surprisingly have no other clients on my list today, so whatever you want, we can do." That was magic to my ears as I began to set the plan in motion.

"I want the right side of my stomach having the happy and sad joker faces. Make is as sick as you want to. Do any detail that you want to. Just make it black and white. I don't want a bunch of fancy bright colors on my skin."

"Cool beans," he said. "Give me about ten minutes here to set up and Jesse can take care of you with the paperwork." It was three in the afternoon, so I figured with the amount of space he was covering, it would be an all night thing.

"How long do you think it will take Jason?," I screamed towards the back.

"MAYBE TWO HOURS!!! THIS SHIT IS GONNA BE SICK!!!" So I was wrong. It wouldn't be an all night thing. Wow. I couldn't believe it. I was really about to get my first tattoo. It would definitely be something worthwhile I hoped. After looking through his portfolio at the front of the shop, my fears were eased and I became more than jubilated for this.

"Come on to the back. What's your name?"

"Star."

"Star. Cool ass name." That was the first time I was told that. I took off my shirt and leaned back in the chair, immune to everything else going on in the world. He wasn't going crazy over my body which was my sign that he was used to seeing women's stomachs, or any other part for that matter. He showed me the design that he had in mind. It wasn't exactly the joker faces, but the evil and happy masks. The shit was sick. If I was going to get a tattoo, however, it was go hard or go home. He traced everything out on wax paper and placed it on my stomach. Meanwhile, I was texting Carl, letting him know that I was in a tattoo parlor. *"What the fuck woman???!!! You getting a tattoo. Sheep must be pissin on bull nuts and flies are Crip walking on water buffalo carcasses."* I would've easily took a good job, go get it babe or something along the lines of that. Instead, he did it in typical Carl fashion with crazy ass statements that only he could think of. As the buzz from the needle rang throughout my ears, I braced myself for the first impact that would occur on my skin.

Not that bad I thought. It felt like he was doing the outline, which was confirmed when I asked him. Really, this shit didn't hurt. The best way that I could describe it you ask? It was like having an irritating ass mosquito on your body that would constantly pester you. The shit actually was cool though, until he hit that spot close to my waistline. Hot damn!!! When that needle hit down there, that shit hurt like a muthafucka. I just gritted my teeth and bared the brunt of it.

"You doing good?," Jason asked me.

"Never felt better," I responded so sarcastically. After an hour, he finally finished up the outline. He took a picture on his phone and showed it to me.

"How's that so far?" I looked at it and was just in awe. He really did the damn thing with some sick artwork. The faces stood out and it wasn't even complete. It went a little bit past my waistline, which I knew would turn my husband on. I was highly anxious for what the end result would be. Jay forwarded the picture to my phone and I sent it to Carl. His response: *What the hell woman. Why you get two of your home girls tatted on your stomach???"*

My response: *"Fuck you."* After a good twenty minute break, and some Wienerschnitzel from right across the parking lot, we were right back on it. Good conversation made the session go by even quicker. By the time I looked up, it was five o'clock in the evening.

"We're almost done. Maybe another 20 minutes if that." I didn't mind the time, but it was music to my ears. I now had a newfound respect for everyone who had some serious ink work on their body. It takes a special kind of person to sit in a chair for hours on end just for some ink therapy. I truly saluted all those who were in the inked the hell up club. Trust, this does not include the prissy women with small lucky charm hearts and butterfly tattoos. Don't nobody give a damn about that small stuff. The crazy thing is that some women actually think that's considered real work. **HA!!!** Yeah right.

"All done Star. Wanna check it out in the mirror?" I got up and Jason positioned me between the two mirrors.

"**HOLY SHIT!!!**," I yelled out. It was indeed some of the best work that I had ever seen. More importantly, it was on me and I felt redefined. I felt like a completely new person. There it was. Two faces, the words resiliency and pain, and a bunch of crazy ass fill in design that just made it stand out to the T. I easily swiped my card for the $150 I was charged for it. This was damn well more than $150 worth of work, so I appreciated the generosity. I sent Carl the pic and his whole reaction was different. *"Girl, that shit turning me on. I know it's gonna drive me crazy in person. I already got your* *healing stuff here at home."* Funny how all his shit talking all of a sudden stopped. He wasn't getting none tonight. Not because of anything he did. This work though was not going to get messed up. He was going to cater to me for a good week or so, because I wasn't having him on top of me. He'd be good for about a week. A few blow jobs and a couple hit it from the back sessions would cure his sexual cravings.

I got home that night and just sat in my parking spot, thinking about how I felt. It was a crazy feeling, but I think getting that ink began a whole new me. I know many things changed my perception on life. Now, with having this reminder of making it through the worst on my body, I could tell my story to someone who didn't quite understand me with something else other than long drawn out stories. I was indeed happy with life and all that it was entailing. I went into the house to eat and spend time with my husband before we both crashed. In the words of Ice Cube, today was a good day.

A few nights later, I had a dream. There we were, Carl and I. We were in our car, traveling through the city. We were two young kids in love. As we laughed and joked, suddenly, things became very dull as we cruised through downtown San Diego. He was still upbeat, but I was starting to get nervous about the surroundings. Suddenly, the people started to look very different. What I meant by that is all of them were staring at us, except they had blank faces. Nothing was there. The lights from the buildings weren't the same as the illumination seemed to die right in front of us. Carl wasn't noticing anything. It was just me. Finally, we hit Pacific Coast Highway. It was barren with no soul in sight. For some reason, Carl hit the gas.

"**STOP!!!**," I yelled to him. "**STOP CARL STOP!!!**" As I looked over, Carl all of a sudden didn't have a face either. When I turned back forward, I screamed as all I seen were lights heading directly for us.

"**AHHH!!!**" I woke up in a huge panic, breathing uncontrollably and crying my ass off.

"**WHAT HAPPENED BEAUTIFUL???!!! WHAT HAPPENED???!!!**" Still intense and in the clutches of my husband, I slowly brought myself down.

"We were there. We were there again."

"Where babe?," as he now had me back down on the bed, head on his chest, rubbing my forehead.

"The accident scene. Something is there. Carl, something is there that we have to find."

"Beautiful, it was just a bad dream. I know October is almost here but." I cut him off.

"No listen. Something is there. We have to go back. Something is there. I bet my life on it something is there." I jumped out of bed and started throwing on clothes.

"Woman if you think I'm driving to a deserted road at one in the muthafucking morning you done lost you damn marbles." I wasn't even trying to hear dat.

"Star."

"**CARL!!!**" I was not to be messed with at this time and place, as I was determined to see what this dream meant. I took off towards the kitchen to grab my keys and bounce. He soon followed me out, still throwing on clothes, pissed off as ever.

"Babe," as he grabbed my arm. "At least let me drive. Okay?" I was tense and anxious, but I let him. I know this isn't what he wanted to do, but that's another factor of a relationship. Doing what you don't want to do sometimes to improve the greater good of the relationship. Lord knows there were nights that I didn't want to be up making hot tea and chicken noodle soup for his sick ass, but I did it. I know there were nights before we were married where he didn't want to hear my rants, but he listened to them anyway.

That's all a part of the relationship process. He took his time on the road as he reassured me of his love and that everything was going to be alright. We didn't even take the freeway. We went through Point Loma and down Harbor Drive by the airport.

It was a slow, methodical drive as I was so focused on what was there.

I remembered the memory like it was yesterday. The car came out of nowhere and plowed into us. Carl came crawling over to me with the little life he had left in his body just to grab my hand and assure me that he was there, even if it may have been the last thing he did in life. It was horrific to think about, but it was something neither one of us could erase.

"Stop right here," I told him. We were back. There was the Jack in the Box. The same one I saw through my blurred vision and the blood pouring from my forehead that night.

"Beautiful what are we looking for? It's been almost a year and it's cold as shit. Nothing is here."

"Something's here Carl," as I exited the car and began scrambling across Pacific Coast Highway, looking for anything that stood out. Carl soon began walking on the other side of the road, looking for whatever had meaning from that night. Common sense would tell me that everything was gone. However, my intuition told me that our lives were about to change. We had been out there 20 minutes and found nothing.

"**YOU FIND ANYTHING BABE???!!!**," he yelled from across the street.

"**NO!!!**," I yelled back.

"WELL I'M GOING INSIDE JACK IN THE CRACK!!! C'MON???!!!" He was right. We had been out here for what seemed like forever and hadn't found anything. Maybe I was delusional. I'm pretty sure the people in the few cars that drove by were wondering why two random humans were running up and down the road at that time of night. Then I remembered that this was San Diego. Nothing was surprising. As I crossed the street to meet Carl, that's when I spotted it.

"CARL!!!" I picked it up and ran towards him. He just stood there with a what the fuck look, not believing that I actually found something.

"Babe what's that?" I handed it to him. As I was looking at him, his eyes became transfixed on what was in his hand. I had never seen him this silent in his life. I didn't even remember him going more than three seconds without saying a word.

"This can't be beautiful. It just can't be." I looked into his hand to see an old watch. The old style ones where you open them up. Inside the almost rusted over silver, there was a picture of a lil boy.

"Is that you when you were younger babe?" He stood there silenced for a few seconds.

"Yeah. Let's go home. I got something I need to tell you." He suddenly walked off towards the car, leaving me perplexed where I stood. I was nervous now, as he had never acted like this before. The news didn't sound good at all. I just had to do my best to prepare for it. We got home and Carl's mood was just down and dejected. Here we were at 2:30 in the morning, drained, yet facing another battle. As he sat on the couch and hunched over, I began to rub his back, hopefully giving him comfort.

"When I was six, my mother gave me this watch. She told me that it would always be some sort of a good luck charm. This picture is from when I was five. She said it was her favorite picture of me. She got this watch from a pawn shop. She couldn't afford too much caring for me and my brothers, so she managed to scrape up some change and get me this. As a kid, I thought it was the coolest shit ever. It made me feel like a grown man. When I seen some shit like this in the movie Life, I really thought I was boss. Anyways, I carried it everywhere with me. From when I went to jail, all the way until I came in the Navy. It's one night though that really changed the way I looked at this watch. You notice how it has a deep indentation?" I looked at it. It was kind of deep, like something had attempted to pierce through it.

"I was 17 and Gary used to have this place called Skate World. It was like a teenage sanctuary for us. In one moment, you would be skating your ass off. The next thing you know, the skate floor was turned into a dance floor and it was juke city. I used to go there with my boys and had a lot of good memories there. Even when this one chick said I popped her cherry, but I didn't, it was still a good memory.

Her jukin skills were just mediocre. One night, we were in there chillin' like always. I think I had kissed some ugly bitch that night whose ponytail was hanging on the back of her head for dear life. I don't know when it happened, but all of a sudden my dude Worm got into a verbal with some lame ass nigga. You would've thought things would be all gravy since we were all Vice Lord, but it didn't play out that way. After the rink let out, these two niggas met in the parking lot. Worm started to beat the breaks off this nigga. I mean, it was almost like watching a UFC exhibition. One of his ol dude's boys jumped in and that's when we all converged. The fight was on and poppin'. We were rippin' these niggas a new asshole. Things didn't calm down until I seen my cousin Big Jo, and I holla'd at that nigga to get the steel. Everyone scattered like roaches and we were on our way home shortly after that. We were on ten in the car, just waiting for next week when we were gonna go back and mob on those same niggas, cause we knew they would be there. So the days passed with the usual teenage gab going on around the halls of school.

"We gone mob on those Eastside niggas."

"They ain't ready for the real."

"Real Almighty bout to ride. On the fin." You heard every line, saying whatever. Niggas were ready. So then came Saturday night. We were headed back to the rink. In the car, I had a bad feeling that something ill advised was about to go down. Something that we weren't prepared for. We mobbed into skate world, dancing it up with the Gary ratchets as usual. As the night went along, we seen those Eastside niggas coming in more and more. I knew it was about to go down. From the looks of it, they had the numbers. As we exited at least 40 deep, cars started to circle the parking lot. From a rough estimate, I'd say it was about a good 70 of them. We were holding our own, talking shit at the cars that were circling all of us throughout the whole lot. Then, there came the shots.

We all scattered like roaches. As I ran towards the homies car, I felt a huge thud hit my chest. I immediately dropped. In shock, I didn't remember much. As I came too, there were a bunch of people surrounding me. **HOLD ON CARL!!! HOLD ON!!!** That's all I kept hearing. I knew I had been shot, but it didn't feel like a gunshot wound. My chest was hurting, but it wasn't burning, nor did I see any blood. As I felt my body over, I hit the left side of my chest where my shirt pocket was. I felt a hard object and reached in too grab it. Lo and behold, it was my watch. It stopped the bullet from entering my chest. Had I not had that, I more than likely wouldn't be here telling you this now." I couldn't put my finger around things. How did after almost a whole year was this emblem of hope still there at the scene? Why was I so ecstatic to head over here? I could easily say the dream was the reason, but I saw nothing in that dream to symbolize what I found. I really started to think about it. Why didn't anyone have faces including Carl? It was because what was meant for me to see, it wasn't meant for them. Why did the city not illuminate like it usually did? Simply because we had to go back into a dark time in order to find something meaningful.

I realized that the answers to many questions are right in front of us. We sometimes try to make things more complicated than what they really are. I hugged Carl on that couch with an embrace that could not be explained. As he continued to sob on my chest, I looked up to the heavens. *"Thank you,"* I whispered to God and his mother. Indeed if I never believed in angels, I certainly did now. I called off work that morning and decided to make his day special. As I seen him off around nine o'clock, I just stared out of the window. Who knew tragedy could turn into triumph so many years later. From Gary and Wichita, to the hills of Cali, this seemed like an unrealistic dream, but it was indeed real. I opened the patio door and took in the crisp fall morning. The last remnants of birds that were still here hummed tunes that became music to my ears. It seemed like the same music that my mother used to play when we danced in the living room. A smile came across my face. I was in a different place. I was happy and at peace for once in my life.

6 OCTOBER

The last month before Carl's ship came back was here. I was determined to make the best of it since he would have to return to sea duty upon their return. They were scheduled to come back November 5th, and I wanted to ensure that these last 30 something odd days would be worthwhile in our books.

We started off the month by taking a weekend trip up to Reno, Nevada. Neither one of us had ever been there, so it was a new experience for both of us. We flew in and were met by slot machines galore. I for sure thought that this would be like a miniature Vegas. We took our happy asses to the Atlantis Hotel where we were staying on this crisp Friday night. Lord knows the word crisp meant cold, as I hadn't experienced a chill like this since leaving the Midwest. I had to remember that we were here in the mountains. We were a hop, skip and a jump from Lake Tahoe.

Later as we cruised their version of the strip, we literally saw why they called this city a poor man's Vegas. It had just enough flare to satisfy you, but merely not enough to compete with its big brother that was about nine hours south. We hit up some of the casinos, but they weren't anything spectacular.

All in all, it turned out to be a trip of just bonding, which was cool with me. Nothing extraordinary happened over that weekend, as all we did was just eat, sleep, workout, fuck and go out dancing. We got home early Sunday afternoon sometime after one, grateful to be back in the great San Diego weather. Instead of heading home immediately, we stopped by Lefty's Chicago Pizzeria over in Mission Hills to indulge our inner fat person. I mashed on some pizza puffs and fries while his greedy ass ordered a whole thin crust sausage and mushroom pizza.

"Babe, how in the good hell are you going to come to a Chicago pizza joint and eat some bullshit ass thin crust?" Stuffing his mouth, he looked at me weird.

"Girl you trippin. I may be from 'round the Chicago land area, but I don't fuck with that deep dish shit." I couldn't believe this clown of a hubby of mine. It was like saying someone grew up in a jungle, but they didn't fuck with monkey meat. Me and Carl literally had it out in that joint. You think husbands and wives always argue about legit shit all the time?

Hell naw. This is what husbands and wives did most of the time. They argued about the small, irrelevant things. You can't be from the Midwest and love New York style pizza over the style of your own home turf. It was crazy. We ate up, but the debate was raging on as other patrons would occasionally glare over at us, probably thinking that we were nutty in the head. I didn't even realize how loud we had gotten. All in all, it was a memorable moment in our marriage. This was something that I knew we were gonna laugh about for years to come. Work came around with the quickness the next day as everything went back to normal. There was the couple who both suffered from PTSD and had to give up their children due to their condition. There were the anger issues of a brand new guy to the fleet.

Then, I was back to dealing with someone else whose wife had stepped out on them while they were deployed. Unlike my case from a while back, he caught his wife's secret life on a radio show out here called "War of the Roses." I couldn't fathom how someone would fall for anyone offering them a free dozen red, romantic roses out of the blue.

As always, they sent it to the side piece and all hell broke loose over the radio. It was quite entertaining to say the least. As my day winded down to the last few hours, all I had on my mind was going home and curling up with a good book. "Star, line 2." Carla snuck in and snuck out. I picked up the phone expecting nothing less than supervisors wanting something else done for the program. Then, my mouth dropped.

"Your husband has suffered a severe heart episode." Those words sunk into my soul with deadly precision like a rattlesnakes fangs.

"Could you say that one more time sir?" I didn't want to believe the doctor on the other end of the phone, but I had no choice. I literally muffed all of my papers into folders and shoved 'em into the drawers of my file cabinet. Then it was off to Naval Hospital Balboa. In critical situations like this, most people freak out and risk death trying to get to their loved ones. Over the years, I had learned to stay calm and keep all of my anxiety inside when bad news arrived. It helped me cope with the situation. Also, if Carl was responsive, the last thing he needed was for me to be freaking out in front of him and giving him an episode.

I pulled up to the hospital about 15 minutes after I got the call. I knew to keep my feelings at bay inside of the hospital, but I was still human. I wept inside the car profusely. Who was I fooling?

This shit was scary. Once again, I was in fear of losing him. The first time was due to my rebellious attitude towards everyone. Now if I lost him, he would never come back. This reminded me all too well of his friend OG Mac. He was the only witness at our wedding, but Carl had told me the story about how he dealt with his heart problems out in Hawaii.

He said that experience had changed his life because it had taught him to appreciate every minute of it. Mac survived his heart ailments. I was hoping that my husband would have some of the same luck. I finally mustered up the strength to get out of the car, wiping my face along the way to the ER from the distant parking garage. As I got to the main desk, the clerk was busy on the phone, back turned to me.

"Excuse me sir?" He turned around in the chair and immediately dropped the phone. My mouth did the same thing.

"Star?"

"Dorian?" I couldn't believe it. My lost long brother. The one who I had last seen in at a rest stop was here. I couldn't believe it. In the midst of all the pain that I was going through, it was like God saw fit to give me comfort through someone who I considered family.

"What are you doing here?"

"Carl. My husband. Carl."

"Husband? Yea it has been a long time?" Immediately Dorian started looking through the computer for people who had come in.

"What's his last name?"

"Jackson." "Yea, he's on the third floor. C'mon. I'll take you up there." As we walked, Dorian went into brother mode and quickly gave me reassuring words so that I could stay calm and focus on supporting my husband through this trying time. It felt good to have this reunion again. We were both in the same place again. Only this time, we were both grown, on our own and doing great things with our lives. Talking with him definitely put me at ease as this brought back memories of a time in which he was there for me in the same way, but in a much more dire situation.

It was my last year in high school and in that house for good. Lord knows I would've rather grown up in the Amityville horror house than that place. Old man Gilman came home one night, drunk and on a rampage. It was only Mama Gilman, me and Dorian in the house. Me and Dorian were in the basement trying to put together dreams of what life would be like if we ever made it up out of here. Suddenly, the arguing from upstairs started. We thought nothing of it. We were used to being in a house with no love. They hated us and each other. The arguing seemed to go on forever until everything went silent. For a good hour, everything was calm. Our dreams were starting to pan out in the basement.

"So where you gone be in ten years?," I asked him.

"I'm gone be saving lives in a hospital. I'm gone be a doc. Somehow, someway. What about you sis?" I had to think about it for a second. I wasn't sure if I would even be alive with the path I was headed down. However, I wanted to think positive because it seemed that I had never done that at any point in my life.

"I want. I want. I want."

"YOU WANT WHAT!!!," he shouted.

"I want a family. I want to love someone. I want kids to hold. I want to see sunsets on a regular. I want to be there at their lowest moments to pick them up. I gotta be alive though bruh." He looked at me kind of crazy.

"Why you say that? I know this ain't the best situation in the world, but why put death on yourself?" That's when I told him everything. I told him about the every now and then drug use, the drinking, the multiple sex partners, the abortions and everything else that I was ashamed of. I just let it all out. I couldn't hold it in anymore. I wasn't so shocked that I was telling him this. I was more so shocked that he had no idea. But when I really had time to think about it, I had to realize that we were two different people. I was rebellious, outgoing and trying to feel loved. Dorian, he put his solace and peace through his love for the arts. Avoiding the outside world at all costs was his safe haven.

"Here sis. Read this?" He handed me a notebook that was folded to a particular page. "Read this and tell me what you think?" I looked at it up and down for a while, trying to comprehend what I was reading.

"Read it out loud?," he asked me. I obliged.

WHERE CHANGE LIES

I once noticed dollar bills lying on the floor

Untouched, unmarked and crisp, waiting to be picked up and spent by the hands that touched them

From my eyes I saw ones, fives, twenties and fifties

I thought I was rich beyond my wildest dreams

I saw big homes, nice cars, dates with movie stars and good eats in my future

I placed the bills in my pocket and went on about my way

And along my way, I saw change

Why is it change that we most look over

Ignoring that it has more value

Than be the paper

That is discarded for the worthless change that is

It wasn't the kind that folded

It was of bronze and silver

Dimes, pennies, nickels and quarters

I thought nothing much of it, so I left it

As I lay to sleep that night, my house caught fire

I had no desire to save anything but my life

When the smoke cleared and the ashes settled,

I saw everything that was paper burnt to a crisp

Including the money that I had found to be crisp

But through the rubble, I still saw the pennies,
and the dimes, and the nickels and the quarters,

They were still standing in their round form

Somewhat charred, but their shape was intact

They had survived the impact

And then that made me question myself

Would I rather be paper?

The one everyone chased

But also the one who could be torn apart so easy

Or would I rather be that change

That no matter how much changed

I still maintained my shape

I still maintained my value

Even when my face was gone

People still knew who I was

So I asked myself

be selfish, or selfless

"I'm not trying to sound dumb brother, but what does this all mean?" That's when he broke it down to me.

"Ok look. When you see paper money, the first thing that comes to mind is I got some bread. If you see some loose change, you really don't get excited. It's just you find a few coins and stash 'em, hoping that they'll add up over time. You don't question whether dollar bills will add up because our society is so focused on spending big dollar amounts with everything. Well, that's sort of how life is. We focus on being the dollar bill. The one that everyone wants to spend. The one everyone robs over.

The one everyone kills over. The one who presidents and rulers of countries sell out their people for. It causes us to be selfish, because we will step on someone else's neck to keep our money growing. Then, you look at loose change. Now, think about it. Have you ever heard of a robber coming up to a person and saying gimme all the pennies in your pocket or that's you ass? Have you ever heard a ruler of a country say to his people that we are going to war for 10 nickels and 2 dimes? When will you ever go to a store and see a sign that says Jordans for .99 cents? I got friends that have been overseas to Malaysia. Them joints over there cost $0.12 cents to make. That's an $0.87 profit if they were $0.99. Yet those things are sold for over 200 times their value in America. It's a shoe. A fucking shoe. It's leather hide that got whooped off a cow's ass and formed into a shoe. People overlook that. Now this is where it gets great. Whenever you make a purchase, any purchase almost, you always see an amount of change in the end.

People never wanna break those dollar bills for the extra change. They always scramble through their wallets or purse looking for that extra 12 cents. That extra 27 cents. That extra two or three cents so you can get an even amount of dollars back. That shows you right there how valuable change is. Star, you are change, but right now you are viewing your soul as merely paper money. I see the good in you, but you are gonna have to be that change."

He smiled after saying that to me and all I could do was put my head down. Before I could respond, that's when we both heard the crash. Furniture or whatever it was had hit the floor. We heard the screaming back and forth. It was scary indeed. The last tidbit we both heard with a huge thud was Old Man Gilman screaming

"**I'LL KILL EVERYBODY IN THIS MUTHAFUCKA!!!**" That's when Dorian grabbed me, telling me to c'mon.

"**WHERE THE OTHER BASTARDS AT???!!!**" He wasn't about to find us.

"Get in here," Dorian whispered. He had led me to a dusty old chair in the dark corner of the basement. He pushed it aside and it revealed a door in the floor. He opened it up.

"Go. I'm right behind you." I climbed down the six rung ladder, not knowing what this was or where it was leading too. He soon followed. Now I was staring in a tunnel that was illuminated to the core. It looked like something that the Mexican cartels would construct.

"Where are we Dorain?"

"Just follow me woman." We kept moving, only stopping when he went to a dark corner and pissed. This was indeed amazing in my eyes. It reminded me of some old fairy tale movie where someone would escape an old witch through a secret tunnel that led to the land of OZ. Ironically, we were in Kansas. We kept walking for what seemed like forever. I mean we literally had traveled some miles underneath the earth. Then, after about 30 minutes of walking, we came to a ladder.

"Here it is sis. You ready to see my getaway?"

"Yea after I catch my damn breath." I put my hands on my knees for a good minute or two as my legs were jello. I'm not going to lie. I was nervous as all get out and scared shitless, even though I was with my brother. He climbed up the ladder first and popped through the manhole cover. It was then that I saw one of the most amazing sights of my life. I saw nothing but stars, and they were beautiful.

"C'mon sis." I was staring up at him, stuck, not moving.

"It's okay. You know damn well I wouldn't take you somewhere where it was dangerous. Climb up." I finally mustered up the courage after about thirty seconds of hesitation and climbed. When I got to the top, I saw yet another sight of sights.

"Dorian, where in the good hell do you got me?"

"It's an old junkyard sis." I didn't know what was so amazing about a frickin junkyard, but it was like magic to him.

"You see. We free over here. Yea, you think this place is nothing that no one would ever pay attention to. You see those mattresses over there? That's what me and a bunch of other outcasts used to play on. We did wrestling moves on each other all the time. That office building right there, it still has power. I got food and pop stocked for days in there. This shit is heaven to me." We walked over inside the office building. Unlike the junkyard, it was well kept in here to my surprise. Dorian grabbed us both a pop and we sat down on a couch.

"This is heaven for me sis. Man. I can't say it enough. All these years when I needed a release, I'd come here. As you can see, I still do. They say one man's trash is another man's treasure. I indeed found that out to be true. It's the same with you. You think you're trash to this world. One day, some man is gonna think you are a treasure. He'll probably have to be a smart ass to you for you to see that you are treasure. But hey. I'm just a dreamer. What do I know besides a 30 minute walk leading to the greatest place on earth?" It's obvious that he knew a lot. Even crazier is that all these years after that story, it finally sunk in that his words actually came into fruition.

"Aight, he's breathing, conscious and in good spirits right now. Let me go back in here and make sure the nurses are good, and then I'll bring you in."

I nodded in agreement as I tried to bring down the anxiety of seeing my husband. I was trying to prepare myself to be strong for him. He needed me stronger than ever right now.

"Aight sis. He's all yours." Dorian whispered those words to me thru the cracked door.

"Carl. You have a visitor brother." I walked into the room and we locked eyes. His pearly white smile lit up the room and my soul. I tried not to cry but I couldn't hold it in.

"Baby don't start that shit." I totally ignored him as I rushed over and hugged him as if my life depended on it.

"Babe, I can't breathe."

"Boy shut up." I wasn't trying to hear it. He was my heart, my soul, my everything. If he died, then I died.

"Carl what happened?," I muffled through my tears.

"Well," as he sat up. "I was at the hazmat desk, kicked back watching TV, looking as fine as I wanna look. Then my heart started to do the macarena in my chest. I told them foolio coworkers of mine to get the doctors down there immediately. It was really my coworker Shakedra who got shit done. Her nutty Chicago ass was cussin' folks out to get help. Hell, she even cussed the docs out who came down there for me. Told them that they were taking too long. I got scans and everything. They say I have a dual AV node and mitral valve prolapse, whatever the hell that means. All I know is that I'm good right now, I'm alive and I'm looking at you. I'm gravy love. And I'm still fine as shit."

"Don't joke with me right now boy." I hugged him again. At this moment, actions meant everything. There was a knock at the door.

"**COME IN!!!**" It was Dorian with a woman. "**CARLA!!!**"

"Oh snaps, how do you know my wife?"

"Your wife? Carla you been married to my brother this whole time and didn't tell me?"

"Well, Star. I didn't know you had a brother until about five minutes ago." What a small world it was. This whole time I had been working with my sister in law and didn't even know it.

"He told me everything Star. I'm so glad you both are okay." The hug I felt from her was different this time. It really felt like family instead of friendship. Hell, it was family. We all spent the rest of the evening laughing and joking, making the best out of a scary situation. I even met Carl's co-worker Shakedra, who he called a pitbull in a skirt.

She was short as ever, no taller than 5'4. However, even I had a fear of her. She just had a look that she would knock you out on sight. Then again, that was how Chicago folks were. They stayed ready to knock someone out on sight. The doctor came in during the visit saying Carl could be released tomorrow with meds, but that surgery would be required to fix his condition. It was scary thinking that his heart would have to be operated on, but it was a risk that he had to take. What I learned in life is that you cannot fear the aspect of fear. It will eat away at your mind much more than your own flesh. I felt fear the day Carl called me beautiful, because I had heard the gimmicks many times before.

Had I stayed in my own shell of a self, I never would be the married woman that I am now. Fear kept me from facing a man who took so much away from me as a youth. When I did finally muster up the courage to face him, it started a transformation inside of me. Fear only attacks what fears it. No longer was I subject to that. I was a revamped woman and I was proud to say it.

As we left around seven, with Carl indulged in a Wheel of Fortune episode, I decided to take an invite with Dorian and Carla for dinner in Downtown San Diego. We hit up Rio De Gado, an expensive, yet filling Brazilian Steakhouse. Carla had never been, so it was an opportunity for her to get her first taste at some good cuts of meat. As for me, I wanted to reconnect with Dorian as much as I could. Not to mention get me some of that fire ass flame broiled pineapple that they were famous for. As we sat over dinner and laughed the night away, with Carl heavy on our minds nonetheless, I turned the conversation to what my focus was.

"So how'd you and Carla meet Dorian?" They looked at each other as if they were lost in each other's eyes.

"Well sis. EHarmony." I damn near spit my drink out. It was romantic but funny at the same time. I saw she was in San Diego and I thought to myself wow, that's a fine Italian sister right there. To make a long story short, when I told her that I was moving out here, she offered to pick me up from the airport. The rest is history."

"So how long did it take for you two to tie the knot?"

"One month," they said in unison. I was amazed. People usually gave it time. I guess when you just have that feeling, then you just have that feeling.

"Yea we didn't waste any time with a big ceremony or any of that. We simply went to the courthouse and got it done," Carla said, as she smashed another piece of that fire ass grilled pineapple." I was amazed that my brother had found love. Hell, we both found love. Coming from the circumstances that we came from, it was an amazing feeling.

"So wait. Carla. Why don't you have any pics of him up at work?"

"The same reason you don't. Military wives and their questions."

"Gotcha." We ended up staying until about nine before we all were getting tired and about to call it a night.

"Hey babe, would you mind it if I talked with my sister for a little while longer? I'm off tomorrow, so only if its cool with you." Carla kissed him on his lips.

"Sure. See you tomorrow Star." Carla headed to her car while me and Dorian took a drive through downtown discussing what had become of our lives as a whole. As we began to head back towards Kearny Mesa, the area that he lived in, one of his stories would turn my life around forever.

"So you know I found out my real pops died not too long ago."

"Damn, I didn't even know you had found him."

"Yea. It was a long, drawn out process, but I finally got a hold of him. I mean, he hadn't been anything in my life but a sperm donor, but it brought me peace to find out who he was. I talked with him for a brief moment, because he was sick and barely able to articulate any words at the time. He did however manage to say one phrase that will always stick with me. He said I'm sorry. As mad as I used to be, I swore that no apology on Earth could restore my soul.

"That just shows you the process of growing up sis. Yep. His name was Jennings. Dontae Jennings." I slammed the brakes right next to Carmax on the middle of Balboa Avenue.

"What the hell are you doing girl? You just stopped in the middle of the damn road for nothin." I was so zoned out that I didn't even hear him.

"Star? What in the good hell are you doing?"

"Tell me that isn't your father Dorian. Please tell me that you're fucking with me." I knew he wasn't joking because of the look on his face.

"I really ain't joking with you and I have no clue of why you flipping out on me. I ain't did shit but tell you about my folks. Is there something that I need to know?" I eased my foot off the brake and continued to drive.

"Just tell me where you stay Dorian?"

"This next street over. But why are you flipping out on me? I didn't do anything but have a conversation with my sister." He was right and I came back to my senses. It was time to open up. I pulled the car up in front of his house, parked and took a deep breath.

"Remember when I told you about my young life? About the man who used to beat my mother and molest me?" I looked at him. He looked back.

"Star, you bullshittin right?"

"Died in the hospital after they took him out the prison right?," I asked him. Right then and there, we found out just how much smaller the world was. We found out how the most different of people could be bonded by one single person. He was in shock and I was just a complete emotional wreck. We sat there quiet for about another five minutes before he finally broke his silence.

"Look, sis. I can't take back what he did. I don't even wanna imagine what he did. I'm sorry. I really am. All I'm asking is that you don't see him when you look at me. Keep seeing me as your brother. I didn't do shit and it would be unfair as hell for you to take the anger you had for him out on me. I don't get mad anymore sis. It takes too much energy. Hell, my Aunt Diane left me on the street and drove away when I was three, but I ain't mad.

"Wait, wait, wait," I asked him. "This is all too much at one time and crazier to boot. She left you?"

"Yea. I was three years old. I know I don't remember much about that time in my life, but I can remember being in that convenient store, crying my eyes out. "Where is your mommy?," someone asked me. I don't know is what I told 'em. The only thing I remember is us being on aisle six and her saying stay right here by the cereal boxes while she runs a meat package back to its section. I never saw her again after that. I don't know if she alive or dead. Quite honestly, I really don't give a shit. All she did was tell me to call her Aunt GG. I figured out over time what that really meant. Good and gone." I completely empathized with him at that moment. We were indeed cut from the same cloth, just in a different field. As we said our goodbyes for the evening, I drove home with more focus on life.

I learned a valuable lesson tonight. I learned that the world is truly not as big as we think it is. The random person that I am looking at over dinner could be the person who may save my life one day. The person I see next to me on the road could be the one who I inspire to live their dreams. I got to the house that night and strolled in to lay it down for the night. Lord, thank you for this lesson. I don't know what would've become of me had I not experienced this night.

I picked Carl up the next night and brought him home. He was on some meds that kept his heart rate down, so I was watching him carefully. In his typical fashion, he wanted to get up and do everything. It damn near took me putting a skillet to his cranial to get him to sit down. We relaxed as he just tried to keep everything normal. We didn't discuss anything about the incident, nor about Dorian, seeing that they had their unofficial meeting last night. As we were watching television early the next morning, we came across Maury. Lord Jesus knows this show was as wild as they come. You already knew what was going to happen. Either the chick was going to be right about the daddy and dance around on stage. Or, she would be wrong and run backstage. I swear it looked like whatever studio they filmed the show in was ten miles long because it seemed like those girls could run forever.

"Beautiful? What would you have done if I died yesterday?" I ignored him and kept watching TV, not even wanting to talk about the incident, let alone think about it.

"Beautiful?"

"Carl, I ain't trying to think about it. Just watch TV." Through my side vision I could see him staring at me, but I wasn't trying to entertain him.

"I saw your mother yesterday." My head quickly snapped around.

"What you say?"

"When I blacked out for a quick moment, it was a woman who kept saying I'm Anita. I'm Anita. She reached her hand out towards mine and touched it. That's when I came too in the hospital room with all those people around me." I tried to act like that wasn't a big deal, but I couldn't contain myself. The tears started rolling down my face.

"What are you trying to do to me Carl?"

"Nothing. But you think you may be pregnant?" I looked at him with a look of disdain. He went from near death experience to asking me if I was pregnant.

"You know what happened. You know I can't become pregnant. It's too risky for me. Don't joke around like that." That's when he said something that stayed etched in the back of my mind.

"Well, they say in order to create new life, someone has to die. Maybe I had to meet death in order to bring new life." I couldn't even argue with what he just said. It was deep and indeed factual.

You look at Lions when a new male takes over the pride. In order for his generation to flourish, he has to kill the babies of the old male. It may sound harsh, hurtful and cruel, but it's something that happens to keep the balance of nature intact. I didn't know what exactly to think in that moment. Maybe, just maybe, his words would hold true. This time, maybe I could sustain nine months. Who knows? Maybe I was just being a wishful thinker. Or maybe, just maybe, my husband was onto something. Time flew throughout the month until Halloween hit.

Carl was still at work while my Friday ended early. We were once again heading out to a Halloween party that night and the memories of the year before kept playing in my head. I tried to block it out, but it just seemed like yesterday. The sound of the metal crunching, the smell of our own blood and the sight of Carl lying in the middle of the street was stirring my emotions up to a point where I almost broke down completely.

It was around one in the afternoon when I hopped in the car and drove down to the docks along Harbor Drive near the sight of where our lives turned upside down. I parked near the U.S.S. Midway and just walked along the oceanside strip to fill my head full of good things. It was more beautiful down here than I had ever recognized. It was funny how the beauty of a place always grew after a life changing event. I started walking north towards the Fish Market where the huge statue of the sailor kissing the woman in World War 2 was. It was flocked with tourists as people took pictures re-enacting the scene.

It actually put a smile on my face to see happiness occurring around me. Lord knows that the world needed more of this. I made my way back north and continued on my journey. I hit the new Boardwalk Pier, which was honestly a waste of money in my opinion. It looked nice, but something better could've been done with the money, like building the Chargers a new stadium.

I got to Anthony's Fish Grotto which was a mecca around these parts. You could just smell the freshness of the seafood as you walked past. It damn near drew you in. As I continued on towards the Star of India, I saw a homeless woman in the distance. She was sitting near a parking meter with an old coffee can, trying to collect loose change. People paid her no mind as they continued to walk past her as if she didn't even exist. I felt bad. If I was ever in that situation, I would hope someone would help me. As I got within steps of her, she said no words. We locked eyes and she simply held up the coffee pot. I stopped immediately.

"Have you eaten today?," I asked her. She shook her head no. Right then and there, I took out $40 and put it in her pot.

"I'll be back in about an hour. I will go get you something to eat."

"Thank you," she said in a soft voice. My mind was now on feeding her instead of healing myself. I continued on past the County building, crossed the street and eventually hit Pacific Coast Highway. The whole road brought me back to what once was. I could literally see me and Carl having a conversation in the car, laughing and joking. As I got closer to Jack in the Box, the accident played out in my mind once again.

I walked with the demeanor of someone who had lost everything. Facing your fears alone takes a whole different level of strength. When I came back with Carl it was for a different reason. Now, I was truly on the search for closure. I eventually made it to Jack in the Box, ordering three egg rolls, two supreme croissants, a breakfast burrito and some curly fries. If that homeless lady was going to eat, then I wanted to make sure that she would indeed have a good meal to sleep on tonight. I got her order and began the long walk back towards the pier.

I swear I felt like I had been walking for ten miles instead of a few long city blocks. When I finally started to approach where the woman was, I noticed she was nowhere in sight. Not panicking, I figured she had just moved a bit of a distance down the pier. I mean, it was warm out, so she found a place with some shade is what I thought. Yes, I said that right as well. It was warm in October out here. That was a blessing about this city.

The winters and fall could reach 40 at night. In the daytime, however, your shorts and t-shirts were still a go. I looked everywhere for this woman, walking all the way down to the Fish Market, but she was nowhere in sight. I was upset to say the least. I purchased all of this food out of the kindness of my heart and now I had no one to give it too. I figured that Carl might eat it when he got home, but then I remembered that he was about to have heart surgery, so fried food was the last thing he needed. I walked to my car to begin the journey home. It was 2:42 p.m. on the dot. I didn't even realize how long I had been walking and meditating on things.

As I exited the Fish Market parking lot and hit the first light on Harbor, I saw her. There she was, standing at the light, coffee pot in hand, waiting to cross. I wanted to scream to her, but being five cars behind at the light did me no justice. When the light turned green for her to walk, she didn't move. I just stared at her, wondering what in the world was she doing. After a good thirty seconds, I turned my focus to the radio, flipping through each and every station, trying to find something to vibe too. Finally, after settling on the old school station, the light turned green. As soon as it turned green, however, it went straight back to yellow in a matter of seconds.

"**WHAT THE HELL!!!**," I yelled. As the car in front of me was making a move for it, I was about to hit the gas and blow right through the light. The glimpse of the woman, however, made me stop. As I hit the brakes and the car in front of me was going through the intersection, it happened.

An out of control truck came barreling through the intersection and hit that person head on. It was the most horrific sight I had seen in my life, as the driver of the pickup flew through the windshield. I knew instantly he was dead. I sat in my car, hand covering my mouth from shock and disbelief. People were flocking to both vehicles to see if anyone was alive in either. In the state of awe that happened right here on Broadway and Harbor, I turned my head to see the old homeless lady crossing the street. As she crossed, she stopped directly in front of my car, smiled and continued on her way.

I followed her until I bullshit you not, at least ten steps past my car, she absolutely vanished. I literally jumped out of the car and ran to the spot where she was. Traffic was at a standstill as no one could move, not even to turn right on Broadway because people had literally blocked it off with their cars trying to help. As I spun around looking in every direction, I saw a card on the floor. I picked it up. On it there were some bible verses. Isaiah 7:11-16. It all seemed strange to me at this time, but I put it in my pocket and walked back to the car.

After a good forty minutes of waiting, police finally started to clear things out and I was headed back home. Carl got in around his usual time feeling upbeat. He was due for surgery on the fourth of November, so I wanted to make sure he would go into it with good vibes. He showered up quickly as we headed to Liberty Station to eat. Afterwards, we hit Old Town and took a tour of The Whaley House, which was supposedly America's most haunted house. He truly didn't want to go, but I was nuts about the paranormal world. I watched Ghost Adventures every Saturday night. I always told myself that if I could get to a real haunted house, I would. When we got there, though, Carl was so freaked out that we didn't even go in. I tried to coax him into it, telling him that everything would be okay. He was so concerned about a spirit coming home with him that he wasn't having that.

"You have seen Sinister right babe?"

"OMG CARL!!! IT WAS A FRICKIN MOVIE!!!"

"Well I'll tell you what," he said. "You walk yo' black ass in there, I'll drive home and you can tell me what y'all did in the morning, cause ain't no way in good hell I'm going in there with you."

"And what if I cut it off?"

"**THEN I'LL JACK OFF EVERY HOT DAMN DAY!!! I AINT FUCKING WITH NO GHOSTS!!!**" That actually was funny. I just wish he would've not put on that front the whole week leading up to today talking that shit about he ain't scared of nothing. I swear men talk with their balls sometimes rather than their minds. We made the short drive home and I was messing with him the whole way back. It was hilarious to me to see him get mad. He messed with me, so it was only right that I messed with him right back. The mess talking even continued as we got in the house.

"Sleep yo' ass on the couch tonight woman." I laughed. I had never heard a man say that, but I was going to oblige. He wasn't going to let me go ten minutes lying by myself. He stayed in the bedroom watching TV. I walked in there with my blue boy shorts and a wife beater.

"Goodnight Carl. Sleep tight." I shut the door and went into the living room, reclining the sectional back and lying under the fan. Not even five minutes later he was in there trying to cuddle up. No man was gonna resist his wife in his favorite outfit. He had sense. The next thing you know, I was out of that outfit. My husband was punishing me for doing what I did to him. It was good being a bad girl sometimes. And by all accounts, those meds had his heart pumping very well.

7 NOVEMBER

November 4th was here and it was D-Day as I called it. We had been briefed on the procedure the day prior. From what the docs said, everything would go well. As a wife, you always have that ounce of doubt in the back of your mind. I was more worried about whether or not the doctors would mess up.

Would they do something wrong? Would they lose their marbles and operate on the wrong part of his heart? Shit, would he go in for heart surgery and end up getting a kidney operation? I didn't want to lose my husband due to any mistakes. Also, considering his treatment was in a military hospital, I was really losing it. The night of the 3rd was something different for me and Carl. We ordered in, eating his favorite meal. Sausage and mushroom pizza, with 16 wings from Wings-n-Things. It was around five in the evening when we did this. There wasn't much talking, as both of our minds tried to downplay what was about to come next. Then, I just couldn't take it anymore.

"How do you feel about tomorrow?," I asked him. He put the slice of pizza he had took a bite in down.

"I'm scared honey. I'm really scared. I got everything I want in life. I got you, the crib and the experiences that no man can take away from me. When tomorrow comes, I realize that the last thing that I may see are lights." He began to cry as I grasped his hand, reassuring him of my love. On the other hand, I wasn't crying. I had learned to be strong and hold it together when he was weak.

"I shot a little bit of hoops today with the fellas and just broke down. I mean, what if that was my last time playing with Corey, Bama, Doc, D and the rest of the crew?" He looked at me with tears in his eyes. I could see the genuine fear instilled in him. It was hard seeing my husband like this.

"You remember when you told me I was beautiful, but ugly as shit? Well those words ended up saving me. Now, I'm telling you that you will be okay. You aren't walking into a grave tomorrow. You are walking in there with me. If I have to do the damn surgery myself, I'll do it. You saved me. Now, let me save you by being the support you need."

I looked him dead in his eyes when I said that, not budging at all. I loved this man and if I had to give my heart to him so he could live, I would. We embraced in a hug that said more than I love you. It said I'm here, I care, your body is my body, my soul is your soul and your fight is my fight. We cut the TV off that night and just cuddled with each other. It was nothing but quietness, embrace and the sound of a fan. We were having our moment.

It was that moment of falling in love all over again. It felt like being back in that hotel in Wichita, the first time he made love to me, and the first time I was ever made love too. The next day rolled around with the quickness. The time was 7:30 a.m. and I was in the hospital room with Carl. He was in good spirits as we laughed over an episode of Sesame Street. It was funny how we were still big kids after all these years and how something as simple as a favorite childhood show could bring us together. We didn't talk about the surgery one bit as we kept our conversations focused on laughter. In the back of my mind though, I had to express something to him. It was something that I knew he would have difficulty accepting. The surgery was slated for 9:30, so I knew I had to tell him before 9:00 rolled around. It was 8:30 and he was starting to get his nerves going.

"Beautiful," he said so despondent.

"Carl don't worry I told you. Don't think like that. You're going to be alright. We're going to be alright. As a matter of fact, I got some news for you."

"Yea, yea, yea. Once again I know that its a line of women outside wanting my autograph. Tell them to holla at me after the surgery." I gave him a quick pop upside his head.

"What you do that for woman?"

"Nigga you ain't getting rid of me." Soon as he got to laughing, that's when I hit him with it.

"I'm pregnant." His laughing became even more severe.

"Aight babe. You got me. That's a good one. Nice way to get me to focus on something I can't have, but don't joke like that. You know having kids is very near and dear to my heart." He kept laughing, but the look I was giving him told him a different story. All of a sudden, the laughing stopped.

"You ain't bullshittin are you?"

"No Carl. I'm not." He plopped his head back on the pillow as I caressed his forehead.

"I have a different feeling about it this time Carl. I don't know why, but I do. Please trust me. I promise nothing will go wrong." He turned and looked at me. I was scared of what he was thinking or what he was going to say. Then, he just smiled.

"If we have twins, name them Immanuel and Isaiah."

"What about Carl Jr. and Carlos?"

"Girl I am not naming a son after me. As crazy as my black ass is. He would be twice as crazy. But I fucks with Carlos. Big Los is what I can call him. Yea." All I could do is smile back at him as we embraced in a kiss that sealed our love for good. About twenty minutes later, I hugged and kissed him goodbye as the doctors wheeled him out to surgery. I sat in the waiting room tense as ever, hoping that the only time the doctors came in here were when they were telling me that his operation went successful.

Three hours later, docs were coming out, saying that everything went well and he could go home tonight. With the technology they had, his chest didn't even need to be cut open. They went right through the femoral arteries in his legs, up to his heart and did what they had to do.

I was beyond grateful and immediately let out a thank you to the heavens for God watching over my husband. I don't know if this was a wound that needed healing personally for me. In my eyes, a bandage had been put over our old love and healed into something new. We once again fell in love after this moment. As long as I was living, we would continue to fall in love each and every day of our existence.

"C'mon love? **PUSH!!!**"

"SHUT THE FUCK UP CARL!!!"

"Stay focused ma'am and breathe," the nurse said. I let out everything on that final grunt, as it seemed I was going through hell with gasoline draws on. I had heard the stories about birthing a child, but it didn't prepare me for this. It literally felt like someone was ripping me open and beating the hell outta me. Then, I heard the sweetest sound that any woman could ever hear. The baby was loud, obnoxious and crying. I was breathless and tired. If this man wanted anymore kids, he had better make 'em with another woman, because I sure as hell wasn't pushing any more out.

"Congrats Mrs. Jackson. You have a healthy baby boy." I was relieved. On this May 12th day in 2015, I had my child. The child that they said I could never have, I had it. There he was, lying there as his daddy cut his umbilical cord. He looked like he had just climbed through a tub of prune juice.

"Here's mommy man." Carl handed him to me. I was astounded. I really couldn't believe it. I had a son. I really was a mother. He was so loving and innocent. It was truly a priceless moment for me.

"What you gonna name him mommy?"

"Immanuel, just like you asked me too."

"I ain't ask you that. I said Carlos was cool. Just not Carl Jr."

"Damn, you right." In that moment, I started to think about how I randomly decided on that name.

"Star? Why do you wanna name him Immanuel?"

"I remember on Halloween I found a card at an accident scene. It said Isaiah 7:11-16. So I googled it and read the verses. I even memorized 'em."

"Ask thee a sign of the Lord thy God; ask it either in the depth, or in the height above. But Ahaz said, I will not ask, neither will I tempt the Lord. And he said, Hear ye now, O house of David; Is it a small thing for you to weary men, but will ye weary my God also? Therefore the Lord himself shall give you a sign; Behold, a virgin shall conceive, and bear a son, and shall call his name Immanuel. Butter and honey shall he eat, that he may know to refuse the evil, and choose the good. For before the child shall know to refuse the evil, and choose the good, the land that thou abhorrent shall be forsaken of both her kings."

Carl was in awe. My husband was truly amazed by the story. Any worries and fears of whether or not he would be the greatest father in the world were nonexistent. As I simply smiled at him, all I could do was reminisce on everything that brought me to this point. Everything in life happens for a reason and there is a reason for everything. Today, on this May 12th day, the last bandage I had came off, never to be put on again. I was completely healed. There was no scar or any evidence of anything negative. My life had finally taken its full course. Two and a half weeks had gone by and Carl was back at work. As I wandered into the bank to deposit some money into our account, I was struck by the handsomeness of the bank teller. I had never seen him here before in all my time, so it was obvious that he was new. I know I was married, but hell, people are still going to be attractive. If you do get married and automatically stop thinking that the opposite sex ain't attractive, something is seriously wrong.

"Next please," he said. I walked over with the stroller. "How are you today ma'am?"

"I'm good. How are you?"

"I'm fine." That's when I noticed he was looking at me kind of funny.

"Have we met miss lady? You look mighty familiar like I have seen you somewhere before." I chuckled at the notion.

"No sir, I don't think so." We shared in a laugh as he asked me for my identification. I happily obliged as baby Immanuel started to cry.

"What do you have?"

"A boy. A bumbling one." As I picked up this big bowling ball of a baby and looked back at the teller, he said my name with a different tone.

"Star? Star?" I was confused. I swear I didn't know this man.

"Ummm sir. I don't think we know each other and this is kind of strange."

"My apologies ma'am. What do you need today?"

"I'm just making a small deposit." I handed him my money, he handled my deposit and again apologized.

"It's okay," I said. As I turned to head out the door, he then said one final statement.

"Have a good day. But let me just say this. I never see you with anyone, so I figured you needed a friend. Hope this carnation makes you smile. Years ago, I saw something amazing in you. That's why I sent you that carnation in high school." I stopped dead in my tracks and turned around. Well I'll be damned.

ABOUT THE AUTHOR

- -SPOKEN WORD ARTIST
- -BEST SELLING AUTHOR
- -MOTIVATIONAL SPEAKER
- -WRITING CONSULTANT

Joe McClain Jr., a.k.a. Joe Mac was born and raised in the Harborside section of East Chicago, Indiana. He faced the perils of gangs, drugs and death, much like all inner city youth. Add the fact that he also grew up in a broken home, and you would expect his story to turn out into one of the  many sad ones we read coming out of the urban environment. However, Joe adapted and overcame to turn his story into a successful one. Staying active in the Boys and Girls Club, he channeled his expression through art and sports. After graduating from East Chicago Central High School in 2002, he enlisted in the United States Navy, relocated to

San Diego and continued to write and perform spoken word. He has released five books to include a national #1 best seller in BANDAGES. In the spoken word genre, he has performed nationally and internationally with some of the biggest names in the industry. At just the age of 32, the quote on quote "50 cent of poetry" is one of the most powerful voices in spoken word, telling raw, unedited tales of the problems that plague this world and all subjects in general. He is indeed one of the top tier performers in the spoken word craft and an inspiring writer whose stories makes readers feel as if they are watching a movie.

You can find out more about Joe McClain Jr. by visiting his website:Joemacuncut.com

IF YOU ENJOYED READING
"BANDAGES 2"
PLEASE LEAVE A REVIEW ON
AMAZON.COM
http://ow.ly/JggvZ

ALSO AVAILABLE ON UPROCK PUBLICATION

When his father passed at 12, Mr. Terrelle Washington grew up fast and survived the dangerous streets of East Chicago, Indiana. After finding out his deceased father left him a large inheritance, he decided to leave for California and achieve his dream of becoming a published Author. However, the land of Hollywood stars was soon transformed into a maze of unforeseen obstacles he never expected on his way to the top. How will it play out??? Will he achieve his dream, or will it be shattered into a nightmare of failure.

UPROCK PUBLICATIONS PRESENTS

BANDAGES

JOE MCCLAIN JR

A hard life in the inner city. Made it through. About to prepare for the next step of most young men. College. That was all until one fateful night to where freedom was taken away. Now, in the battle of his young life, a young man has two options. Die in prison, or snitch and possibly get another chance. Either choice will draw consequences, but what will he choose??? What wounds will be healed, and what wounds will be re-opened???

Ricky Walters grew up in the gritty streets of San Diego California. Upon quitting his security job, he meets an ex pimp name Trust who teaches him everything about the pimp game. Ricky ends up turning out a young Asian girl name Yuki, changes his name to Jackpot, and jumps knee deep in the pimp game. Jackpot makes a conscious decision to become the biggest pimp to ever play the game and goes cross country. Here, is where Jackpot finds himself getting money, ducking the police, feuding with haters, vindictive females, snitches, and eventually doing time in the penitentiary.

Let Me Pimp Or Let Me Die 2, tells the story of a few female workers in the "Game," told through their lives as you see and find out what motivates a woman to start ho'n and sell her body. Re-visit some of your favorite characters from part 1 and see what drove them into the lifestyle that they chose. Each story different but ultimately the same.

Graphic and not for the faint of heart, the scenes take place in a realistic setting with many twist n turns you won't see coming. Find out how F.A.B Killed Sunshine and what happened in those last moments. How Green Eyes got hooked on drugs and the real reason she left Jackpot for dead in prison. Or the number one question...Will Jackpot Return To The Game?

Xavier Sands and Danielle Seville meet at the grand opening of Xavier's nightclub, and it happens to be his birthday. Not to be left out, Danielle is celebrating her birthday as well. As the two grow closer, wedges are driven between them behind the scenes, by their own mothers!

Xavier and Danielle both work for King Kole Konners, in different venues, but when the King is shot, all bets are off. The kingdom having just survived the Chase St. John mutiny in South Nubia, is rocked once again. The assassin begins picking off the King's top people, leading to Danielle being kidnapped...

"Freeze mother fucker!" a cop spat, but the Skyline hardhead wasn't trying to hear it. He blindly reached on the floor for his gun as he slowly regained his eyesight. Jail wasn't an option for the young rida. He knew he had done too much to turn back. Fuck it, he was gonna hold court in the streets. As he placed his hand on the gun that laid dormant on the floor, that would be as close as he got to picking it up and letting off a shot...

Lamar Atteley III has made out a good life for himself. He has turned Las Vegas into his own personal playground after surviving the rough environment of Detroit, Michigan. However, with a new job offer, he now has to prepare for a new chapter of his life that will either make or break him. His adventure will take him to the other side of the world......to Guam. Now, he will be tested harder than any other point in his life. With all new surroundings, more money, women at his disposal and a different breed of people in general, the question is can he handle it all. When its all said and done, you will understand why we sometimes sleep with the lights on.

Wake n Bake the natural way. Weed consumption through digestion is a lot healthier than smoking it, which is why we put together this book of tasty meals with a 420 kick to keep you happy, smiling and feeling good! From breakfast, lunch, dinner to dessert we got you covered. Enjoy some weed laced french toast for breakfast. Craving a light snack? Try some of our weed hummus. End the night with a homemade weed pizza and cheesecake for dessert. We even have a recipe for cooking oil and weed butter. Over 30 different recipes to choose from. Meals so quick and easy to make, you'll wonder why you didn't pick up this book sooner. Simple everyday recipes made easy will have you feeling like a pro in the kitchen! No more having to buy overpriced edibles from the dispensary. Now you can make all those delicious treats yourself.

With the P.E.E.R.S. five step system towards achieving greatness, you will see how your inner voice and what you do can affect your outcome in not just your life, but many people around you as well. Much like the friends we choose, it is truly a reflection of us. Your work ethic and what you are willing to do to succeed is a reflection of you.

By the end of this step by step guide, you will learn the tools of what it takes not only to speak powerfully, but to achieve greatness overall.

How does a man survive his toughest challenge
when the battle is against his norm
How does he conform to something he is not accustomed to
when he never accepted it
Why does a man see a bigger picture
even if it causes him to lose his own frame
Why does he still put blame on himself
even when it is not his responsibility
How does he find humility in situations like these
How can one ever question his heart
How can he stay on a path
when even the path he's on can lead him astray...

Don't have the time to read? Well, we have the solution. Pick up your audio version of "Let Me Pimp Or Let Me Die." The book by Caujuan Akim Mayo that started it all. Listen to this action pack audio book, loaded with special sound effects and cinematic music for dramatic effect, like no other audio book you've ever heard before. This is the audio book, that changed the game and set the bar.

Website: www.uprockpublications.com
Emails: uprockp@gmail.com
Facebook: uprockpublications
Twitter: uprockpub
Contact: (619) 259-0298

www.ingramcontent.com/pod-product-compliance
Lightning Source LLC
Chambersburg PA
CBHW071051250626
47159CB00002B/436